MW01700405

Freddy Frieda Goes to War

A Labrador Native's Story

by

Earl Pilgrim

DRC PUBLISHING
3 Parliament Street
St. John's, Newfoundland and Labrador
A1A 2Y6
Telephone: (709) 726-0960
E-mail: staceypj@nl.rogers.com
www.drcpublishingnl.com

© Earl Pilgrim, 2012

Library and Archives Canada Cataloguing in Publication

Pilgrim, Earl B. (Earl Baxter), 1939-

Freddy Frieda goes to war : a Labrador native's

story / Earl B. Pilgrim.

ISBN 978-1-926689-49-4
1. Soldiers--Newfoundland and Labrador--Fiction.
2. World War, 1914-1918--Newfoundland and Labrador--Fiction.
3. Newfoundland and Labrador--Fiction. I. Title.
PS8581.I338F74 2012 C813'.54 C2012-904590-X

This book is a work of fiction. Names, characters, places, events and incidents either are the product of the author's imagination or are used fictitiously.

Cover design by Randy Bailey Rock 5 Studio Inc.
Box 196, Roddickton, NL, A0K 4P0
www.rock5studios.com
randy@rock5studios.com
phone 774-0102

Layout by Becky Pendergast

Published 2012
Printed in Canada

We acknowledge the financial support of the Government of Canada through the Canada Book Fund (CBF) for our publishing activities.

We acknowledge the financial support of the Government of Newfoundland and Labrador through the Department of Recreation, Tourism and Culture for our publishing activities.

ALL RIGHTS RESERVED. No part of this publication may be reproduced, stored in a retrieval system or transmitted in any form or by any means without the prior written consent of the publisher.

Dedication

In memory of Burton Winters, age 14, who tragically lost his life on the sea ice near his home community of Makkovik, Labrador, in 2012.

Burton was reported missing on Sunday evening, January 29. He was last seen leaving his grandmother's house on a snowmobile earlier that afternoon. The young boy walked 19 kilometers in the dark and cold trying to find his way home after his snowmobile became stuck on frozen sea ice. His body was recovered February 1.

Table of Contents

Foreword

I am thrilled that Earl Pilgrim is sharing the story of Freddy Frieda through his new book "Freddy Frieda Goes To War, A Labrador Native's Story." Freddy's story is a fascinating and intriguing one that illustrates but one of the many connections the Labador Inuit had with the world around them. The use of Freddy's life as the basis of this fictional historical narrative incorporates aboriginal culture and global events to create an innovative reader experience. Stories are a big part of the Labrador Inuit culture. For millennia people have been gathering together throughout the Nunatsiavut coast sharing myths and legends, and learning lessons from each story-telling. The story of Freddy Frieda from Hopedale continues with this story-telling tradition. The communities of Nuntsiavut, both present and past, have an untold number of stories still waiting to be shared. I am very excited to see that one of these stories has made its way onto your book shelf. I hope you enjoy Freddy's story and through the process feel a little more connected to Hopedale and the life of the Labrador Inuit.

Happy Reading.
Johannes Lampe, Minister,
Culture, Recreation and Tourism Nunatsiavut Government

For more information on Nuntsiavut, please visit
www.tourismnunatsiavut.com

Special Thanks

Special thanks to Iris Fillier, Alvone Sutton and Maxwell Snook for editing and advice, and thanks to Ross Decker for his work on material.

Special thanks to Frederick Frieda's daughters, Nancy Morris of Hopedale, Labrador, and Susan Frieda of Calgary, Alberta. Thanks to Eleanora Godwin of Goose Bay, Labrador, grand-niece of Freddy Frieda, who supplied material.

Thanks to Ian Winters of Hopedale for supplying information. Thanks to Natasha Fudge, Patty Tuttle, Max Kinden, Norman Pilgrim, Kevin Aylward, Bruce Humby, Eric Kinden, Don Gillard, George Humby, Roger Canning, Baine Pilgrim, Lister Richards, Captain Robert Gillard of the *Northern Ranger*, Harrison Hopkins, and Jimmy Snow. Also thank you to Gary Newell and the Grenfell Foundation, St. Anthony.

Thanks to Jimmy Tutauk of Hopedale for help with research. Special thanks to Mr. David Lough of the Nunatsiavut Government in Nain, Labrador, for advice. A special thank you to David Adey of St John's, who is a master at supplying material and giving advice. Thanks to Peter and Jean Edwards Stacey of DRC Publishing for their assistance. Without the help of my wife, Beatrice, this story would not have been written. Thank you, Beatrice. And lastly, a very special thanks to all my loyal readers.

CHAPTER 1
Start of War

It was September 15, 1915, and the sun had not yet gone down in Hopedale, a small community on the north coast of Labrador. The tranquil evening peace was suddenly shattered by the sound of a ship's horn blowing three times. The captain of the *Strathcona* was letting the people of Hopedale know that the hospital ship had safely arrived.

Doctor Wilfred Grenfell, the Northern Doctor as he was known by people around the Labrador coast, came on deck and looked at the evening sky. "Are we in port yet, Captain?" he asked.

Captain Trevize, a Cornishman who had been sailing with Grenfell for more than 20 years, nodded his head. "Yes, we are about to let down the anchor," he said. "We are close to our usual anchorage but the tide is out and it could be somewhat dangerous docking at the Moravian wharf right now. We'll wait an hour or two for the tide to rise a little higher, just to be on the safe side."

"That's a marvelous idea. It will give us time to have a cup of tea and a chat before the patients begin coming aboard. I am sure there will be quite a few. This is usually a busy village for us."

The captain grinned. "I'd say it won't be long before people start coming aboard. It's a clear evening and I'm thinking the people spotted us a long distance off and recognized the Doctor's Boat."

After the *Strathcona* was safely anchored, the cook quickly made a pot of tea. Dr. Grenfell prepared his medical bags and then he and the captain and the mate sat at the table and waited for patients to arrive. It wasn't long before the three men began talking about the war that had started in 1914.

"It appears England is going to have a hard time defending herself, if at all," Grenfell said as he sipped his cup of tea. "Germany has a lot of powerful weapons to unleash across the English Channel, and probably the greatest army in the world. There's no doubt that England is going to need every man she can get to fight for her, and that's the reason I am going to enlist in the army as soon as I can get back to St. John's. I have a nasty feeling this could be a long war. There's no doubt it could be a bloodbath like we've never experienced."

Captain Trevize frowned. He was not happy to hear what Grenfell was saying. He didn't want to see the fifty-year-old Northern Doctor go to war. In his opinion it was much too dangerous for a man of his age.

****

On June 28, 1914, in Sarajevo, capital of the Austro-Hungarian province of Bosnia, a Serb nationalist assassinated Archduke Francis Ferdinand, heir presumptive to the throne of Austria-Hungary. On July 28, Austria-Hungary declared war on Serbia. Russia, which was bound by treaty to Serbia, then began mobilizing its troops. On August 1, Germany, which was allied to Austria-Hungary, declared war on Russia. On August 2, Germany demanded free passage through neutral Belgium territory for German troops attacking Russia's ally, France. Britain retaliated with a demand that Germany withdraw its troops from Belgium. When their demand was ignored, Britain declared war on Germany. On August 4, 1914, Sir Walter Davidson, governor of the British colony of Newfoundland, received word that Britain was at war with Germany. What that meant was that all of the British Empire, including Newfoundland and Labrador and Canada, were also at war. What would later be called the Great War went on to become a global conflict involving more than 30 countries.

****

And now, in September of 1915, as the captain and the mate and Dr. Grenfell sipped their tea and ate their lunch the conversation turned from the war to the Moravian Missions along the Labrador coast.

German missionaries with the Moravian Church – a Protestant denomination dating from 1457 and officially known as Unitas Fratrum, or Unity of the Brethern – established their first Mission on the Labrador coast in Nain in 1771, and went on to establish seven more, including the one in Hopedale.

"I wonder what the Moravians are saying about the war?" the mate asked Grenfell. "They have wireless sets and they get the news every night."

"You don't have anything to worry about as far as the Moravians are concerned," said Grenfell. "They are completely neutral; I have had many conversations with them about Kaiser Wilhelm of Germany."

"I wonder what the people on the coast think of it all." Captain Trevize asked. "It's sad hearing about people being killed every day by the Germans then going to church on Sunday and listening to a German preaching the love of God."

"The Moravian Church and their missionaries are one hundred per cent against what the German Army is doing in Europe," said Grenfell. "They have told me that and they have expressed it as well to the Newfoundland Prime Minister and the Governor. I saw the documents while in St. John's attending a meeting and we had a long discussion about this matter. In fact, the Governor asked me to try and recruit young men in Labrador for the Newfoundland Regiment."

There was silence for a few minutes and then Captain Trevize addressed Grenfell. "There is something I have to ask you on behalf of our crew, Dr. Grenfell, do you mind?"

"If you think it's that important then go ahead," Grenfell replied after a moment's pause.

Trevize tried to be brief and to the point. "From the time you got on board the ship in St. Anthony you haven't been the same as other times," he said. "I've noticed you staring into space, like something is bothering you. Is there something we've done that's bothering you?"

"I didn't think you noticed and it's nothing to do with any of you," Grenfell said as he looked at the captain. "But, yes, there is something weighing heavily on my mind and I am bewildered and worried about the outcome. Close the door and I'll tell both of you what it is."

****

After World War 1 broke out in 1914, the whole of the free world suspected every German in every country that was supporting Germany of being a spy for the Kaiser and his regime.

One day in August, 1915, Dr. Grenfell received an urgent telegram from Newfoundland Prime Minister Richard Squires asking him to immediately come to St. John's for a meeting with Governor Davidson and himself at Government House.

Grenfell knew it was no small matter; it was something more important than matters pertaining to medical work or the skirmish he was having with the fish merchants over their unfair treatment of fishermen.

Not wanting to wait for the coastal steamer to come from Corner Brook, he made arrangements for the *Strathcona* to take him to Lewisporte where he could connect with the train going to St. John's. He notified Government House of the time of his arrival.

When he arrived in St. John's he was met by a government vehicle and driven directly to Government House where the two top men in the country were waiting.

Grenfell was taken to the governor's inner office, where Governor Davidson, Prime Minister Squires, and two other gentlemen were waiting for him. He knew both the other gentlemen, they were Ambassadors from the United States and Canada. He hadn't the slightest idea why he was here to meet them. The only thing he knew with certainty was that war was raging in Europe, and he had volunteered to go overseas to serve with the British Forces.

Governor Davidson welcomed Dr. Grenfell and apologized for having him come to St. John's in such haste.

And then he immediately began to explain the reason for the meeting: "A very serious matter has arisen regarding the Moravian missionaries along the North Labrador Coast. It is so serious that the Newfoundland Government doesn't know how we are going to deal with it, which is the reason we have called on you."

Grenfell stared at Davidson wondering what was coming next.

Davidson continued, "I'm now going to ask the American Ambassador to give you their findings. Mr. Ambassador?"

"Gentlemen," the American Ambassador began after thanking everyone for allowing him to meet them on such short notice. "As you know, the Government of the United States has had our intelligence people working around the clock trying to infiltrate the German spy ring. We've had a great deal of success, however, we have only scratched the surface as far as finding out what they are really doing and planning to do. Approximately one week ago our agents and the New York police raided a rooming house in that city and seized documents of vital importance. After we decoded the documents, we saw what the German High Command is planning. I have a copy of the documents here. They are classified, of course, but I will tell you what they said."

The Ambassador cleared his throat as he thumbed through the papers in front of him and then resumed speaking: "It has been learned from documents seized from German agents operating in the United States, in the New York area, that the German military is planning to establish submarine bases in North America, namely, in the Colony of Newfoundland and Labrador and along the Quebec North Shore. It has also been learned that there are German agents operating in these areas. The President and Congress have been briefed on the seriousness of this matter. From the documents seized we have discovered that the Moravian Missions may have German spies on their staff. If this is the case, then they'll probably head the program to help establish submarine bases and put in place wireless communication stations so that Germany can communicate with submarines patrolling the North Atlantic. If these submarine bases get established along the North Labrador Coast and the Northern Peninsula of Newfoundland, no transport ship will be safe in the North Atlantic. Our supply lines to the United Kingdom will be in grave danger."

The Ambassador paused before beginning to read from another page.

"The briefcase seized in the New York apartment contained the following information," he said. "A base of operations will be established at Great Harbour Deep on the east side of the Great Northern Peninsula of Newfoundland and on Grey Islands (South Grois Islands), and several places along the North Labrador Coast.

In areas beyond the regions fished by the Newfoundland fishing fleet, this will be north of the Turnivik Islands. This area is the center of where the Moravian Missions are established. From what we can gather this is a well thought out plan by the German Navy in order to use these people to disguise their agents."

The Ambassador took another file from his briefcase and placed it on the table before continuing: "We have had this area under surveillance for over a year. We've had an agent in that area collecting information on Mission personnel. Although no one has yet been named as a German spy, several people are under suspicion. The Canadian Ambassador and I were told today by Prime Minister Squires that the Newfoundland Government has sent two patrol boats to the Northern Peninsula, to the Harbour Deep-Grey Islands areas, to patrol there for the rest of the war. And we understand two more patrol vessels are on their way to the North Labrador Coast."

Prime Minister Squires confirmed what he was saying with a nod.

"As you know," the Ambassador went on, "a patrol boat can only patrol the ocean, what happens on land is the responsibility of other people who must work hand in hand with each other. For this reason we have to take matters in our hands and control what's around these bays and in the towns. Mr. Squires will now tell us what the plans are and what he intends to do about it."

Squires opened his folder and started by saying: "We have for some time been looking into reports that German spies are operating along the north coast of Labrador. In fact, even before the American and Canadian governments contacted us, several reports had been received from fishing captains of schooners coming off the Labrador of sightings of submarines surfacing in the deep bays. Without doubt they are there for a special reason; they are engaged in a war. The Moravian supply ship *Harmony* was on the coast in July. At the same time it was reported by fishermen that three German subs were sighted in the area of Hopedale. We were not able to confirm this. However, after seeing the reports presented by the two Ambassadors, it confirms reports made by credible fish merchants that the presence of German submarines off the Labrador coast is true."

Squires shifted in his chair and looked at Grenfell who said nothing.

"Gentlemen, we don't have naval ships capable of engaging German submarines," Squires continued. "The four patrol boats we have are in the areas doing what they can. However, as for the Moravians along the North Labrador Coast, we intend to do something about them." Squires paused for a moment and picked up another sheet of paper before continuing. "It has been decided by my government that every Moravian missionary along the North Coast of Labrador will be arrested and brought to St. John's and put in a concentration camp in Mount Pearl and kept there until the end of the war. We will start as soon as possible."

Grenfell was so shocked by what Squires was saying that he was rendered literally speechless, but he continued to listen intently as the Canadian Ambassador stood up and gave his comments.

"I have been in contact with our Prime Minister and he will be sending a war ship to the Quebec North Shore within twenty-four hours," said the Ambassador. "We have permission from your government, Mr. Squires, to patrol the Strait of Belle Isle and that will benefit everyone on this side of the Atlantic."

Governor Davidson, who was chairing the meeting, asked Grenfell if he would like to give his opinion. Grenfell put his elbows on the table and wiped the perspiration off his forehead before he spoke.

"To tell you the truth, gentlemen, I am shocked to say the least," he said. "I am not shocked to hear about sightings of German submarines around our coast. Germany has the capability to have submarines here but we have not sighted a single one, and I have not talked to one single soul who has sighted one. I have been from Hebron Bay in the North to Green Bay on the Island of Newfoundland. We have three hospital boats operating all the time and not one has sighted a submarine. I would have been told if they had."

Grenfell paused then continued, "I am prepared to put my head on the block on the matter of any Moravian missionary being a spy for the Germans. I don't believe it for a minute! I know all the missionaries personally. Most of them have been there for a lifetime. They love Labrador, the same as I do, and the people love them. They are more against what the Kaiser is doing in Europe than anyone I know. For you to gather up these missionaries and throw them in a prison camp would be a disgrace to humanity, a deed talked about for generations and a black mark on the consciousness of this colony that will never be erased."

Prime Minister Squires wasn't pleased to hear Grenfell's words. He'd had an idea the physician would not agree with his plan even before he invited him to St. John's. He had mentioned this to Governor Davidson, but he insisted that Grenfell have an input in the decision in case there was a diplomatic outcry. Grenfell was a close friend of several European kings, including King George V of England, and for this reason Davidson was uneasy.

"What do you propose we do in this case, Dr. Grenfell?" the Governor now asked.

"For one thing, Governor Davidson," said Grenfell. "You could not possibly take these elderly gentlemen who have been in Labrador for some sixty years and throw them in a prison camp. It would break their hearts when they are innocent. If you do imprison them, may I ask who will bury the dead, who will baptize the children, who will marry the people and pray for the sick when they are dying? Who will help the needy when they have no boots to wear during the winter, who will hand out medical supplies during the winter when no medical help can be obtained, when there's a frozen ocean for a thousand miles? The Moravians are life-givers for the Labrador people and have been for over two hundred years. They have sacrificed their whole lives. They are not spies for Kaiser Wilhelm. Someone has made a grave mistake."

The four statesmen, along with the two secretaries who were taking notes, stared at Dr. Grenfell. They hadn't been aware of his oratorical abilities until now. They had forgotten that the Northern Doctor had lectured to kings, presidents and prime ministers.

"You will have to come up with a better plan for those Moravian missionaries, gentleman," Grenfell went on. "It's only natural for our authorities to suspect people of German nationality to be on the side of Germany. However, most of the people you are accusing have lived longer in Labrador than Kaiser Wilhelm has been on this earth. They hate what the German Armed Forces are doing to humanity. I know that is true because I have talked to them. Because someone found a document in a briefcase in the United States declaring an escalation of the war in Labrador, it doesn't give you or anyone else the right to throw the Moravians out. I am sorry, gentlemen."

Governor Davidson called for a break and during the break Dr. Grenfell was asked how his medical mission was going in Labrador, on the Northern Peninsula, and on the Quebec North Shore. He replied with enthusiasm that everything was going well.

"When are you leaving for the British Isles?" Governor Davidson asked him.

"Sometime around the last of October, I'll be going to the battlefront in France. I have already signed up," he told them. "I'll be with the Royal Army Medical Corps."

Squires asked who would be replacing him and Grenfell said it would be Dr. Little, who had been with him for some time and had already agreed to fill in for him while he was away.

Later on at the meeting it was decided to leave all the Moravian missionaries as they were, at least until the following spring.

By then, everyone agreed, the war might be over. And, if the war was still ongoing, another decision could be made at that time.

And now, after telling his story to the captain and the mate, Grenfell sat in the galley of the *Strathcona* and looked out through the porthole at the barren hills above the houses of Hopedale and wondered out loud what was going to be the end of it all. Nothing further was said regarding the Moravians or the war as the three men finished their lunch.

****

The people of Hopedale were very happy to see the green and white hull of the hospital ship coming their way with its canvas sails gleaming in the breeze. They called the *Strathcona* a gift from God, and referred to Dr. Grenfell as a saint.

The villagers had heard the Doctor was somewhere along the North Labrador coast, and even though several people were very ill, yet they had to wait patiently for him to arrive. There was no other way.

Before Dr. Grenfell had finished his tea one of the sailors reported small boats were coming to the vessel with patients.

"Let down the gangway and remind everyone to be careful," Grenfell said as the mate headed up on deck.

The mate was followed by Nurse Clementine, who had accompanied Grenfell, and wanted to be on hand to welcome the patients aboard.

The captain went on deck to see what was happening and came back to tell Grenfell he thought they should immediately move the boat to the Mission wharf where it would be safer for arriving patients.

About twenty people were already aboard the hospital ship.

More than twenty small boats with sick people on board were heading for the ship when the captain returned to tell them to go back to shore and wait until the ship was docked at the wharf. He said getting aboard then would be less dangerous than walking the gangway. Dr. Grenfell came on deck and waved to everyone and assured them all patients would be treated. He said to spread the word to come to the Mission wharf.

When Grenfell went into the ship's waiting room, eight patients were waiting for him and Nurse Clementine was taking information relating to their ailments. Some of the patients had crude bandages wrapped around their hands, others looked very weak; one elderly woman had to be helped along by two men.

Grenfell knew it was going to a very busy afternoon as it was more than two months since his last visit. He worried about his medicine supply. He was sure the medicine he had left with the Moravians had run out by now. He sighed as he thought about the real need for a doctor or nurse to be stationed at Hopedale.

Even before the *Strathcona* was securely tied to the dock, more people began gathering. They came in droves, some were carried on hand-barrows, children were carried on the backs of relatives, some of the sick arrived in wheel-barrows. It was a grueling evening for the staff aboard the hospital ship as they treated patients until late into the night. One of the most common ailments was toothache. People suffered terribly with bad and infected teeth and Grenfell pulled dozens of teeth during the evening.

Near midnight, a servant from the Moravian Mission arrived with a letter for Dr. Grenfell. He opened it right away and smiled as he read the following words:

Dear Dr. Grenfell,

It was a welcome sight for all of us here to see your hospital ship enter the harbour. We have been anxiously looking forward to your arrival for weeks and we all thank God you arrived safely.

This letter is an invitation for you and your staff to dine with us tomorrow evening. I would also like to have the pleasure of meeting with you at your convenience.

Thanking you,
Yours truly,
Reverend Helbig.

Grenfell hastily wrote a reply and gave it to the servant:

Rev. Helbig,

I want to thank you for the invitation. I will notify you in the morning regarding when I can visit you. I have to get a better idea of the work load before I can decide anything. We will be here tomorrow, Saturday, and plan to leave for Nain Sunday afternoon, weather permitting.

Wilfred Grenfell

****

Well before 8 a.m. Saturday Dr. Grenfell had a great many patients waiting to see him. People in the outlying coves had heard the Doctor was in Hopedale, and they started out before daylight in small rowboats with their sick folks aboard. Patients coming to the hospital ship ranged from elderly people to infants, and there were as well quite a few pregnant women. As always, it was a hectic morning.

Grenfell was notified that there were several people who were too ill to be carried to the ship and he was requested to visit them in their homes.

In the afternoon, he and Nurse Clementine packed up their medical bags and set out along the footpath to visit the sick and dying. They were accompanied by a young man who led them to the homes they needed to visit. As they traveled along the dusty road Grenfell asked his name.

"I'm Freddy Frieda," he replied.

"Is this your home, young man?" Grenfell asked.

"Yes," Freddy replied, and then added, "We live here in Hopedale, but we spend the early summer out at the Turnivik Islands fishing with the Newfoundlanders for salmon and cod. We return here in August and Mom goes to work with the Hudson Bay Company until Christmas. During the fall I spend my time in the country trapping. After Christmas, we move to the back country, to our winter tilt about thirty miles back. We find it better there; it's closer to the firewood supply."

"It sounds like a very interesting life," said Grenfell.

"A busy life, sir. I think you knew my father, he was Michael Frieda."

"Yes, I knew him, I met him several times. Your father was a good man, his accident was very unfortunate." Grenfell remembered back when Michael Frieda fell through the ice and eventually died of pneumonia. He was forty-seven at the time of his death.

Grenfell was amazed at how well Freddy spoke English. He asked him if he'd gone to school in Hopedale.

"Yes," said Freddy. "I went to the Moravian school, completed the Royal reader, that's as high as you can get here."

"Well that's very good, young man, I am happy to hear that." Grenfell would have asked him more about himself but just then they arrived at the first house they had to visit. At the end of the afternoon, Grenfell thanked Freddy very much for his assistance and said he'd like to talk to him before he left Hopedale. He invited Freddy to come visit him on the ship at 2 p.m. the following day.

CHAPTER 2

Dinner with the Moravian Minister

After Dr. Grenfell had visited a couple of houses, he wrote a note to the Moravian minister informing him he would be able to attend a late dinner at 7 p.m. if that was convenient. Freddy delivered the note for him.

It was 6 p.m. when Grenfell arrived back on the hospital ship. Two patients were waiting to be seen. One man had something in his eye, the other wanted advice on how to treat dysentery.

After seeing the patients, Dr. Grenfell and Nurse Clementine went on to the Moravian Mission for dinner. Captain Trevize was already there. They were welcomed with open arms by Reverend Helbig and his wife, Marie, who spoke with a more distinct German accent than her husband. A delicious caribou roast was served and Dr. Grenfell commented on its mouth-watering aroma. Marie was pleased he enjoyed dinner. Reverend Helbig asked him about his day while they ate.

"Busy as usual, Reverend," replied Grenfell. "The village is much in need of a permanent clinic staffed by a nurse year round. That is one of my greatest priorities for the North Labrador coast. I will be meeting with Prime Minister Squires and Governor Davidson when I go to St. John's in a week or so and I will bring the matter up then."

"I hope someone will listen to you," said Reverend Helbig. He was pleased to hear that Grenfell was going to lobby for a clinic for Hopedale; he knew it would be a blessing to the whole area.

"I doubt if anything will happen now. It probably won't happen until the war comes to an end," said Grenfell.

Helbig thought for a moment before answering. "We have special prayers every morning asking God to make the leaders of Germany give up the insane cruelty they are involved in and live like civilized human beings before God puts a curse on the whole nation."

Dr. Grenfell decided to tell Reverend Helbig he was planning to go overseas to fight the Germans. He could see the missionary was opposed to the war and against everything the Kaiser stood for. Grenfell wanted Helbig to know his plans because the Moravian missionary was his contact person in Hopedale.

"It is possible, Reverend Helbig, that this could be my very last trip to the North Coast of Labrador, or maybe even my last time seeing the Labrador forever, because I'll be leaving for England as soon as I get back to St. John's," he said. "I've been asked by the War Office to come home to the British Isles and do my part."

Reverend Helbig was lost for words. He hadn't expected to hear that Grenfell was going to enlist. He had heard the call for volunteers, for young men to join the military, on BBC-Radio almost daily, but he never thought Dr. Grenfell would be among those going overseas.

"I am sorry," he finally said. "I never thought this dirty war would reach the land of Labrador, but in this case it has."

Grenfell knew this man was speaking from his heart, however there was very little he could do or say. If he told him what the Government was planning to do with the Moravian missionaries in Labrador it would break his heart, therefore he kept silent.

But there was something he wanted to say.

"I have been asked by Prime Minister Squires to try and recruit as many young men from Labrador as I can to join the armed forces, preferably the Royal Newfoundland Regiment," he said. "They want all the volunteers they can get before they start conscripting them."

"There are not many young men in Hopedale who would qualify," said Helbig. "For one thing, they need a certain level of education in order to be able to read orders and take notes."

"All they have to know is how to use a gun and obey orders, everything else will come naturally," said Grenfell.

"In that case, everyone around here qualifies. They are all trappers, handy with guns."

"I just met Frederick Frieda. He appears to be a fine young man," said Grenfell.

"Freddy, everyone calls him." Helbig smiled. "He went to school here at the Mission and, in fact, he can speak German fluently. We use him as an interpreter if one of our German members comes here and can't understand the native language. But Freddy's mother would never allow him to leave Hopedale. He's the only one she has to provide a living for their family."

"I see," said Grenfell.

He knew it would not be wise to continue talking about recruiting young men. The Moravians were against people going to war no matter what side they were on. However, he decided he would approach Freddy Frieda about joining the war effort before he departed from Hopedale.

By 9 p.m. Grenfell and his party were back aboard the *Strathcona*. It was Saturday, 1915, late September.

CHAPTER 3

About Freddy

Frederick Frieda grew up in Hopedale. His father, Michael, had a house in the town. Freddy said he was from Hopedale, but he spent most of his life out on the land trapping during the winter and fishing for cod at his father's premises on the Turnivik Islands in summer. Freddy was tall for a Labrador Inuit, 5'8" in height. He was strong and could move with the skill of a wild animal. He was also fearless, and his fearlessness almost cost him his life several times while traveling on bad ice. Freddy was known around the Hopedale area as someone willing to take chances, especially when traveling in winter storms. If someone got lost in winter storm they could count on Freddie to do a search. He was known as a very dependable young man in the Hopedale area.

Whenever Freddie was at home he visited the Moravian Mission. He was close to the missionaries, who were mostly Germans, and his mother played in the church band. Freddie respected Dr. Grenfell, just as every other native person living on the Labrador Coast did.

Everyone on the coast looked forward to Grenfell coming to their community, and they were all willing to give him anything and go anywhere he asked. Freddie appreciated Dr. Grenfell's work more than most young people, maybe because he was more mature than others his age.

After Freddy's father died, his mother, Nancy, was asked by Dr. Grenfell if she would like to take her children and move to St. Anthony, the headquarters of Grenfell's Mission on the Island of Newfoundland.

Nancy refused, saying she preferred to have her children follow in her husband's footsteps.

And now Dr. Grenfell himself had invited Freddy to visit his hospital ship. Freddy was excited. It was good news and he could hardly wait to tell his mother about it.

****

Dr. Grenfell was asked to speak at the Sunday morning service at the Moravian Church.

Close to the entire population of Hopedale was in attendance as he talked of God's love for mankind and the urgent need for permanent medical needs in Hopedale and along the North Labrador Coast. He told the congregation that Hopedale was at the top of the list of communities needing to have a doctor or nurse stationed there year round.

When the church service was over, Grenfell and Reverend Helbig stood at the door to shake hands with all who had attended. That included Freddy, and Grenfell reminded him of their meeting that afternoon. Freddy said he would be there.

Dr. Grenfell knew he had to soon begin his trip south due to the early freeze up. He asked the captain if they should proceed further north or start heading back to St. Anthony.

"Tomorrow is the 25th of September," said Captain Trevize. "It's dangerous to venture further north into the bays for fear of getting frozen in the ice. I don't think it's wise to go any further north."

"The only thing is that we have medical supplies for the area around Nain and Hebron, and their only hope of getting it is for us to bring it," said Grenfell.

"Maybe we could leave the medical supplies with the Moravians here. I thought Reverend Helbig said a boat from Nain was expected tomorrow. We could leave everything here for them to take back to the three towns further north," suggested Trevize.

"Alright," said Grenfell. "We'll stay here until they arrive so that I can talk to them and give someone instructions."

"I suppose we could delay our departure for a day but no more," said Trevize.

Grenfell had no other choice but to agree with the captain. Trevize was responsible for the ship. His priority was to make sure the ship and those aboard, including Dr. Grenfell and the crew, didn't get frozen in on the North Labrador Coast and have to stay there until June.

"Twenty-four hours will be fine," said Grenfell. "If the boat from Nain doesn't arrive by then we will leave the supplies with the Moravians to be transported by dog team later this winter."

It was a little before two when Freddie arrived at the *Strathcona*. He was shown aboard by one of the sailors who had been briefed by Grenfell. Freddy introduced himself and said Dr. Grenfell was expecting him.

"Come aboard, young man, the Doctor asked me to watch for you." The sailor, an older man, reached out to shake Freddy's hand. "You stay here for a moment, I'll tell the Doctor you are here."

Freddy was nervous, he couldn't figure why Dr. Grenfell wanted to see him. He wasn't sick, the rest of his family was fine, he wasn't in possession of anything, and he had done nothing wrong. He was puzzled. His mother was concerned when he told her the Doctor wanted to see him, but she insisted Freddie go as requested. It seemed only a minute before the sailor came back and signaled Freddy to follow him. He was taken down a flight of stairs and into the study of Dr. Grenfell. The Doctor rose from the chair behind his desk and took Freddy's hand. He asked him how he was and his distinctive British accent made Freddy pay special attention to what he said.

Dr. Wilfred Grenfell was not only a medical doctor. He was also a master at whatever he set out to do, whether it was dealing with the highest officials of Government, fighting the fish merchants, or soliciting financial support at a public meeting in New York. He knew what he wanted and most of the time he succeeded in getting it.

As he sat behind the desk and sized up the young Labrador native who nervously sat in front of him with wondering eyes, Grenfell could only think of what this young man's future would be if he ever had to go on the battlefield and face flying bullets aimed at him as though he was a wild animal.

"Freddy, do you know much about the war that's going on in Europe?" he asked. "I mean the war between Germany and England, and that of course includes Newfoundland and Labrador. None of us will be safe if the Germans win this war. We're all in it together, and that's why I'm joining up as soon as I get to St. John's."

"I know about the war, Doctor. The Moravians keep us informed as to what is going on."

"The reason I wanted to talk to you is that the Empire needs fighting men," Grenfell began. "I've been asked by the Governor to recruit young men for the army wherever I travel, especially along the coast of Labrador." Freddy was silent as he stared at Dr. Grenfell. "I asked the Moravian minister about you after I met you yesterday on the road. He said you were an outstanding young man, and due to your ability to speak the German language he felt you would be a perfect candidate for the British Army, especially for the intelligence branch. Men like you are badly needed." Freddy shifted nervously in his chair as Grenfell continued. "Although this may come as a shock to you, it would be much worse if it came to the point that the authorities came here and to other small communities and conscripted people without their consent."

"I have never thought about joining the army," said Freddy. "I have thought about what it must be like to be a soldier, but I have never thought of becoming one."

"It's the same for me," said Grenfell. "I have been to many different countries around the world, but I have never been a military man. With what's happening now, though, I feel I have to join up and try to do my part. How do you feel about it?"

"Doctor, I don't know what to say or how to answer you. It's something I'll have to talk about with my mother and the rest of my family," said Freddy.

"I understand. It's a decision you don't want to make lightly. You can let me know as soon as you make up your mind. I won't be leaving until tomorrow noon so if you decide to sign up I can take care of everything as I'm qualified to administer the oath. If you enlist, you will go to St. Anthony with us then travel to Lewisporte on the coastal steamer and take the train to St John's," said Grenfell.

Freddy had heard of Lewisporte and St. John's and he knew about the coastal steamer, but he had only ever seen a train in the lantern slides.

"Dr. Grenfell," he said, "it's a shock to be asked to join the army. I may not be physically qualified."

"If you decide to join I will give you a physical examination and we will know then if you qualify or not," said Grenfell.

He didn't say it, but he felt quite certain Freddy would qualify, the boy was young and healthy and strong.

"If you don't mind, I could come and visit your family in about an hour and talk things over with your mother. She may have some questions she wants to ask."

Freddy agreed. As he left the hospital ship and stepped onto the dock his mind was in a swirl. The thought of leaving Hopedale and going to places he had never heard of before was a little too much for him.

After he passed the Mission church and started following the footpath to his home questions began popping into his mind. He wondered what his mother would have to say about him going off to war. How would she survive if he went away? What would happen to his fishing gear and his trap line? Who would cut wood to keep the stove going? I am going to have to get all of those questions answered, he thought to himself.

****

Nancy Frieda had also wondered why Dr. Grenfell wanted to talk to Freddy. When Freddy left for his meeting she watched him until he went aboard the *Strathcona* and disappeared from sight.

Freddy was breathing hard when he arrived back home. His mother knew there was something wrong when she saw him coming towards the house.

"What did Dr. Grenfell want you for?" she asked as soon as he came through the door. Freddy shrugged his shoulders. She asked him again, demanding an answer.

It wasn't every day that Dr. Grenfell, the most popular man on the North Coast, the man everyone referred to as God, asked to have a private meeting with anyone, and especially with a young fellow from Hopedale. Freddy smiled as he closed the door, he knew his mother was anxious to hear what the meeting was about.

"He asked me to join the Army, to go overseas with him and fight in the war," he bluntly said.

For a moment it didn't sink in, however when Freddy looked his mother in the face, she knew it was true. "Join the army, and fight in the war, is that what you said?" she blurted out.

"Yes, that's what he wanted me for," said Freddy.

For a moment his mother was silent, she had not been expecting that. As far as she was concerned, the war was far removed from Labrador. Nancy went to the stove, lifted the cover and put a piece of wood on the fire.

"What did you tell him, Freddy?" she asked.

"I told him I would have to talk to you first."

"What did he say then?"

"He said that was fine, but he would like an answer as soon as possible because he's leaving in the morning. He said if I enlisted I would leave with him. He said he's already signed up and this is his last trip here till after the war."

Nancy Frieda was not happy. She didn't want to hear anything about her son going to war. Without him there was no way for her and the family to survive; he was their provider.

"He's coming to see you later this afternoon. He wants to know what you have to say about this," said Freddy. "I suppose he wants to ask you if I can go with him in the Newfoundland Regiment. But really, Mom, it's up to me. I'll soon be nineteen. I can make up my own mind about what I'm going to do."

"Freddy, don't let it even come into your mind about leaving. If you go, we will be finished. You can't go." Nancy sat down at the table and thought if only her husband Michael was still around he would straighten this matter out. She looked at her son as he came and sat at the table with her. She couldn't bear the thought of him leaving. If he went away, if he went off to war, it would break her heart.

"Mom, don't worry about it, I'm not gone yet," said Freddy.

"I hope you never go, my son. The Germans will never come to Hopedale," she said.

"They are here now, Mom." Freddy raised his eyebrows and nodded at his mother.

"The ones who are here are missionaries, Freddy," she said as she looked back at him, her face very serious. "They are men of God. They won't hurt us."

"I know, but it's like the pastor told us a while ago, old Kaiser Wilhelm wants to rule the world and he is killing everyone who stands in his way and that is why England is crying out for men. It's the reason Dr. Grenfell is going to war. I don't think we are any different here in Labrador than they are in England. Soon, the Germans will be over here after us," said Freddy.

Maybe Freddy is right, Nancy thought, he may have to go to war. Then she thought about what she would do, how she would continue to provide a living. She worked part time at the Hudson Bay store helping to tan skins in return for food, but it would not be enough to meet all her needs. She was used to a good living from the fish Freddy caught and sold to the Newfoundland fish merchants during the summer and the furs he caught and sold during the winter. If he went off to war she knew it would be tough.

Nancy had done volunteer work with the Moravian Church ever since she was a young girl. After she got married she continued to play a big part in church activities. She brought Freddy with her and that was when he began learning to speak the German language. The missionaries thought highly of Freddy. He played the trumpet and saxophone in the church band with his mother. He also helped maintain the Mission buildings.

It was late in the afternoon when Dr. Grenfell and Nurse Clementine arrived at the Frieda home. The Doctor knocked before they entered, then called "Hello."

He was warmly greeted by Nancy who welcomed him into her humble home and introduced him to her daughters, Sarah, fifteen, and Blanche, thirteen. Freddy was sitting on a daybed next to the stove. He smiled at Dr. Grenfell.

"I'm pleased to meet you and your girls, Mrs. Frieda," Grenfell said as he held out his hand in a friendly handshake.

Putting out her own rough and calloused hand, Nancy very delicately shook hands without looking him in the eye. Grenfell noticed this and realized she was shy.

Although she carried scars from hard work and possessed a determination that had been carved out of the cruelest environment on earth, below the surface lived a heart and soul that loved the very ground that Dr. Wilfred Grenfell walked upon, so much so that she didn't feel worthy to look into his face.

"I want you to meet Nurse Clementine; she is the staff nurse on our hospital ship," Grenfell said in a friendly tone of voice.

Nancy held her hand out to the English nurse and managed to say she was pleased to meet her.

Grenfell told Nancy it was Nurse Clementine's first trip to the North Coast of Labrador. He said the nurse would be visiting the coast for at least the next five years, and he would make sure she dropped in to see Nancy every time she came to Hopedale. Nancy thanked him. There was some discussion about Nancy's health, and that of her family.

"We have always been well, Doctor," she said. "Michael was the only tragedy we've had. I suppose if he had not fallen through the ice he might be still around." Tears filled her eyes as she spoke of her husband.

As he looked sympathetically at Nancy, Grenfell was aware that taking her son away from his safe home in Hopedale and off to the war in Europe would no doubt change his life forever, even to the point he might never return. Young men were being killed every day on the field of battle in defense of their country.

"It's a terrible thing to lose a loved one, especially when it's an accident such as the one your family experienced," he said with deep sincerity. "There's no doubt we would all go to any risk or make any sacrifice to save a life. Whether we are young or old, life is sweet to us all."

There was silence in the kitchen broken only by the ticking of a clock on the wall over the table as Grenfell surveyed his surroundings.

The Frieda house was spotlessly clean. There was no canvas on the floor, only bare boards that showed white from cleaning with a scrubbing brush. There was no fancy furniture, the table and chairs were homemade, but they were well constructed by someone with great patience and a good knowledge of carpentry. Standing on one side of the kitchen was a well polished Waterloo stove.

Just then, the kitchen door opened and a young woman entered. Nancy introduced her as Emily Bromfield, Freddy's girlfriend.

"This is Dr. Grenfell and Nurse, ahhh sorry, I can't remember your name," said Nancy, stammering.

"I'm Nurse Clementine, how do you do?" The nurse held out her hand and Emily politely shook hands with her.

"Emily lives next door," said Nancy.

Emily sat down on the daybed next to Freddy. Grenfell was pleased to meet her. He knew her father and had heard him speak highly of his daughter. He knew Emily was seventeen. He could see she was part native, but not Inuit. She was Innu, a very beautiful Indian girl.

After things settled down and everyone became more at ease, Grenfell started talking about the war and the need for young men to join up and fight to keep Britain free.

"I don't know if you are aware of the fact that I have the authority to sign up members for the armed forces, that is, to recruit young men and women for the army and navy," he said, looking around at his audience.

No one said anything and he continued. "I was told yesterday that Freddy can speak German fluently and this makes him a very worthwhile candidate for the Royal Newfoundland Regiment. The army badly needs men with Freddy's qualifications." Nancy Frieda was silent as she stared at the floor. "If he volunteers to go overseas he will travel with me. As soon as I get back to St. Anthony, I will be leaving for St. John's to go in the army as a medical doctor. If Freddy comes with me we will travel together to St. Anthony and then it will be on to St. John's and from there to England."

Emily looked at Freddy with wide, tearful eyes as if to say, 'You're not going to the war, Freddy, you're not leaving me.' Freddy gave her a shy smile and continued to listen to the Doctor.

"It is a possibility, if this war is not won by the Allies, that Labrador could be taken over by the Germans," said Grenfell. "We are all part of the British Empire. If England gets defeated then Newfoundland and Labrador gets defeated too. None of us want that to happen. And that's why we have to go to war. We must defend Britain."

Nancy was not convinced.

There were other people besides her Freddy. Why should he have to go? Grenfell looked at Nancy and then glanced at Freddy. He noticed that the look on his face had suddenly changed.

Freddy saw Grenfell look at him and immediately spoke up.

"Dr. Grenfell," he said, with determination in his voice. "I have made up my mind about going to war with you. I am going to join the army and I'll sign up immediately. I don't want the Germans coming to Labrador and killing everyone."

Grenfell was surprised that Freddy had made up his mind so quickly, but he was glad to hear his decision.

Freddy told his mother he had to get packed as he would be leaving with Dr. Grenfell in the morning.

Nancy Frieda looked surprised.

Freddy had so many responsibilities at home she was sure he would decide not to go to war. She didn't want to create a scene in front of Dr. Grenfell and Nurse Clementine, but she felt certain she could convince Freddy not to go after they left.

Grenfell was well aware that Freddy's mother and girlfriend might persuade him to change his mind after he and Nurse Clementine had left. If Freddy was going to join the army he would have to get signed up right away, before someone talked him out of it.

"I am going back to the ship now," he said briskly to Freddy. "I want you to come along and sign the necessary papers. After you do that you can return and straighten out the things necessary to your being absent."

"I want to talk to Mom for a few minutes before we go," said Freddy.

"Yes, that's quite all right, we'll wait outside," said Grenfell.

When he was alone with his mother and sisters and girlfriend, Freddy said he was convinced of the need to help protect Labrador.

"Someone has to go and it might as well be me,' he whispered, not wanting Grenfell or the nurse to hear what he was saying. "If everyone waits until next year it may be too late. According to the Moravians, the world is being torn apart by a madman, this Kaiser Wilhelm, and the Moravians should know because they are Germans. Mom, you have heard them say that."

"I know, Freddy, but why should you have to go? It will break my heart if you leave. It's too sudden," Nancy whispered back.

"This is my only chance to get off the Labrador this fall. No other boat will be coming this way until next spring after the ice melts."

Nancy looked at him with wide eyes.

"What about our six Husky dogs, do you think I'll be able to handle them hauling wood this winter, and what about the trap line, who will trap your area?"

"Mom, don't worry about that. You're capable of driving twenty dogs, and as for the trap line, the animal population will have a chance to increase. I will only be gone a couple of years, if that. Everything will be okay. You have a part-time job with the Moravians, and another one at the Hudson Bay store. I've got our winter supply brought in and there's enough dog food to last until spring. There's a year's supply of firewood outside, so everything should be fine."

"What about after a year, Freddy?" Nancy asked.

"I'll tell whoever is in charge to let me come home to get firewood and food for the dogs," said Freddy, laughing.

His mother didn't laugh and neither did Emily.

Freddy's girlfriend was crying. Tears streamed down her face. All of this was too sudden for her to grasp.

"I can't believe it, Freddy. You're going away," she sobbed.

"I didn't intend to stay in Hopedale all my life, Emily. Even if we had got married, we would have moved somewhere for a few years. We would have had a change," he said as he put his arm around her.

"I know, but a year or two is a long time for us to be apart."

"You dry your tears now, my love," Freddy gently patted Emily's shoulder. "I might be back again the first thing in the spring if the war ends. Don't worry, everything will be okay."

Emily and Nancy started weeping again.

"I am not leaving till tomorrow morning, so don't cry now," Freddy said as he tried to console them.

"Freddy," said Emily, wiping her eyes and looking at him. "I want to go to the ship with you, if Doctor Grenfell will let me."

"I'll ask him if you can." Freddy stood up and made for the door, looking relieved.

Dr. Grenfell said he would be pleased to have Emily accompany them to the *Strathcona*; she could witness the signing by adding her signature to the papers Freddy had to sign in order to enlist.

CHAPTER 4
Freddy goes to war

It was only a ten minute walk to the *Strathcona*, but it seemed like an hour to Freddy. The Doctor led the way, talking all the way about the voyage across the Atlantic.

"The troops usually go on a large ocean liner that will be considered a troop ship. We may have to go to Halifax, Nova Scotia, to join the ship," he said.

This was like a foreign language to Freddy; he had never been past the Turnivik Islands. He wondered where this Nova Scotia was, but kept silent. As they came aboard the *Strathcona* Captain Trevize greeted them and then turned to speak to Grenfell.

"I think it's going to be frosty tonight, hope it doesn't interfere with our departure in the morning," he said. "But if all goes well I guess we'll depart shortly after daylight."

Grenfell agreed and then went directly to his office where he took out the necessary forms for Freddy and spread them on the table.

Nurse Clementine asked Emily if she would like to accompany her on a tour of the hospital ship.

After they left the office Grenfell got down to the business of filling in the forms needed for recruitment into the Royal Newfoundland Regiment. It didn't take long to gather the information.

Freddy had more than the necessary education needed to qualify and no criminal record and Dr. Grenfell gave him an excellent bill of health.

"All we need now is your signature and a witness to sign next to yours and then I'll swear you in," said Grenfell.

Captain Trevize said he would witness the signing but Grenfell said he thought Emily wanted to do it. Trevize called Nurse

Clementine and Emily back down to the office and Grenfell had Emily sign the papers. He got a Bible and had Freddy repeat the oath of allegiance to the King.

"Congratulations, Freddy, you are now a soldier," he said as he shook Freddy's hand after everything had been signed and sealed.

The captain and the nurse shook Freddy's hand too, but Emily stood as if frozen stiff, with tears running down her cheeks. She was saying goodbye to the one she loved and it was breaking her heart.

Captain Trevize told Freddy to be at the dock at 6 a.m. as he planned to depart at first light. Freddy promised to be on time.

"You can have breakfast aboard ship. You are one of us now, you're a military man," said the captain.

****

The first thing Freddy did was go home and let his mother and sisters know that he had enlisted.

When the news reached the first house that Freddy Frieda had joined the army and was going to war with Dr. Grenfell, it only took a few minutes for everyone in Hopedale to know. The news spread like wildfire.

Some people came to Freddy's house and shook his hand and wished him well, while others cried and said he would be killed by the Germans on the other side of the world, or go down to a watery grave somewhere in the briny Atlantic.

This Sunday evening was a sad time in Hopedale.

When Reverend Helbig heard the news about Freddy, he and his wife came to see Nancy and encouraged her to be strong.

"We pledge you our support and will do anything to help you while Freddy is away,' he said. "Someone has to stand in for us, Nancy, we don't have to be ruled by madmen, so don't take it too hard. We all have to be strong."

From his own house, Freddy went to the Bromfield home with Emily, who cried all the way. As they walked along the narrow footpath she clung to him.

"I can't believe it, Freddy, you are going away, going to the war, leaving me, and I may never see you again." She choked back tears and made him stop for a minute. "Freddy, what will I do without you? I will go crazy after you leave." Her voice rose to a wail.

Emily's father, Charley Bromfield, was a tall man, maybe six foot three or four with a very dark complexion. He was part Montagnais Indian; people referred to him as a mountaineer Indian.

Charley was sitting quietly at the kitchen table in his sister's house sewing binding on a dog's harness when he heard the sound of his daughter crying.

"Good grief," he yelled as he dashed to the door. "Emily, what happened to you? Has someone attacked you?" His yell was loud enough for most of the people around Hopedale to hear him.

"No, Mr. Bromfield," said Freddy calmly. 'No one attacked her."

"Then what in the devil's name is the matter with her?" he yelled again.

Freddy didn't answer; he waited for Emily to explain to her father what she was crying about.

"Freddy is leaving me, Dad, he's joining the army and going off with Dr. Grenfell," she sobbed.

Charley told them both to come in. After closing the door, he went to his daughter and put his arm around her.

"It's the best thing Freddy could ever do is join the army," he said, with a smile for both of them. "I wish I was younger and I'd be going with him if they would take me."

Freddy smiled at Charley as he pulled a chair near the table. He was not a stranger in this house; he had been coming here for two years, the length of time he had been going out with Emily. Charley had been away for most of that time. He worked as a herdsman for Grenfell's reindeer herd back in St. Anthony.

Charley had married a white woman from Cupids, Conception Bay. She had died not long after giving birth to Emily and a broken-hearted Charley brought his baby daughter home to Hopedale.

Charley's sister, Rachel, raised Emily in Hopedale. Rachel thought of Emily as her own daughter. She was fond of Freddy too and pleased that Emily loved him. She could see that he was good to her.

"I'm going back to St. Anthony with you on the *Strathcona* tomorrow morning," Charley now said to Freddy. "We are moving the reindeer herd next week. I've got to get back, been here for two weeks already."

"Well, Father, if you go tomorrow morning, then I'm going with you. I'm going to start packing right away," said Emily. She spoke with determination as she dried her tears.

"Yes, you can certainly come with us if Dr. Grenfell is okay with it. I'll ask him, but I know he will say yes. You can stay with me in St. Anthony till Freddy comes back from the war," said Charley, smiling at his daughter.

Freddy was happy; things were working out just fine. Charley asked Freddy to finish binding the dog's harness while he walked over to the *Strathcona* to talk to Dr. Grenfell.

After her father left, Emily came and stood behind Freddy as he sewed the cloth around the rope.

"You had better behave yourself, Emily." Freddy grinned at her. "I have to finish this first because if I don't your father will hang me with it. So, you get packing your clothes. You may be leaving Hopedale for a long time." Freddy tried to push her away, but it was too much for him. He had to put down the sewing needle and put his arms around her and hold her tight.

Charley was back in less than half an hour looking pleased with himself.

"Emily," he said, "Dr. Grenfell said he is delighted you are coming. He said he has a job for you as soon as you arrive in St. Anthony." Charley was very happy that his daughter was coming with him.

CHAPTER 5
Leaving Hopedale

Freddy went home and packed up his few clothes and returned to spend the night with Emily.

Her Aunt Rachel, who had raised her from a small child, was broken-hearted to see her go. But although she was going to St. Anthony, Rachel thought, at least she wasn't going off to war.

"I'll be back next spring, maybe on the first mail boat that arrives from the south," Emily told her aunt. But even with that promise, Rachel spent a sleepless night, weeping as she prepared Emily's clothes and packed them in a suitcase.

Freddy told his mother he was going to have breakfast aboard the hospital ship, but she wasn't having any of that.

"Freddy, you are going to have breakfast with us this morning," she insisted. "It may be the last meal you'll have with us for a long time. I am going to cook watered fish and scrunchions."

Freddy kissed his mother; he knew there was nothing on the *Strathcona* that could compare to her home cooking.

"Yes, Mother," he said as he gave her a hug. "I'll have breakfast here."

Before he left, Freddie went to say goodbye to his six dogs. He went out to where they were chained up and called each one by name.

The dogs jumped up around him and licked his face as if to say, 'Goodbye, Freddy.' It was an emotional experience for him. It made him wonder if he was doing the right thing.

It has always been said that the stars over Hopedale shine brighter than anywhere else in the world. Maybe it's the position of the land that makes them appear much larger.

The stars seemed to shine even more brightly as Nancy with her family of three and Emily with her father and aunt walked along the dusty footpath towards the ship that waited with its lights blazing in the frosty September morning.

No one spoke as they trudged along in the chilly morning air.

Their silence made it seem as though they were heading for an execution or some other dreadful event.

They got quite a surprise when they drew near to the wharf.

Almost all the people of Hopedale were there, waiting to say goodbye to Freddy and Emily.

When people heard Freddy was going to war and leaving at 6 a.m. they wanted to be on hand to see him leave. Even the Moravian missionaries were there.

Freddy and Emily shook hands and hugged everyone on the dock, and just about everyone wept as they said goodbye. Before the lines were cast off Dr. Grenfell came to the railing. He stood between Freddy and Emily as they waved to the people they were leaving. Reverend Helbig stood tall and proud as he led the people in singing:

God be with you till we meet again,
By His counsels guide, uphold you,
With His sheep securely fold you,
God be with you till we meet again.

Refrain:

Till we meet, till we meet,
Till we meet at Jesus' feet;
Till we meet, till we meet,
God be with you till we meet again.

God be with you till we meet again,
'Neath His wings securely hide you,
Daily manna still provide you,
God be with you till we meet again.

God be with you till we meet again,
When life's perils thick confound you,
Put His arms unfailing round you,
God be with you till we meet again.

God be with you till we meet again,
Keep love's banner floating o'er you,
Smite death's threat'ning wave before you,
God be with you till we meet again.

It was a moving moment as voices soared into the clear morning air and tears rolled down the face of Freddy Frieda.

CHAPTER 6
Going Overseas

The *Strathcona* had to break the ice in order to get out of the harbour. There was no doubt navigation was closing in around the small villages along the Labrador coast. Everyone would soon be locked in by ice until the following spring.

It took the little ship three days to reach St. Anthony on the Northern Peninsula of Newfoundland. St. Anthony looked like a city to Freddy and Emily compared to their small village of Hopedale. It was the largest town they had ever seen.

They left the *Strathcona* with their meager belongings and went with Charley to his home.

At the Grenfell Mission there was lots of activity. People were bustling around everywhere. Even Grenfell's reindeer herd was roaming around in the town as they waited for Charley, their head herdsman, to arrive. Charley told Freddy and Emily that Grenfell had imported 300 reindeer from Norway in 1908. He intended that the herd, which by now had reached over 1,800 animals, would be a source of food and fur for local people and could also be used for hauling wood.

During the voyage, Dr. Grenfell had informed Emily she would be working in the laundry at the hospital, and accommodations would be provided for her at the annex. She was to start work immediately.

Charley was happy his daughter was going to work in St. Anthony and that he would be able to see her quite often. He had not yet told her he was seeing a lady by the name of Mary Ann and was planning to get married before Christmas. When he finally did tell her, the news had hardly any effect. Emily was so much in love with Freddy that the thought of him going off to war occupied her mind both day and night.

Freddy spent three busy days in St. Anthony waiting for the arrival of the coastal boat going south. He visited the reindeer herd and was amazed to see the mature does being milked. Back in Labrador he had hunted and shot caribou on the open barrens; the closest he ever got to one was not less than fifty yards, but here he could lead the reindeer around with a rope. Some even had harnesses and were hooked to sleighs pulling wood. It was all truly amazing.

Finally the coastal boat arrived. It was the *Prospero*, which carried mail and freight and passengers around the coast. The ship docked in St. Anthony all night.

Dr. Grenfell invited Freddy and Emily to come to his home and meet his wife. Anne MacClanahan Grenfell wanted to know all about Freddy, and all about the Labrador and its people. She said he was certainly the right person to ask about people's lives in the north because he had lived there all his life. Freddy told her all about the people and their way of life and finished off by saying, "You may not think it, Mrs. Grenfell, but if there was to be no more food carried to Labrador by the boats we would not starve; we could live off the land and from the ocean."

Freddy spent his last night with Emily. He promised he would marry her when he returned from the war.

"Wait for me, darling," he said as he softly kissed her lips. "No matter how long I'm gone I'll come back and marry you and then we'll live in Hopedale and raise a family."

"I'll wait for you to return, supposing it's forever," she promised.

****

Early the next morning, the *Prospero* blew its horn, indicating it would be sailing in an hour. Everyone in town knew Dr. Grenfell was going overseas. They knew about the war raging in Europe and they wondered if he would ever return again. Many young men from St. Anthony and the surrounding area had already gone off to fight and several had been killed. When people heard about Freddy Frieda of Hopedale, Labrador, going to war with Dr. Grenfell, they thought he must be a special young man to volunteer.

People came to the Grenfell Mission wharf to say goodbye to the Doctor and his wife. He told them he would be back.

"Just keep supporting the mission as you've been doing, God will reward you," he said. With tearful eyes the people cheered as the *Prospero* slipped its lines and moved out of St. Anthony harbour. It was the 15th of October 1915.

It took the *Prospero* more than a week to make the run to Lewisporte. After leaving St. Anthony, it ran into bad weather and had to stay anchored in Harbour Deep, a fishing and logging community on the east coast of the Northern Peninsula, for four days.

Freddy was having the time of his life aboard the coastal boat. Dr. Grenfell had a movie projector and showed several films while the ship was storm-bound at Harbour Deep. The films were shown in the Anglican Church and everyone in the community came to see them. Grenfell also had lantern slides that he showed aboard the ship to the passengers and crew.

Lewisporte was a very busy place. A town in central Newfoundland situated in a bay close to the mouth of the Exploits River, Lewisporte was the center of operations for all freight going north. Arriving trains were filled with passengers and freight to be distributed along the east coast and the Northern Peninsula. Freddy watched as a train pulled into the station not far from the dock and thought it was obvious there was a war on because soldiers and sailors were everywhere.

Dr. Grenfell was a celebrity. He had established a hospital not far away, on Pilley's Island, and the staff was there to meet him. Freddy could only follow along and take it all in. Grenfell had a short meeting with the hospital staff and then quickly boarded the waiting train. Whenever anyone shook hands with him and his wife, he would introduce them to Freddy and they would shake hands with him as well. He felt like a young Labrador Ambassador. It was quite an experience for the Labrador native and served to boost his confidence.

On the train, Dr. Grenfell and his wife had a suite next to the dining room. Freddy was placed in the day coach, which was filled with other army recruits and soldiers and sailors. When the troops discovered Freddy was from the North Coast of Labrador they were all interested in finding out what it was like to live there. Freddy wasn't shy in telling them about the country and the people.

"We eat all raw meat and blubber and sleep out in the open when the weather gets cold," he said with a grin. He had everyone's attention as he continued. "We also shoot everything that moves with just one shot. We don't get a second chance and we make sure it's dead."

One of the recruits asked Freddy which part of the forces he was joining, the army or navy.

"I am not joining either," he said, and when they looked surprised he added, "I am going to war as a bodyguard for Dr. Grenfell." They all laughed. This Freddy Frieda had a great sense of humour and they were enjoying his company.

Before the train arrived in St. John's the next morning, Dr. Grenfell sent a steward to get Freddy. He wanted to talk to him before saying goodbye.

"Freddy, I guess this is where we part," he said. "You'll be going into training and I am going to tell the adjutant in charge of training about your ability to speak German. There's no doubt he will be in contact with you personally."

"When will you be going across the Atlantic, Doctor?" Freddy asked.

"On the first ship going that way, I expect," he replied.

"Will I see you again before you go?"

"You may not, but all you have to do is remember what I told you after we left Hopedale. Do what you are told, work hard, and keep your mouth shut. If you do all of that, you'll get through okay."

"I'll never forget it, Dr. Grenfell."

When they arrived at the station in St. John's, they all said goodbye. Freddy hugged Mrs. Grenfell and shook hands with the Northern Doctor as they departed.

****

Training was grueling at the boot camp set up in Pleasantville, an area in the east end of St. John's next to Quidi Vidi Lake. There were a hundred and forty five recruits and they were broken up into five platoons. Freddy was in "C" (Charley) platoon. After two weeks of hard training the instructors introduced the recruits to the weapons they would be using as a fighting group. Freddy was no stranger to a rifle. He had been using one since he was a boy and he was immediately made a marksman. His greatest problem was learning how to wear a uniform properly and how to salute. Freddy got along well with the men of his platoon. Most were fishermen or sons of fishermen, and when they discovered he could speak German it made him a celebrity with them. Even the instructors were impressed.

One day, after a month's training, the platoon lieutenant sent for Freddy and told him that he would be going overseas immediately to train for a special assignment.

He said Freddy's keen interest in training and his ability to get along with other men had been observed, and that, along with his ability to speak German, made him ideal for the reconnaissance section.

The lieutenant said Freddy couldn't receive training in St. John's for his upcoming assignment. He would have to go to England to take the necessary training.

Freddy asked the lieutenant if he had any idea when he would be leaving.

"No," he answered. "But as of today you have finished your training here. In fact, you will be promoted from a recruit to a private soldier. We don't usually do that without a promotional ceremony, but none of the other men will know about our meeting and what we've discussed is top secret. You will tell the men of your platoon you are going back to Labrador on an urgent matter. Have your gear packed and be ready to go at six tomorrow morning. Remember, no one knows about this, not even the platoon sergeant, so carry on as usual. The sergeant major will give you special orders later today, so go back to the barracks and wait there."

Freddy saluted the lieutenant and marched to the barracks. He arrived shortly ahead of the men of his platoon who were coming for lunch. They had been surprised when Freddy was told he had to see the platoon lieutenant. They knew it had to be something important to be called to see him.

Freddy told everyone he was going back to Labrador on an urgent matter and would be gone for a week or two.

No one believed him, but they asked no more questions.

When the men left for lunch, Freddy quickly packed his kit-bag and in half an hour he was ready to roll.

While he was waiting he decided to write Emily.

He told her about his training in St. John's and how much he liked it. "I think I could run all the way back to St Anthony without stopping. All of us here are in excellent shape," he wrote. He said he loved her very much and he asked her to tell her father he would like a job with him as herdsmen for the reindeer when the war was over.

At 2 p.m. the lieutenant and the sergeant major came to the barracks with further instructions. Freddy stood up and saluted when they entered.

"Are you ready to go, Private Frieda?" the sergeant major asked.

"Yes, sir. I'm all packed. I've even had time to write my girlfriend."

"You have just written your girlfriend. Where is the letter?" asked the lieutenant. His voice was sharp and suspicious.

"Right here, sir," Freddy said, taking the letter from his inside pocket.

The lieutenant read the letter and then grinned.

He was pleased with what Freddy had written and realized the young man could keep a secret.

He passed the letter back to Freddy and said the sergeant major would mail it for him.

The lieutenant then asked the sergeant major to step outside saying he wanted to give Private Frieda a few instructions, top secret stuff.

"You'll be going aboard a ship tonight after dark, dressed as a civilian," he told Freddy when they were alone. "On board, you'll work as a steward and a janitor. You'll be instructed by the captain what you'll have to do and where you'll have to go when you arrive in England. Don't let anyone aboard the ship know you can speak German, not even the captain." He paused and then added, 'No one on this side of the Atlantic knows where you'll be going or what you'll be doing, not even me."

****

At 4:30 p.m. when the recruits arrived back at the barracks Freddy's bunk was empty and he was nowhere to be found. Freddy had been taken to a clothing store on Water Street and changed from his uniform into civilian clothes which he purchased there. The bill was paid by the sergeant major. Freddy was then taken to the *S.S. Florizel*, which was loading for England. On board, no one had any idea he was in the military.

The trip across the Atlantic took three weeks in rough seas. Freddy was a hard worker and got along fine with everyone aboard. After the *Florizel* entered the Irish Sea it was met by an escort of three naval cruisers. The ship was boarded and searched at gunpoint. Freddy didn't know what to think of this action, however he realized a war was raging and suspicion was the order of the day.

The ship was escorted to the city of Douglas on the Isle of Man. Freddy disembarked there and was taken to King William's College near Castletown. This is where he would receive his training as a spy for the British Army.

Freddy realized full well what he was getting himself into. He was being trained to go behind enemy lines and tap into German intelligence activities somewhere in Belgium or France. The training activities and identities of all involved were classified as top secret. The men were told not to make friends with anyone outside of their group. The news of the war was not good and there were fears Britain would be invaded, especially after the Germans went into France.

During his training, Freddy received several letters from Emily. She told him how much she loved him and missed him and couldn't wait for him to return. "I will never love anyone else but you," she signed her letter, "Yours forever, Emily."

CHAPTER 7
Isle of Man

Training on the Isle of Man was wet and cold, and that was especially true at night. Freddy and his fellow troops usually did four man patrols in the night and in complete silence as they went cross country. They were surrounded by trip wires with flares attached, and sentries using blank ammunition were posted at certain points. Every second day they ran to Douglas and back, a distance of more than twenty miles, in full battle gear. Freddy soon became an expert in cross country maneuvers. His job was to get the patrol safely from point A to point B. Maps became his specialty. He only had to look at a map once and get the lay of the land and after that he could travel anywhere. He was also blessed with a photographic memory.

During training, he met a young soldier from western Newfoundland named Peter Benoit, from the Port au Port area. Benoit knew telegraphy and was an authority when it came to maps and compasses. He was also a demolitions expert and spoke both French and English.

He had been transferred from the Royal Navy to the Newfoundland Regiment to train as a spy. Benoit was open about his dislike for the Navy. "I am a land man, spent all my life in the woods. The rolling ocean was only made for whales and sharks, not for the likes of me who comes from Port au Port," he said to anyone who would listen. Then he would start singing a French song about the way of life around the Port au Port Peninsula.

Benoit possessed great skills. The men in the barracks called him The Ghost because he could hide in places where not even a tom-cat would look. He was able to make himself invisible almost anywhere. He was also quite a ladies' man. None of the women he came in contact with turned him down. They all loved him.

Benoit was assigned as part of Freddy's five man team. The captain said his ability to speak French was very important due to the work they would be doing with the French underground. Two other members of the team were Dutchmen from the London area. Franz Arink and Anton van der Welle were both engineers and they looked so much alike with their blond hair and blue eyes that Freddy had difficulty telling them apart. The last member of the team was an Irishman. Sean Mahon, known to everyone simply as Irish, was a wireless operator.

The five man team received orders to move out. They had fifteen minutes warning to pack and be on the move in the dead of night. Freddy had everything he owned in a duffle bag, including his Newfoundland Regiment uniform. He was told to hold on to it and be ready to use it. The men were driven to the north end of the Isle of Man to the town of Ramsey, a distance of twenty-three miles, over a bumpy dusty road. Ramsey was a farming town where raising sheep and horses was the main industry and the stench of horse manure filled the air.

****

When they arrived in Ramsey it was after dark. They were put in a cattle shed and told to wait for further orders. The captain who had driven them to Ramsey informed them they would not be going back to Castletown and then left them. It was the last time they saw him. Approximately an hour after they arrived at the shed they heard a noise outside.

"Someone is coming," Freddy whispered. The door opened and a man entered, he had a long white beard and wore glasses. "Three of you men come with me. They don't want the five of you traveling together. It might look suspicious," he said with a Scottish accent. Benoit and Freddy stayed in the barn, the others quickly left.

It was cold in the barn.

During the night Benoit and Freddy wrapped themselves up in whatever they could find to try and keep warm. As dawn approached, they heard someone coming. Freddy had been peeking through a crack in the wall, watching the barnyard and the house for the last hour. Benoit was sitting up, having slept covered in an old horse blanket that stank to high heavens. It was freezing cold. The person approaching was whistling an old Irish tune that the two men recognized.

The door squeaked open as the person came inside.

"Good morning, sheep," came a woman's voice that sounded Irish. The sheep had started baaing the minute the door opened. The two horses also started to make a noise. The animals knew breakfast was coming. The two soldiers were silent. After the hay was fed to the animals the voice said, "Gentlemen, I don't know where you are hiding, but you can come to the house as soon as I leave." Freddy and Benoit didn't say a word as the person left the barn.

"I suppose this is our contact, but the captain didn't say it would be a woman. What do you think?" Freddy whispered to Benoit.

"She knows we are here. It must be part of the plan," said Benoit.

They grabbed their kit bags and ran to the house, trying not to be seen. They stepped into the dark porch and Benoit fumbled around looking for the doorknob, but found none.

"There must be a latch, look for a string, should be on the side," said Freddy, thinking that is what he was used to back home in Hopedale.

"Got it," said Benoit as he pulled down on the string, lifting the latch inside.

The door swung open into a room containing a man and woman. The smell of toast was in the air. The man asked Freddy where he was from. When he did not answer, he asked Benoit the same question.

"I'm from Quebec, Canada," said Benoit with a heavy French accent.

The man spoke a little French, enough to say good morning. "Can your friend speak English?" he asked. Benoit said Freddy was from Norway and couldn't speak any English. The man and woman both grinned.

"Don't worry. You can trust us," said the man. "I am a member of the 2nd battalion Royal Scots Fusiliers, part of the 28th Brigade. I'm Major Ian Bundy, Head of Intelligence for the Irish Sea area. And this lady who was just out feeding the animals is my assistant,

Lieutenant Grace. She's a nurse at the Royal Southern Hospital in Liverpool. She's been here for a couple of days and is now on her way back."

Benoit saluted. Freddy pretended he didn't understand the conversation. However, the major wasn't stupid. He gestured towards Freddy as he said, "You're Frederick Frieda of the Newfoundland Regiment. You're from Hopedale, Labrador, and you're age nineteen, almost twenty. Would you like me to tell you more about yourself?"

Freddy realized the major was someone connected with what they were doing and he saluted him. Benoit spoke quietly to Major Bundy, "Sir, I'm disappointed because we should be operating with a password," he said. "Because you know a great deal about us doesn't give us the assurance you are part of our operation. We have to have something more than a handshake and an introduction."

Major Bundy moved the kitchen table and pulled back the floor mat underneath, revealing a small hatch. He lifted the hatch and brought up a strongbox about a foot square. He unlocked the box, removed two envelopes, and gave one to each man.

"Your instructions are in the envelopes," he said. "I have not seen what's in them but we will deliver you to the boat as soon as it gets dark tonight. After that, you will likely never see us again."

Lieutenant Grace left the kitchen and went upstairs. Moments later, they heard the dots and dashes of a wireless set. Benoit paused for a moment and listened, he knew Morse code.

"You got the message, Benoit?" asked the major.

"Yes, sir," replied Benoit. "What about the weather?"

"Yes, I'm glad you mentioned that. This operation depends on the weather, of course. There's not much more I can tell you only wish you luck. After you have breakfast you can go upstairs and rest. Make sure you stay away from the windows. Study your instructions, then burn them after you memorize what's in them. That's all I have to say." Major Bundy said nothing more as he put on his coat and left. As he went out the door he really looked like an old farmer.

****

Lieutenant Grace came downstairs and sat on a chair next to the stove. She was probably no more than twenty-five but looked older because of the way she was dressed. Freddy paid particular notice to Benoit and saw that he had his eye on her.

"If we are going to stay here all day and part of the night, we should bring in more wood for the stove, don't you think so, Lieutenant Grace?" he said as soon she sat down.

"Yes, we should," she answered, looking at Benoit with a grin on her face. "We certainly do have to keep the fire going."

"We should probably get the wood now." Benoit smiled as he spoke.

Lieutenant Grace stood up and smoothed her skirt over her hips. "Let's you and I go get the wood," she said. "I will show you where it's stored."

Freddy watched as the two of them left for the barn. It took them an hour to get the first load of wood.

While they were gone Freddy made breakfast. He fried up the eggs and bacon that had been left on the table next to a loaf of bread that he cut in slices and also boiled the kettle to make tea.

He wanted to make a comment when Benoit and Lieutenant Grace returned, but he was afraid the lieutenant might take offence. After breakfast, the two men went upstairs and settled in for the day with the window covered. Lieutenant Grace went to the small bedroom off the kitchen and shut the door.

"What message did you pick up from the wireless?" Freddy asked Benoit.

"It was a message for us from the captain who dropped us at the barn. It said that we will be picked up by a fishing boat sometime after dark tonight and taken to an unknown destination, provided the weather is okay. Our password is number three."

The men opened the envelopes Major Bundy had given them. They found passwords they were to use for the next eight days. The envelopes also contained English currency.

Freddy fell asleep and didn't wake until late in the afternoon. He noticed right away that Benoit had a guilty look. The house was cold and it seemed they were alone. Freddy suggested Benoit go downstairs and take a look around. Benoit crept down the squeaky stairs. He found the fire in the kitchen stove was almost gone. He looked in the small bedroom next to the kitchen where he had spent half the afternoon with Lieutenant Grace and saw the bed was empty. She must have left in a hurry, he thought, although she'd said she was going to stay until dark. Benoit searched the house and found no one around. He shouted to Freddy to come down. He said they might as well stoke the fire and get the kettle on.

When Freddy came downstairs he didn't say anything, but he had heard the goings on between Benoit and the lieutenant earlier. He'd also heard Lieutenant Grace leaving about twenty minutes earlier. But none of that was his concern. Freddy looked around the kitchen. There was a loaf of bread on the table and a block of butter next to it. It was not much of a meal, but it would have to do.

"If we only had a salt dried codfish boiled, wouldn't it be something?" Freddy licked his lips.

"Don't go talking about anything back home, especially dried cod, or I may go AWOL," said Benoit, and the two men laughed.

"You know what we should do? We should go out and butcher one of the sheep. I hear sheep taste like caribou," said Freddy.

"It tastes something like it," said Benoit. "I've eaten caribou but I was reared on mutton. The Port au Port Peninsula is alive with sheep."

"I've never eaten sheep, but I think I'd rather have seal. There's lots of fat on seal meat, don't even need it cooked," said Freddy.

"It's a bit too early to talk about raw seal meat," said Benoit. "Let's just put some bread on the stove and have hot buttered toast and tea."

Not long after they finished eating, a blizzard came on. Shortly afterwards, a horse and wagon pulled up and a person got out carrying a bag. Freddy opened the door and Lieutenant Grace came in. She passed him the bag as she waved goodbye to the driver of the wagon.

"The boat you were supposed to leave on arrived an hour ago, but due to the storm it is delayed for twenty-four hours," she said as she took off her coat and unpacked the bag. "I have a few groceries here, enough to last us till tomorrow evening. There's cheese and ham and fresh bread. You can help yourself to it."

"Will you be traveling with us on the boat?" Freddy asked her.

"I'm not sure yet. We'll have to see what happens," she said.

"If we stay here tonight, I should move my cot downstairs so that I can keep the fire going. That's better than tramping up and down those noisy stairs and keeping everyone awake," said Benoit.

Without looking up, Lieutenant Grace nodded in agreement.

Not much happened during the night except that the fire in the stove went out around midnight due to Benoit's neglect.

At daylight, Freddy got up and dressed and went downstairs. After lighting a candle, he restarted the fire and put the kettle on the stove. Benoit, who had been in the bedroom with Lieutenant Grace, immediately came into the kitchen with his pants in his hand and whispered to Freddy to be quiet. Freddy said the storm was over and maybe they would be moving. He said they should have an early breakfast and be ready to go. Benoit went upstairs to get the rest of his things.

When Lieutenant Grace appeared, Freddy noticed the wedding ring on her finger and Benoit's beard marks on her face.

"Good morning, Lieutenant Grace," he said brightly. "It looks like the storm is over."

She turned toward him with eyes blazing. "What does that mean, Private Frieda?" she blurted, thinking he was making a wisecrack.

Benoit heard her as he came through the door.

"The snow and the wind have stopped. The storm is over," he said to her. She told Benoit afterwards she thought Freddy was poking fun at her appearance after spending all night in bed with him.

Just as the three of them finished eating breakfast, they heard the sound of a horse and wagon arriving at the door. The driver burst in and informed them the boat was sailing within the hour. Freddy and Benoit had their bags packed and ready.

As Freddy went out the door into the porch, he saw the shadow of the two lovers embracing and he heard Lieutenant Grace say to Benoit, "I'll see you tomorrow night in Liverpool. I'll arrange for you and me to be together. Just keep your mouth shut and your friend under control."

"Don't worry about Freddy, he won't talk to anyone," Benoit assured her as he waved goodbye. He and Freddy climbed into the wagon and the driver covered them with straw. They were now simply freight to go across the Irish Sea.

CHAPTER 8
To Kent

The two soldiers went aboard the fishing boat as part of the crew. It took two days to get to Liverpool. Benoit pretended he was seasick. This was part of the plan, an excuse to leave the boat upon arrival in Liverpool. After the boat docked, a man came aboard asking if anyone needed a taxi. Benoit told him he would as soon as he told the captain he was not going to stay on the boat due to seasickness. And Freddy wasn't going to stay if his buddy left. The two retrieved their bags and went ashore.

Once they got in the taxi, the driver gave them the password and informed them they would be going to Sheffield, a city in Yorkshire approximately an hour's drive away. This was not good news for Benoit. He had his heart set on spending the night in Liverpool with Lieutenant Grace. Freddy noticed his glum face but said nothing. He didn't want his buddy to see him smiling. As they drove through the countryside, Benoit asked the driver if he had any news of the war.

"There's lots of war news," said the driver. "It appears the Germans are going to take over the world. And things on the Western Front are not very good."

"How close are the Germans to the English Channel?" asked Benoit.

"They are getting close," said the driver. "The cities along the west coast of France have all been captured, thousands of civilians have been killed, and the war in the Mediterranean Sea is not going very well for the Allies. You'll be briefed on the latest battle-fronts when we arrive at the base."

"Have you heard any news about the Newfoundland Regiment?" asked Freddy.

"Reports have been circulating that they are returning from Gallipoli in order to go to the Western Front. It looks like most of the fire power will be centered around France and Belgium. Air power is becoming the main thing now," said the driver.

"Are you in the military yourself?" asked Benoit.

"Yes, I'm a sergeant in the service corps," replied the driver.

It was midnight when the taxi reached Sheffield. At times, it had looked like they wouldn't make it because of drifting snow and high winds. They arrived at the depot and signed in. After they were assigned their room and settled away, they met up with the three other members of their team. They saw that Irish had a black eye.

"What happened to you, Irish? Did a horse kick you?" asked Freddy.

One of the Dutchmen spoke up, "Irish was lucky he didn't get killed. He fell down a flight of stairs on board the boat."

The other Dutchman laughed. "He was drunk, met up with a passenger, you know, one of them with long hair. She gave him the booze. I knew what was going to happen but he wouldn't listen. But when she struck him he had a different tune afterwards."

Freddy and Benoit laughed. "Nothing like that went on where we were, I mean no black eyes, although early this morning I thought I was going to have to call an ambulance," said Freddy with a laugh.

"What happened, tell us what happened?" demanded the Dutchmen.

"If you make one squawk, Freddy Frieda, war will break out right here," said Benoit, shaking a clenched fist.

"Don't worry, Benoit, a deal is a deal," said Freddy. "My lips are sealed."

****

At 6:30 in the morning, the five soldiers were sitting at the table in the kitchen dressed in their uniforms. At seven, they were back in their rooms after a hearty breakfast and wondering where they were going to go next. At 7:30, a runner came to get them. He told them to follow him in single file, which they did, all the way to a large stone building not far away. They marched through the door and halted inside.

"You men stay here for a few minutes while I check with the sergeant major," said the runner, adding sarcastically, "If an officer comes by, for God's sake salute him, if you know how."

While they were waiting, an officer came down the hallway. Freddy called the men to attention and saluted.

"Are you men waiting to see me?" asked the officer.

"We are not sure, sir," Freddy replied.

"Are you the group who came from the Isle of Man last night?" he asked. Freddy nodded yes. "Then you are the men I want to see. Come to my office." After they were inside, the officer introduced himself. "I'm Colonel Stick, head of intelligence for the Newfoundland Regiment. Good to see you." The men saluted him again. "I want you men to relax. Shut the door and make yourself at home," Stick said as he filled his pipe. Turning his chair, he opened a metal safe and took out what looked like a cash box. He unlocked the box and retrieved a brown envelope marked 'Classified.' After he opened it, he placed the document inside on the table.

He ignored the document as he looked at each of the men. "That's quite a shiner you've got there," he said to Irish. "I bet it was very slippery getting around that vessel you were on in the rough seas."

"Yes sir, it was. But in this case it was an elbow that got me. My opponent should have been disqualified," grinned the Irishman.

"You'll know better the next time," laughed Colonel Stick. And then he stopped and again looked intently at each of the men. "How well do you men know each other?" he asked. "Are you familiar with each other's background?"

Benoit was the first to speak. "I know something about Freddy, where he's from, his age, the language he speaks and his abilities. As for the other three, I don't know much about any of them," he said. The others agreed they knew very little about each other.

"One of the first assignments I am going to give you is to live together, eat together and tell each other everything you know about yourselves from the time you were ten years old. I will give you two days to accomplish that. And keep in mind that you are not to leave the base unless ordered to do so," said Colonel Stick.

The five men stood and saluted as they prepared to leave. "Just a minute. I have another envelope to open," Stick said, slitting the envelope with a knife and taking out a sheet of paper. He glanced through it for a moment then said to Freddy and Benoit, "Your outfit, the Newfoundland Regiment, is returning from the Mediterranean. They will be going directly to the Western Front. This, of course, is classified information and you are sworn to secrecy."

****

Over the next two days, the five men had a very interesting time as they got to know as much as they could about each other. They talked a lot, but a lot of secrets were not revealed, especially about their private lives. When the two days were over the men had a deeper respect for each other, they felt as though they were part of a family. Late on the afternoon of the second day, the runner came and told them to report to Colonel Stick at 7 p.m.

When they arrived in his office, Colonel Stick was sitting at his desk flanked by two other officers. A large map was on the desk and it was obvious they had been studying it. One of the officers was wearing the uniform of the Newfoundland Regiment.

"I'm Captain Alex O'Brien," he said as he smiled and came over to shake hands with the five new arrivals. He paused when he came to Freddy. "When I saw Frederick Frieda's name on the list, I asked where he was from," he said. "I was happy to find he was from Hopedale, Labrador. I fished with my father at Indian Tickle, Labrador, and it made me think of home."

Colonel Stick cut short the social talk.

"Gentleman, you are about to go into action," he said abruptly. "Captain O'Brien will outline the details of what you are supposed to do."

O'Brien didn't seem bothered by the colonel's brusque as he continued speaking pleasantly.

"The five of you men are a team, and each member is a key in the puzzle that's planned," he said. "The two Dutchmen, Franz Arink and Anton van der Welle, are trained in railway repairs. Benoit speaks French and is a wireless operator. They also say he can be as slippery as an eel and he is a well known ladies' man."

O'Brien laughed.

"Irish is a wireless operator too and he is also as good as any medic when it comes to first aid. Oh, and Irish has another great qualification. They say he can pick the pockets of the King of England right in his own home."

Colonel Stick scowled and felt in his back pocket for his wallet. They all laughed.

"I wouldn't be that foolish, sir," the Irishman said with a grin.

"And Freddy," O'Brien continued, "can speak German fluently. I doubt if he will ever have to use his native language in France, although Dr. Wilfred Grenfell told the War Office if we sent messages in Inuktitut they would never be decoded by the Germans. Freddy is also a sharpshooter and is known to be able to withstand very cold temperatures." O'Brien paused. "You'll be leaving by train within the hour for the port of Folkestone, on the English Channel. You'll change to civvies when you get back to the barracks. Your uniforms will be stored in a locker in Folkestone before you board the vessel for Antwerp. You will be going as a rail and bridge repair crew. The Belgians have agreed to supply you with all necessary papers. You will get them when you arrive in Antwerp."

Colonel Stick opened the safe and took out an envelope. He opened it and passed the paper inside to O'Brien who scanned through the orders for a few minutes then said, "You will contact the underground movement at Antwerp. We'll give you their location and contacts and you'll get your orders from them. We don't know what they have planned. They will set you up with everything you need to get your messages through to headquarters here in London. If you don't get the wireless equipment, I suppose that is where the Irishman comes in. He'll have to steal what's needed."

The Irishman grinned and nodded.

O'Brien continued, "As we speak, the German Army and the French forces are in a fierce battle around the city of Verdun, which is more than two hundred miles from the English Channel. If the Germans break through there they will have free-wheeling all the way to the English Channel. Most of the railway lines and bridges east of Verdun have been blown up by the underground. The German authorities are anxious to get the infrastructure repaired in order to get their heavy artillery pieces to the Western Front. The Belgian government that is under German control promised to send experts to oversee the repairs. That is where you men come in. You'll go in as repair men under the supervision of the German Army."

The captain and Colonel Stick exchanged glances and then Captain O'Brien resumed talking.

"There is something else we want you to do as well," he said. "We want you to keep a sharp eye out for anything you think may be of particular interest to our side. And that includes watching out for cylinders of gas in particular. We want to know if the Germans are stockpiling cylinders of poison gas anywhere. We are very concerned with the effect of poison gas on our troops, and we greatly fear another poison gas attack. I don't know if you men are aware of it but the first time the Germans used poison gas on a large scale on the Western Front was on April 22 in Ypres. The Germans released more than 150 tons of chlorine gas and approximately 6,000 French and Colonial troops died within ten minutes as a result. Men were blinded or died from asphyxiation. It was absolutely devastating. We don't want something like that to happen again, so we are hoping your sharp eyes will be able to detect anything at all suspicious and let us know immediately."

Captain O'Brien paused for a minute and looked at his watch.

"Benoit," he said then, "you are aware of the code we will be using each day, keep your dates and passwords straight and for God's sake don't give any secrets away." O'Brien took a small piece of paper from his shirt pocket. "Your code name will be, and don't forget this, 'Flat Land.'" After saying this, he lit a match and burned the piece of paper. (Note: Captain O'Brien was wounded at Mericourt L'Abbe, France, in 1916 and died six days later).

"One last piece of advice, men, before you depart," said Colonel Stick. "If you get captured by the Germans, you only have to give your name, rank and serial number, nothing more. Men, I wish you luck."

****

The train roared through the night, blowing its whistle every few minutes, and stopping at assigned stations for passengers who were mostly servicemen. Freddy and his team sat not far from each other. They were very poorly dressed. They looked like local labourers on their way to work. When the train arrived in London, they had a three hour stopover. They used some of their English money to buy a sandwich and a cup of tea in the station. After a wait that seemed endless, they were notified that their train was leaving for Kent. It was now noon. Security was very tight. Guards were everywhere, especially as they got close to the Channel Coast. The train stopped often but no one got on or off. Finally, the conductor announced they were in Folkestone.

CHAPTER 9
Getting orders

Folkestone, Kent, was a small town but a busy one. The waterfront was alive with people and almost every make of ship and small craft you could mention. During the First World War, the town was the main embarkation point for soldiers leaving to fight in the trenches of France and Belgium. Throughout the war years, ten million men passed through Folkestone either on their way to the Western Front or returning after leave.

The five men walked into the dirty noisy station.

Benoit knew what he was looking for: an elderly man with one leg sitting at a table in the canteen and reading a newspaper. Telling the others to wait, Benoit went into the canteen. He immediately spotted a man with one leg sitting at a table drinking coffee or tea and with a newspaper in front of him. He approached the man and whispered the password. The man responded without even looking up.

Benoit went to the counter and pretended he wanted to buy something by getting in the lineup. When he saw the man leaving he followed him. The other four tagged along at a safe distance. The five of them followed the man out of the station and onto the street. They saw him head for a small shop with a sign that said 'Needleworks.'

The man disappeared inside the shop with Benoit close behind him. The Irishman went in next followed by the two Dutchmen. Freddy was the last to go inside.

They followed the man to the back of the building and up a flight of stairs. When they entered a room at the top of the stairs they were surprised to see two British Army officers sitting at a table. One looked to be in his forties, the other was about sixty. As they spoke their Scottish accents were evident.

There was no saluting, no yes sir or no sir. The two officers held up their hands and said hello. They told the five arrivals to take a seat as their contact person left the room. The older officer introduced himself as Captain Bob Riley. He said to call him Bob. The other officer said to call him George.

"Very good then," said Captain Bob. "We shall start our meeting. George, lock the door before we begin. Men, it looks as though this will be a good night to cross the Channel. We're going to have wind and rain, visibility will be zero."

Captain Bob spread a large map on the table. "Gather around, men. You're going to have to remember a few details, especially concerning distances. When you leave here you'll become fishermen. We have a boat at the dock half loaded with fish all ready for you. When you leave you'll be heading to Antwerp. Right here." He pointed on the map to the city of Antwerp, Belgium.

"The boat you'll be on is a navy vessel but you won't recognize it by its appearance and crew. Remember, everyone aboard is a fisherman including you. When you get to Antwerp you'll receive another ID from the Belgium government, or one that will look like it's from the Belgium government. You will also have papers issued by the German Army giving you authorization to travel through France to oversee repairs on railway crossings between Dendermonde, Belgium, and the city of Lille, France. The German Army has all of that area captured.

"At Antwerp, you'll be transferred to a smaller boat and travel inland for close to twelve miles. When you leave the boat you'll have another six miles to get to Dendermonde. There's fighting going on there now between the French and the Germans and it's a dangerous place. The German Army is trying to get its heavy artillery brought in. The roads have almost been destroyed by the underground and the Germans figure it's better to repair the railway than the roads. And that is precisely why you fellows are going there, to oversee repairs. When you get to Dendermonde keep in mind that the place will be swarming with German troops. One wrong move and the Germans will capture you."

George spoke up then.

He told them he was an information officer.

"I'm the person you have to contact with the information you gather," he said. "You realize, of course, it's not going to be easy trying to get information about the strength of the German Army in this area here," he circled an area on the map, "and relaying it back to our headquarters in London. Any questions so far, gentlemen?"

"Yes sir," said Benoit.

"Go ahead with your question," said George.

"Where will we get a wireless set to send messages? Will we have our own equipment?"

"Good question. The French and Belgium underground will have those items hidden somewhere. They'll let you know where they are located, and they will have a code book for you."

"I don't know if you have heard any war news within the last day or so, but it doesn't look very good for the French Army," said Captain Bob. "They are taking an awful beating around the city of Verdun. If the British Army doesn't counter attack soon, the French Army will have to surrender or be wiped out. That is why you are going into the Dendermonde-Lille areas. The British counterattack is going to take place somewhere here," he indicated the area on the map.

George drew a large circle on the map between the city of Lille and the coast of the English Channel and to the west.

"This area here is known as the Somme," he said. "If we can push the Germans further to the west their heavy artillery won't be able to strike us from across the Channel. If they reach the French coast near Dunkirk, they will be right on our doorstep. The Newfoundland Regiment will be occupying the area near Beaumont Hamel soon. We want you to report every night where the German front lines are, and all the details you can get about their strength, especially around the Beaumont Hamel area."

One of the Dutchmen asked Captain Bob if there was an alternative route if the river west of Antwerp was frozen over and the smaller boat could not be used.

"Yes, we have discussed that possibility," Captain Bob answered. "And if that should be the case you will be taken overland as far as

Dendermonde, where most of the bridges are out. However, you will not remain there; you will go on to the city of Lille. That's the area where we require all the information we can get about the Germans, the location of their front line on a daily basis and their strength. We know only one of you can speak German but that shouldn't be a problem. Freddy will be able to communicate with the Germans. He will be the key person in this operation."

"When you arrive in the city of Lille you may have to link up with the underground. If you find out the Germans suspect anything, get out of there as fast as you can," said George.

Captain Bob folded the map and said, "Gentlemen, we can only wish you luck. In a few minutes the padre will come to see you. It's routine when we send out fellows like you. Sometimes the men want to give him messages for loved ones back home."

Bob and George shook hands with each of the men before leaving the room. When they were gone, Freddy began to laugh. Irish asked him what he was laughing about.

"You know, Irish," he said, "this assignment is pretty near as dangerous as rowing out to the Turnivik Islands with a load of salmon nets aboard through pack ice in the spring of the year."

Irish was in no mood for joking. His life was on the line.

CHAPTER 10
Antwerp

The boat carrying the spies spent two days battling the North Sea.

They were told by the captain of the vessel to tell whoever checked them they were fishing on Thornton Banks for a company in Antwerp. After arriving at the entrance of the bay near Vlissingen they were stopped by security patrols. These were German patrol boats flying the Dutch flag.

The two Dutchmen and the captain convinced the patrols they were fishermen and they were allowed beyond the submarine nets that were in place across the bay.

After being thoroughly searched, they were given clearance to proceed all the way to Antwerp under escort.

The city of Antwerp is about forty miles inland from the North Sea. The city lies on the banks of the River Scheldt, which was frozen over except for a channel that was being kept open by ice breakers patrolling the area. As they got closer to Antwerp they saw columns of smoke billowing up, a sign of fighting on the Western Front.

After dark, everyone got off the boat and they were taken by truck to a house in the countryside. One of the Dutchmen said they would be saying there all night as a snowstorm was brewing and roads might get blocked. He said they would likely have to continue overland. One of the crew from the boat prepared dinner, a tasty meal of meat and potatoes with black bread.

Shortly before midnight, the men were awakened by hard knocking on the door and someone calling in German to open up. Freddy got up off the floor where he was sleeping and opened the door.

Two German soldiers stood outside.

Freddy asked them to come in.

One soldier asked Freddy what he and the others were doing.

"We are fishermen, came into port late this evening. This is a company house and we were provided with accommodations for the night while our fish is being unloaded. We have all our papers," Freddy told him.

The soldier asked to see everyone's papers and after checking them out and looking especially carefully at Freddy's documents he asked him to go into the next room.

Freddy did as he was told.

When they were out of hearing of the other men the soldier spoke part of the password for that day. Freddy quickly gave the other half of the password.

The soldier shook his hand and said he and the other soldier with him were part of the French underground. He said he was Rene and the other man was Henri. He said Freddy and his four comrades would be leaving with them immediately. They had to get through to Lille as soon as possible, before snow blocked the road.

Rene said the boat crew would be told that Freddy and his men were being arrested. The crew would then be put in another room and Freddy and the others would change into German uniforms the men from the underground had brought with them.

When he and the others were dressed in the German uniforms, Freddy held up his hand in a mock salute and Henri said, "Hail to the Kaiser," then spat on the floor.

"We'll explain what we are doing as we drive along," Rene said, then asked, "Do any of the other four speak any German at all?"

"Not a word," said Freddy, as he and the others climbed into the two waiting trucks. Immediately, the five man team and their two French escorts were on their way.

CHAPTER 11

The underground

The streets of Antwerp were deserted and dark as the trucks proceeded along the main thoroughfare. Benoit kept saying how impressed he was to be driving in a truck instead of being pulled along in a wagon by a mule. Things were quiet as they drove except for the German checkpoints which everyone leaving or entering the city had to go through. The trucks were waved through when the sentries caught sight of the men inside wearing German uniforms. After the two vehicles got outside Antwerp the weather improved. There wasn't as much wind.

A few miles before they got to Dendermonde they encountered a lot of German vehicles. Apparently there was a skirmish not far from the road off to the right.

The German soldiers who checked them said the British had staged an attack on the main road not far from Lille. They had blown up the bridge and traffic was being diverted.

"We are a repair crew heading that way and we can check it out," said Freddy, speaking perfect German.

"That's good news, we wish you luck," said the German guard.

"You know, you speak better German than I do," said Rene, grinning as they drove away. Freddy didn't comment.

As dawn broke they arrived on the outskirts of Dendermonde.

German soldiers were everywhere, waving rifles and shouting.

Panic was in the air.

Freddy and Benoit were shocked to see the devastation of the city. Houses and building had been turned into rubble as far as they could see. It was the first time they had seen the real horrors of war. It seemed like every few minutes they heard a volley of gunfire as people ran for cover and sirens screamed. They finally reached the outskirts on the west side of the city.

"Are we on the right road to Lille? Have you seen any signs?" Rene asked Franz, who was familiar with the area.

"Yes, we are on the right road," said the Dutchman. "I have traveled over this road many times when things were civilized. When you get to the next intersection, take the road to your left and it should take you on through to Lille."

"What's the road like? Is it passable?" asked Rene.

"It was a very good road before the war," replied Franz. "I would say now the heavy war machinery has it rutted. But the snow may have the ruts filled up, giving us a chance."

Freddy asked Rene if they had any extra gas for the trucks. He said they had ten jerry cans full in the back and that should be enough to take the two vehicles all the way to Lille.

As they traveled further away from Dendermonde the road conditions weren't as bad. In places, they saw what looked like prisoners of war being shepherded along by German soldiers. After moving very slowly for about a mile, they were stopped by two German soldiers who demanded to know the names of everyone in thie truck and where they were going.

"We are heading to the city of Lille," said Rene. "I have a bridge repair crew aboard. We have been sent by the German High Command to help repair the bridges west of Lille."

One soldier looked at the identification on the front of the truck and called the other soldier to look at it. They had a discussion. The first soldier returned to Rene and said, "Beaver."

Freddy immediately recognized the password and answered back, "Neck." The soldier told them to take the road to the right, a couple of hundred yards further ahead.

He also spoke to Rene and said he had a message for him and his partner to immediately go back to Antwerp.

With a curt 'So long and good luck' the two of them left.

The Dutchmen volunteered to take over the driving. The two pseudo German soldiers climbed into the trucks, one in each vehicle, and directed the Dutchmen to a small village not far away.

****

The Dutchmen did as they were told and turned off to the right. Not long afterwards, the trucks arrived in a small farming village where they could barely get through the snow. They pulled up to a house that had shutters on the windows. Freddy saw smoke coming from the chimney. There were tracks around the house, most leading to a barn not far away.

One of the pseudo soldiers went to the door and knocked twice then gave the door a hard thump. It immediately opened and the soldier went in. It wasn't long before he came out and told the others to come inside.

On entering, Freddy could hear someone speaking in a language he did not understand. Someone asked him in German if he could speak French. He told him he couldn't, but he said another one of his group named Benoit could. There were close to twenty people in the dimly lit room.

Someone asked Benoit the password and when he answered correctly it was then the conversation started. The people in the room wanted to know what was happening with the war and who was winning. Were the French and British beating the Germans?

Benoit said he and the others with him had been on the move for five days with no communication with anyone. He said they didn't expect to be in contact with any of the Allies for a while due to their assignment.

"Maybe there's another group operating somewhere that you are supposed to contact," Benoit suggested. "We are heading to Lille to repair bridges west of the city. That's our orders."

"You won't be able to get past Lille. Every bridge is blown up, every railway is out of commission, the roads are in shambles and the city has been leveled. We came from there last evening," said one of the men.

A man sitting at the table in the corner held up his hand to get everyone's attention and then said, "How well are you men informed about the battle that's raging near the city of Verdun between the French troops and the German Army?"

"We haven't heard any war news for five days, we have been operating under cover, afraid to ask questions for fear of attracting attention from the Germans. Our objective is the area northwest of Lille and the Channel, which is Calais, Amiens and Beaumont Hamel," said Benoit.

After the group at the house were satisfied their visitors had no information to give them they offered them food and black coffee.

While they were eating, Benoit asked them where the German front line was and what was their strength. He also asked them if the Germans had heavy artillery in place and where.

The man sitting at the table told them the Germans were going to be heading for the French coast as soon as they flattened the French Army at Verdun. He said if the British didn't counter attack somewhere to the east very soon, it would be useless for them to try and land an army between Dunkirk and Normandy and be successful. He said even if they did land there they would have to go further to the west and encounter the German Army around the Somme.

"That would result in a slaughter for the British forces," he continued. "The Germans would be entrenched on high ground. They would also be too far away from the coast for firepower from the Navy to affect them. They would have everything to their advantage. That is why the British should land a strong force somewhere to the east and do a counter attack near the Belgium border. Doing that would weaken the German ability to fight a major battle around the Somme by spreading their forces on two fronts."

The man seemed to know what he was talking about. As he spoke, everyone listened. Benoit figured the man was in charge and he looked at him as he spoke.

"We have been given a job to do and we cannot jeopardize our plans or go off on some tangent with everyone who asks us for help," Benoit said. "We can't assist you with something we are not familiar with. Sorry."

The man at the table seemed as though he was turning things over in his mind. He was silent for a few minutes and then he said, "The German Army has their headquarters for the Western Front set up in Lille. They also have an interrogation officer there. We had a man escape from there a few days ago and he reported that after the Germans get the information they need from prisoners, the officer in charge shoots them in the head in front of everyone. I tell you this to make you aware that it's better to die fighting than to be captured."

The five man team said nothing, and nothing more was said to them as they prepared to leave. The people at the house wished them well as they departed.

CHAPTER 12
Behind the lines

As suddenly as they came, they were gone, back on the highway. Benoit rode in one truck with Freddy and Franz. Anton and Irish were in the second truck. While they drove, Freddy wondered if it was true about the killing of prisoners and if what the people in the house had said about the Somme was correct. If it was correct, maybe they should relay the information to the War Office in London. It could save a lot of lives. Freddy wondered how he could get the information to London. Maybe they could get access to a wireless transmitter in Lille.

"We know where the German front line is located, we also know about their heavy armour. What we don't know is the condition of the roads and the rail line west of Lille and how fast they can move. From what we've been told, the German Army intends to move west of Lille toward the fishing ports of Ault and Le-Treport," said Benoit.

"There's only one thing left for us to do as far as I'm concerned," said Freddy. "We have to try and contact London and relay the information we have been given."

"The sooner the better," agreed Benoit.

Franz said he thought he knew where they could get their hands on a wireless set in Lille.

As they drew closer to the city, the scene was one of utter confusion. German soldiers were everywhere. It was obvious the battlefront was not far away. The sound of explosions filled the air and smoke could be seen rising from every quarter of the city.

"What should we do? Do you think we could get through the center of the city, or would it be best to go around it?" Freddy asked Franz.

"I don't know," said the Dutchman.

"We can ask someone," said Benoit.

As they passed a group of German soldiers, Freddy motioned to one of them to come over to the truck.

"We are on our way to an area west of the city to start repairs on a couple of bridges," he said. "Is it possible to go through the city center or should we go around the city?"

"I think every street is blocked. And to get around the city you are going to need an escort," said the soldier. "It's very dangerous. You may find a way through on the west side, but the east side is close to the front line and the French Army is creating a lot of resistance. There are a lot of casualties on both sides." He paused for a minute. "Our army is pushing towards the Somme area. You fellows will be a welcome sight seeing you are going to repair some of the bridges. That's what is hanging everything up."

"Maybe we can go back and take the road going around the west side of the city. It may be a quicker route," said Freddy.

The guard nodded and saluted very smartly and then said, "Hail to the Kaiser."

Freddy saluted and said in a faint voice, "Hail to the Kaiser."

After the two vehicles had turned around, Freddy waved for the other truck to stop and then he got out in order to talk to Anton. Irish was sitting next to the Dutchman, not making a sound. Freddy leaned on the window on the driver's side as he spoke.

"The streets in the city are all blocked with rubble. We are going to try to go around to the west. The guard said the east side the city is very dangerous, but that's where we have to go. The guard also said the German Army is heading for the Somme area so we will try and avoid that area." Then he added with a grin, "Hail to the Kaiser." Neither Anton nor Irish thought it was funny.

It seemed everyone was anxious to get moving to the east of Lille, towards the Somme. A little later when they were once again stopped by German soldiers, Freddy repeated that they were a bridge repair team and asked which way they should go to begin their work. The German officer waved to a young soldier and asked him if he knew the route to Nord-pas-Calais via Carvin. The young man pointed out the way and they moved on.

CHAPTER 13
The Haussers

There is yet another side to this story about Frederick Frieda of Hopedale, Labrador. Although the exact date is not recorded and the old timers' memories may be blurred somewhat, there are enough details available to piece together certain facts.

In about 1890, a young Moravian missionary by the name of Albert Hausser came to Hopedale. He was from Berlin, Germany. His father had served for many years in Labrador with the Moravians.

Young Albert came to Hopedale following in his father's footsteps. During the same time, a fellow Berliner was also attracted to the Moravian Mission in Labrador. Her name was Maria Anna Kipple. When she and Albert met in Hopedale, it was love at first sight. They courted for a year and married while they were on a holiday back home in Berlin.

Maria Anna was a teacher. She encouraged her young students to learn the fundamentals of the German language, especially by singing songs and Christmas carols.

One year after she and Albert married, Maria Anna gave birth to a baby boy in Hopedale. The couple and their child went back to Germany for the christening and to make sure the baby was recorded as a German citizen. The baby was named Karl after his grandfather Hausser.

When the Hausser family returned to Hopedale on the Moravian supply vessel in August, Albert was asked to take over the church there and he accepted.

Around this same time, a son was born to a young Inuit couple by the name of Michael and Nancy Frieda. The couple from Hopedale christened their son Frederick. He would be known to everyone as Freddy.

Due to the fact that Michael and Nancy Frieda were members of the Moravian Church and that Nancy was in the church band and also a paid cleaning lady for the Haussers, Freddy became almost like a member of the family.

Karl and Freddy grew up together as brothers until Freddy was eight and Karl was ten. At that time, Albert and Maria Hausser were suddenly transferred back to Germany.

Neither the Friedas nor the Haussers ever saw each other again.

Albert Hausser and his wife became well respected ministers with the Moravian Church at many places in Germany.

When Karl finished high school he went to university in Berlin and obtained a degree in psychology. He graduated at age 21 in 1914.

Karl decided to join the army even before he finished university.

Albert and Maria were not happy with their son's decision. They told him they didn't like him being in the army because they didn't agree with war.

"Vater and Mutter, I'm not in a regiment that goes out on the battlefield and kills people. I'm in a special wing of the army that looks after the psychological part of the troops. If someone loses their mind or becomes disoriented or something, they call on us to assist them, that's all," Karl lied.

Albert was no fool. He knew what it was all about.

"Karl, you are involved with the interrogation of prisoners," he said. "You know that and naturally you are not going to admit this to your mother and me. But I'm going to warn you, every deed you commit, God will record it, and no matter where you go in life it will follow you because you know the difference."

Karl shrugged off his father's words. He had no intention of having a fight with his parents over the war. He loved them too much for that.

Albert said, "Listen to me, Karl, I had a letter from one of our ministers who is stationed at the place where you were born, Hopedale, Labrador, the quietest place on earth. Let me tell you what he wrote."

Albert took down his Bible and opened it. He took the letter from it and unfolded the pages. He skipped over most of the paragraphs until he came to the part about the war which he read aloud to Karl.

****

"Dear Brother Albert,

We are at a standstill right now because of the war. Dr. Grenfell came here two days ago and met with me and he tried to explain what was going on. I read between the lines about what was going to happen to the Mission and the missionaries along the coast if the war continues. We are all under suspicion because we are Germans. You can't blame the Government of the Colony for thinking this way because there have been sightings of German submarines all around, even here along the north Labrador Coast.

Young men, even from here in Hopedale, are going off to the war in Europe to fight the Kaiser. Do you remember young Freddy Frieda? I believe you christened him. He is gone off to the war in Europe and his mother Nancy is broken-hearted. They are taking many young men from Labrador for the war. Dr. Grenfell himself has enlisted to serve as a doctor for the British. He is now somewhere in Europe. It's just awful, Brother Albert, the only thing we can do is pray for the souls of all these young men who will lose their lives in this useless slaughter."

****

Tears were falling from the old man's eyes as he finished reading the letter.

"I don't have the heart to read the rest of what's contained in this letter, Karl," he said. "Even along the Labrador coast, people are suffering because the supply ships are afraid to venture on the ocean for fear of being sunk by German submarines." Karl squirmed in his chair; it was clear he was not comfortable. Albert went on to say, "What breaks our hearts is to know that our son, our only son, the one whom we love dearly, is taking part in this senseless war, and we can't do anything about it, only pray." Albert put his hands to his face and wept.

Karl looked at his father. He couldn't understand why the old man was unable to see the big picture, that Germany was going to rule the whole world, and how good things would be when that happened. For the first time in his life he realized he had no sympathy for his father. His feelings for him were gone.

Karl became an interrogation officer and very quickly rose to the rank of captain. Not long after being promoted, he went home to tell his parents about his next move.

"I am going directly to the Western Front, Vater and Mutter. I don't know how long I'll be gone this time."

His parents were quiet as he spoke. Karl put on his tunic and cap and looked at himself in a large mirror that hung over the couch.

"What a difference in you now, Karl," a voice inside him said. "You are a man, strong and powerful. Your father is a weakling. He cries when he thinks of war." Karl flexed his muscles as he admired himself.

Karl turned to his mother, who had tears in her eyes. He gave her a hug then turned away. Maria Hausser knew her son had changed. He usually kissed her and told her he loved her whenever he left home, but now he had a problem even giving her a little hug that had no warmth. As she saw him leaving in the military jeep with his driver, she knew he was involved with something more than he was willing to admit.

"May God have mercy on his poor soul," she said.

After the sound of the jeep faded, a deathly silence settled around the elderly couple. They had spent their lives as volunteers in the service of the Moravian Mission and had been happy and satisfied with their lot, up until Karl joined the Kaiser's army.

"It would be better if Karl had died when he was born. At least God would have taken him then. Now he could die on the battlefield a murderer, and go straight to hell," Albert said sadly.

Maria Anna took off her glasses and wiped them with the tail of her apron. She was broken-hearted. She looked at her husband and saw that he looked haggard and worn out and older than his years.

"Maria," he asked, "did you get a close look at the tattoo on the back of Karl's hand?"

"Yes," she replied.

"What was it? I thought I saw a cross or something that looked like a cross?"

"Yes, it was a cross. He showed it to me. Under the arms of the cross he has two letters. One side is A for Albert and on the other side is M for Maria. He said he had it put on his hand to remind him every day of us. No matter where he goes or what he does he will always remember us," she said as she broke down and wept.

CHAPTER 14
To Lille

Freddy and his team decided to try and get in contact with the underground in Lille. It was impossible to advance any further west of Lille due to the destruction of the roads. There was no point in continuing as undercover agents disguised as a bridge repair crew. They felt they already had enough information about what the German Army was intending to do. They were entrenching themselves around the Somme area with the hope of controlling the French side of the English Channel, from the seaport of Le Havre all the way to the Belgium border.

"I think we should ditch these German uniforms," said Freddy. "We could get shot by some Frenchman because everything with a German badge on it is a target. It's shoot now and ask questions later."

"You're right," Franz agreed. "At least without the uniform the Germans could tell us to halt first and shoot later."

The first chance they had they pulled off the road and changed into the civilian clothes they had in their duffle bags. Freddy still felt they should try and get in touch with the underground and pass along the information they had. The others objected, saying it was too dangerous.

"If some crazy soldier decides to fire a mortar at us or if we happen to run over a mine on the road we will have had it," said Franz.

"Anything is possible, but let's hope that won't happen," said Freddy.

"We may have to split up, three will go one way and two the other," Benoit suggested.

"Let's go a bit further and see if we can get away from the fighting," said Freddy.

The two vehicles continued on and soon came to a farm road that led to a barn. A German officer came running out of the barn, yelling and waving his hands.

"You better watch out, boys. He looks like he's going crazy. I wonder what he wants?" said Benoit.

Freddy called out, "What's wrong? What do you want?"

"Go back, go back. The French are coming," the officer yelled as he came and jumped on the running board. "Are you Germans?"

"Yes," replied Freddy. 'We are a bridge repair team."

"My platoon got wiped out just beyond the hill," the officer pointed to a small rise not more than two hundred meters away.

"Where are the French troops now?" asked Freddy.

"Just over that rise. They broke through our line, several hundred of them."

When Freddy told the German officer they weren't going anywhere, that they were trying to get further west to repair bridges, he became very upset and pulled out his revolver and ordered them to retreat.

"Okay men," said Freddy. "Turn around and go back towards Lille. This officer will take the responsibility for whatever happens."

The German climbed into the truck with Anton and Irish.

The two trucks had not gone very far when they were stopped by a truck coming towards them at a high speed.

They pulled off to let it pass, but instead the truck stopped next to them and the driver asked in French who they were. Benoit replied in French that they were a bridge repair team and asked them if they were part of the German Army. The two men in the truck cursed, then laughed.

"We have a German officer here we picked up running from the French Army," said Benoit.

"Where and when was this?" one of the men asked.

"About ten minutes ago, just up the road," said Benoit.

"Hand him over to us. We take care of these fellows," one man said.

Benoit signaled to the driver to get out of the vehicle.

"I want to talk to you, it's important," he said.

The driver got out and walked to the rear of the truck. Benoit said the password and was relieved when the man answered.

"Okay, okay, now we know you are with the underground," said Benoit. "We have to get our hands on a wireless set. It's top priority to dispatch a message to London, it's extremely important. Do you know where we can send a message?"

The men hesitated then one of them said, "I'm not going to travel with that German in the truck, leave him here with us."

"No, you fellows will kill him when our backs are turned," said Benoit.

"We can't take you to our headquarters when you have a German officer with you. You must think we have gone mad," said the Frenchman.

Benoit went back to inform the group they had to ditch the German officer. He said the French underground had a hideout not far away where they kept prisoners and some of their people would take the German there. Freddy had no objections, neither did the Irish, but Anton and Franz were aghast.

"They'll kill him the minute our backs are turned," they said.

"This is the deal and unless we are prepared to accept it we don't get our information out," said Benoit.

The Dutchmen suggested letting the officer out of the truck and allowing him to walk back to his regiment. The Frenchman nodded okay.

"We'll take him down the road a little way before we release him," he said. "He won't know where we are going to turn off. You go on, we'll catch up."

The German officer disappeared with the Frenchmen. Benoit had no doubt what happened to him when they were out of sight.

Benoit climbed in with the two Frenchmen after they caught up. The three trucks traveled on a road through forest that had been burnt sometime earlier, maybe in early fall or summer. There were a lot of burnt out vehicles and wagons strewn along the highway, it was obvious a major battle had been fought sometime earlier.

"Where does this road lead?" asked Benoit.

"To Paris, if there was need to go there. We turn off not far from here and take a road to a farmhouse. We have our headquarters set up there," the Frenchman answered.

****

As the trucks continued on the snow was getting deeper. Finally they turned off and headed toward a farmhouse in a clearing. All the windows in the house were shuttered. The three trucks stopped by the farmhouse. It was getting dark and they could hear cattle bawling in a barn not far away. The French driver went to the door and gently tapped. Almost right away the door opened and a woman came out. She carried a pitchfork in one hand, and in the semi-darkness it appeared she had a hammer in the other.

"Who's there?" she asked in a trembling voice.

"It's me. You're lucky we didn't shoot you, coming on the scene carrying weapons like that," said the Frenchman.

The woman recognized his voice and told him to get inside.

The other Frenchman told Benoit he would take the Dutchmen down the road where they could hide two vehicles close to the road and bring one back. He said that was the best thing in case it snowed and the road to the farmhouse got blocked.

The remaining men stepped into the dark porch and the woman barred the door. Freddy was surprised to find himself in a brightly lit room with heavy dark blankets covering the windows. Four men were sitting near a big iron stove and the aroma of roasting beef filled the air. On the stove was a large boiler, steam was escaping from around the cover and shooting halfway to the ceiling.

"We have meat and potatoes for supper and it's almost ready. I don't expect anyone wants to wash their dirty hands. There's a war on and water is scarce," said the woman in French.

Benoit grinned and so did the French driver, who then introduced him to Jules St. Pierre, the man in charge of the group.

"I would like to have a word with you, it's important," said Benoit.

"Certainly," he said and motioned for Benoit to go to an inside room.

After they had been in the room for a few minutes Benoit came out and motioned for Freddy to come in.

"What do you want to say on the telegram, Freddy?" asked Benoit.

Freddy borrowed a pencil from the Frenchman and started writing down the message in code for Benoit to send to the War Office in London.

He told about the entrenchment of the German Army around the high ground southeast of Beaumont Hamel and the build-up of German troops in the Somme area.

The message also had a request from the French underground that a counter offensive be launched near Dunkirk to split the troop build-up. After the messages were sent, the evening meal of roast beef and potatoes was served along with lots of black bread.

"You men can spend the night here with us," said St. Pierre. "But you have to be gone before daylight regardless of the weather. The German Army is on the move. They could be coming here any day for more beef. That's the only reason this farm is still standing."

Benoit promised they would be gone before daylight. During the night Freddy and his companions figured it would be best to try and work their way back to Antwerp. There was no use trying to go further west.

"The next major battle will be fought in the Somme area or close to it," said Freddy. "We have to get back and rejoin our units. I figure our job has been completed here."

An hour before dawn Freddy and his companions had more of the roast beef along with bread and strong coffee. St. Pierre had one of the drivers ready to transport the five man crew to their vehicles. No goodbyes or thank yous were said. It was a matter of out the door and gone.

"We don't have far to go," said the driver, who told Benoit his name was Guy. "Your two vehicles are in an old gravel pit we use all the time. I hope no one followed the tracks last evening."

"Do you live around here?" Benoit asked him as they drove along.

"Yes," said Guy. "My father used to own the farm we just left. We raised cattle for years. The woman you met is my mother. The Germans killed my father about four months ago when they set fire to the forest. They said he was caught in the fire, but when we found his body he had three bullet holes in his back. After what they did to my father, my brother and I kill every German we can get our hands on."

"War is a cruel monster. I suppose no one ever gets even," said Benoit.

"My brother got a little revenge yesterday, thanks to you gentlemen," said Guy.

"Why, what did we do?" Benoit asked.

"You handed over that German officer to him, and my brother had the privilege of blowing this brains out. He wanted to thank you after he arrived home, but he didn't know how you would react."

Benoit didn't comment. He translated everything that had been said for the others and they were quiet. It was coming on dawn when they reached their trucks. The vehicles had not been disturbed. No one had been around. One truck was hard to get started due to the cold, however with a little coaxing it got going.

Before they left, there was some debating about whether or not Freddy should put on a German uniform. They had just one uniform left, having given the others to the underground to destroy or use as they saw fit.

"I am afraid some Frenchman will take a shot at me, especially with only two vehicles traveling together," Freddy objected. "If this was a convoy then I might take a chance on wearing the uniform. But there's really no need for me to wear it. We'll keep on pretending we are a bridge repair team that was forced to turn back due to the heavy snowfall."

CHAPTER 15
Captured

Before leaving the gravel pit they checked their papers to see if everything was in order. After studying a map Guy had given them showing which bridges had been destroyed, they figured they were twenty-seven miles west of Lille.

"Should we attempt to go back the same way by scouting the east side of the city, or should we go through the center of the city. The streets might be cleared now," said Freddy.

"Let's go back the way we came," suggested Franz.

The two trucks moved slowly toward the western side of the city. Up ahead a heavy column of black smoke rose in the air, and further on it looked like a convoy of German troops was stopped along the road. Off in the distance there was the sound of gunfire and loud explosions. As they edged their way forward, a German officer, a lieutenant, waved them over. He saw the Belgian identification on their trucks and came to the window and asked to see their papers.

Freddy explained that they were a bridge repair crew and told him what their mission was. Freddy went on to say it was impossible to get any further west. The vehicles couldn't get through the heavy snowdrifts and there was nothing to keep the roads open. Freddy said they were returning to Antwerp, if it was at all possible.

"Show me your papers," the German demanded.

They showed him their papers, but when the officer spoke to Irish he didn't understand and couldn't answer.

The German became suspicious and ordered them out of the truck. He called another lieutenant to come and assist him search the trucks. The five man team lined up near the front of the trucks as the two officers searched. They dumped out the contents of the bags in each truck, and in one of them they found Freddy's German uniform.

There was no way Freddy could explain it.

He was not a German soldier.

If he was, he would be wearing the uniform.

The ID he produced showed him to be a citizen of Belgium.

"You are a spy, a spy for the French," yelled one of the German lieutenants. He waved his pistol in the face of each man and swore viciously. "These men look suspicious. I think they are part of the French underground. Why do they have a German uniform?"

"Let's have a patrol take them to headquarters. Let the fellows there deal with them. We haven't the time to do a proper search," said the other lieutenant.

The two vehicles were seized and the five man team was loaded into the back of a wagon with armed guards and sent on their way to the German headquarters at Lille.

Freddy knew he would not be able to explain why he had a German uniform.

As much as he tried he could not come up with a good reason.

But what worried him most was the paper he had hidden in the leg of his boot with numbers spelling out the code he was operating under now. If some German was smart enough to figure it out and could line the figures up properly they could break the code and that would create a big problem. Freddy knew he somehow had to get rid of the paper before he arrived at German headquarters.

The wagon headed towards the city. It was cold and the ride was very rough. The two German guards were complaining about the war and why they were fighting in France.

"Imagine fighting over this God forsaken hole when we could be back home," said one.

"I'll be glad when this mess is over," said the other.

"It won't be over for a while from what the captain said last night, especially if they get to the English Channel," said the other.

"Do any of you speak German?" one of the guards asked. Freddy, who was the only one who could speak German, said nothing.

"I don't think any of them can speak German. Maybe they speak English," the other guard said.

Benoit leaned over to Freddy and whispered, "I wonder where they are going to take us when we reach the city. From what we were told the streets are filled with rubble and it's impossible to get anywhere. Maybe they have a place on the outskirts of the city." Benoit finished on an optimistic note. "After they are finished searching us and asking us questions we should be on our way again in a very short time."

They were going down a steep hill when the wagon came to an abrupt halt. The two guards jumped out with their rifles at the ready. Freddy seized the opportunity to get the piece of paper he'd been worried about out of his boot. He tore the paper into small pieces and gave a piece to each man to swallow. In training they had been taught the safest way to destroy a very important document was either to swallow it or burn it.

Hearing shooting outside, they crouched low in the back of the wagon, not knowing if they were going to be shot any minute. At one point they could hear bullets whizzing overhead. After a few minutes the shooting quieted down and they heard loud shouting. Something serious was going on up front because people were running in that direction. Freddy peeked through a seam in the canvas and saw several vehicles burning. He wondered if it had been a mortar attack.

After much confusion the two guards returned and got in the back of the wagon. They were obviously shaken up. Freddy listened as they spoke to each other, saying they were lucky they didn't get hit. One said the attack had come from the French underground. The other said the underground was very sneaky and had every angle covered. The first guard said the underground had to be destroyed before the big German force moved into the area. If not, he said, they would not be able to advance very quickly.

It was late afternoon when the wagon started moving again and snow was beginning to fall. The driver came back and told the guards it would be late before they got into the city.

"We may even have to leave the wagon and walk, unless we can get a ride with someone else." The driver looked at the prisoners and shook his head. "Why don't you let those prisoners go? They don't even have rifles. What language do they speak?"

"We don't know. None of them speak German," answered one of the guards.

"What about English? Did you ask them if they could speak English?"

"No, we can't speak English either," said the guard.

"The fellow in the cab with me can speak a little English. I'll get him to come back and have a talk with them."

"I don't know if it's worth talking to them," said the guard. "The lieutenant told us to deliver them to the interrogation officer at headquarters."

"That's okay if we don't get hit with a shell on the way in," said the driver. "The countryside from here on is crawling with the French underground. Those fellows like to operate at night."

"We can't take a chance letting the prisoners go," said the guard, sounding perturbed. "The lieutenant is convinced they are spies, maybe for the British, so we'd better take them in."

"Okay, but if it was me I'd let them go or shoot them and keep my mouth shut," said the driver.

The guard looked at the prisoners and said, "I'd like to be done with them, but I'm afraid to take a chance. They're not worth getting in trouble for."

Freddy listened to everything that was said. It was nerve-racking to hear someone debating whether or not he should live or die. For the first time he realized the power of man. It was only a matter of yes or no and his life would have ended on a snowy road in France.

Then he thought about what might happen to him and his crew in the hands of the German interrogators. British training had stressed not to tell the enemy anything, to die first. And they had heard the German Army interrogators would shoot you after they got their information anyway. Freddy thought back on his nineteen years. He'd had it so good on his trap-line back in Labrador. Now he might never see the dear old hills of Hopedale again. He might never again see his family or Emily. He thought about his dear Emily and wondered what would happen to her in St. Anthony if he didn't return.

CHAPTER 16
The German Captain

It was almost midnight when the wagon reached the German headquarters near the center of Lille. Every light was out and no one was in the streets except for German soldiers with rifles ready for action. Horse drawn wagons had cleared away enough rubble to get traffic through a few of the main streets. The wagon was stopped on every street corner and there were warnings about gangs of French resistance everywhere, including on the rooftops armed with rifles and mortars. "They could pop out anywhere," warned one soldier.

Several times they had to stop because of shooting across the street. Each time, the two drivers and the two guards got out and hid low near the ditch or took shelter near a rubble pile. There wasn't any thought given to the prisoners in the back. No one seemed to care whether they got hit with bullets or not. They were no more than animals now. When the gunfire ceased, the four Germans boarded the wagon and they moved on.

The wagon finally came to a stop in a compound and voices were heard outside. Freddy heard someone yelling, "Prisoners, prisoners. Get them inside. I think the shooting is going to start again in a few minutes. Get that truck out of here." The guards jumped out of the wagon and ordered the five prisoners to get out. It was a quick exit from the back of the wagon. No sooner had they touched the ground than they were whisked inside.

Three soldiers with flashlights led them into a cold room which looked to be a former office. One of the soldiers said he would kill all five of them in the morning if they made a move or spoke one word during the night. Another soldier took a candle from his pocket. He lit it and placed it on a chair near the wall. The floor in the room was wet and slippery. The soldiers left them alone. As their eyes adjusted to the dull candlelight, they could see a closed door and two windows that were shuttered on the outside. Benoit started exploring the room and quickly realized the wet substance on the floor was blood. He tried the door. It opened and he peered into a small room where he saw a desk and several chairs and a shuttered window. He tried the main door they'd come in through and found it was locked.

"What do we do to get out of here?" he whispered to Freddy.

"I don't know," Freddy shook his head. "There's no sense trying to go through windows. They're facing the street and there are soldiers everywhere out there."

"We could try to get the back window opened," Benoit said. "You stay here and keep your ears open. Irish and I are going to take a closer look."

Benoit and Irish took the candle and went into the small room where they found yet another locked door. They tried to open the window but couldn't; it was closed with a crank. They searched the desk for the crank but couldn't find it. Several manuals were in the desk drawer. Benoit looked at them. "German or French, can't read them," he said, throwing them back into the drawer. In one corner of the room they found a small woodstove with pipes protruding through the ceiling.

"This is probably where they interrogate people," said Irish.

"I would say this is it," said Benoit. "That's why there's blood on the floor out there." The Irishman said nothing. He knew what Benoit said could be true. Benoit took another look around the room and said, "Don't disturb anything in this room, not yet. If we have to burst out we may have to go through the window in here."

"I'm for doing it now," said the Irishman.

"Not yet. Let's talk it over with the others first. Maybe there's a better way," said Benoit.

They talked to the others, but no one could decide what to do. "Suppose the window leads to a back yard full of German soldiers. We'd be shot on sight," said Freddy.

"Let's wait and see what happens in the morning," suggested Franz. "We'll try to convince them we are a bridge repair team and they may have a job for us to do."

"Where are our papers?" Irish sounded worried. "They didn't give my papers back."

"They didn't give any of our papers back. The German lieutenant kept all of them," said Freddy. "Irish and Benoit, you had better remember the address that was on those papers. If not, you had better go through that window in there right now."

"I know the address," said Benoit.

"Me too," said Irish.

"We have only one choice," said Freddy. "Wait until morning."

The five men found the cleanest place on the floor and sat down. There was a rotten stench in the room coming from the partly dried blood on the floor. Freddy was afraid to talk about it for fear of driving the other men crazy, especially the two young Dutchmen who were really just boys. This was nothing more than a butcher shop, he reminded himself.

It was a long cold night, but light finally started to show through between the shutters on the windows. They waited for sounds of someone coming. Finally, they heard the key turning in the lock and three men in uniform entered. The ray of light from the open door lit up the room. The five men inside had to shade their eyes with their hands as they stood up.

"Holy hell in heaven," said one of the Germans. He had three stripes on his arm and Freddy figured he was a sergeant. "What a stink. Someone must be dead in here. Do any of you prisoners speak German? Does anyone speak French? Well by God, you'd better understand English. If not, I'm going to start shooting."

Irish spoke up and told him all of them spoke English.

"I see you've had a very good night. Lots of room in here," the sergeant barked. Then he added, "We'll see what kind of a day you'll have." One of the Germans laughed as the three of them walked to the door of the other room and looked inside. "Why haven't they lit the fire yet? Where is the man who is supposed to light the fire? Go get him," the sergeant yelled angrily.

"He has probably gone to the Western Front," said another soldier. "The big brass came here yesterday evening in desperation and took twenty of our men without even asking. They just herded them into a truck and left."

"Well, you'd better get the fire going and the room warmed up before the captain arrives. If not, there will be trouble," said the sergeant.

With the main door opened a few inches and light streaming in Freddy and the others could see around the room where they'd spent the night. The floor was covered with bloodstains. There were even spatters on the wall.

"Open the shutters in the other room so you can see to light the fire," ordered the sergeant. He walked to the open door and drew his pistol and aimed it at the five prisoners. "I'll shoot the first man who makes a run for it," he said in German. No one spoke! He repeated it again in English. Still no one spoke.

"The captain is coming," said the soldier in the other room.

"I hope the fire is burning. He won't like it if it's not," said the sergeant as he went into the other room and closed the door.

The five prisoners stood shoulder to shoulder near the wall looking at the armed soldier at the entrance. They heard much noise and confusion coming from the inside room. Freddy heard swearing and complaining about the cold room. The sergeant was saying, "It's not our fault, Captain. They took the soldier responsible for the fire last night and we didn't know about it till a few minutes ago. Sorry about that."

"I'll be back when this office warms up," the captain said as he stormed out, slamming the door behind him. The sergeant immediately returned to the other room. He wasn't happy as he ordered the prisoners to lie on the floor.

"You miserable dogs," said the sergeant."It's your fault we're here this morning. If only for the information you have, I would shoot you now."

"The captain is not in a very good mood, Sergeant. I wonder what's eating him this morning. He usually likes interrogating prisoners before shooting them. Something very important must be bothering him," said one of the soldiers.

"Nothing bothers him. He was born for this job. I suppose he can't stand the cold and you can't blame him for that," said the sergeant.

The soldier laughed and said, "It's a funny thing, Sergeant. He can shoot a man anytime, yet he can't stand the cold."

"I suppose that's the reason he's a captain," the sergeant replied.

There was a pause. The sergeant put his hand to his nose and said, "You need a gas mask in here this morning. The soldier who was supposed to keep the fire going was supposed to clean this place up after what happened yesterday."

"No, he wasn't. Remember what the captain said? He told Lieutenant Hau he didn't want the blood cleaned up for a while as it might help to get the prisoners talking sooner. I think it's all part of his tactics," said the soldier.

"I can't remember it all. There was a lot said yesterday," said the sergeant.

Freddy understood the whole conversation. "At least the other four can't understand what's being said," he thought. "I suppose we don't stand much of a chance. This could be our last time seeing the dawn break." His thoughts were interrupted when the office door slammed open. The captain had returned. The sergeant dashed into the office leaving the door to the main room open.

"Sergeant, I want to get this over quickly," Freddy heard the captain say. "I'm leaving within an hour for a week's leave, going home. My father is ill, and my mother has sent for me. I don't have much time. I'm catching the next train to Berlin."

CHAPTER 17
Karl

Karl Hausser was the interrogation officer in charge of the office at Lille. He was known for his cruelty to prisoners while prying information out of them. There was nothing he wouldn't do to achieve his goal and ninety percent of the time he was successful.

He usually traveled with his staff, staying well back of the fighting columns. He went to the Front only to interrogate prisoners. If they couldn't be brought to him he would go to the holding compounds and deal with them. He was greatly feared!

On this occasion he was very busy doing what he liked best, having men become traitors to their superiors or their country. Before coming to the compound this morning, he had looked over the papers of five prisoners who had been captured last evening coming from the Somme area. Which was where the big operation was being planned before the German Army was to make a dash to the English Channel. If these prisoners were spies for the British, then he was the one to find out what they knew and if they had relayed any information to their superiors.

While going over the information he saw the name Frederick Frieda, described by Lieutenant Hau as white, resembling Japanese or Chinese, and approximately twenty years old. Karl wondered where he had heard the name before, it sounded familiar. Suddenly he had a flashback. Freddy Frieda, his childhood friend in Hopedale, Labrador.

"No, it couldn't be, not Freddy," he said out loud. Then he thought about the letter his father had read to him the last time he was home, regarding a young man from Hopedale going off to war with the Newfoundland Regiment. Would this be the very same

Freddy? "No, it couldn't be," he said, and then added, "I will soon find out." He had a plan!

"Just a moment, Sergeant. I need to have another look at the papers and identification belonging to these prisoners," Karl said as he shuffled the papers until he came to Frederick Frieda's name. He looked again and wondered if the person in the next room was really the Freddy Frieda he'd known as a child in Hopedale. He was sure neither of them would recognize each other now.

Karl told the sergeant to bring in one of the Dutchmen for questioning first.

Anton went in through the door followed by the sergeant. There was loud shouting in the room as Anton denied being a spy for the British. He tried to convince Karl he was part of a team sent to help repair bridges for the German Army.

"You are a liar, we know all about you, and so you deny it?" Karl shouted.

"Yes, I deny that I am a spy," said Anton.

"Ok, Ok, then you're not a spy. That's all," Karl spoke quietly. He wrote something on a slip of paper and handed it to the sergeant who read it and gestured for Anton to leave the room. "Sergeant," Karl barked, "when you are finished with him bring in the other one."

"Okay, Captain," said the sergeant as he followed the Dutchman out into the center of the room. "Turn and look at the window," the sergeant said in English to Anton.

The Dutchman turned and looked at the window. Just then, the office door opened and Karl came out with eyes blazing. He walked towards the young Dutchman and drew his pistol and shot him in the back between the shoulder blades. Anton hit the floor before the sound of the shot died away, releasing a terrible scream that echoed through the building. Karl laughed and the clicking sound of his pistol was heard as he took aim and shot the helpless Dutchman in the back of his head. The bullet came out through his left eye. Anton took one deep breath and was still.

It was something the remaining four men thought they would never see. Someone killed before their very eyes. In cold blood. Without having the slightest chance to defend himself. They all groaned in horror and fear!

Freddy felt sick. He had often shot caribou on the barrens of Labrador, but never in his wildest dreams did he think he would see a human being killed right before his eyes. He felt as if he would go mad. He wanted to run, but he knew if he as much as stepped out of line he would get gunned down like a wild animal.

"Not bad, Captain, but try and make it with one shot the next time," said the sergeant.

"I'll do my job, Sergeant. Make sure you do yours." The captain curtly commanded the sergeant to bring in another one of the prisoners. When Franz was ordered to go into the other room, he refused. Franz made a desperate dash for the door. He was shot dead before he got halfway across the room. He dropped in a heap in the middle of the room. The captain came to the door and inquired about the pistol shot.

"Captain, one of the prisoners decided to try and escape and we shot him dead," said the sergeant.

"Who was it?" Karl asked.

"I don't know his name." The sergeant asked Freddy in English who it was. Freddy answered that it was a Dutchman named Franz.

"Ah, that's okay, bring in another one," said the captain angrily. "You," he pointed at Irish. "Get inside." Irish hesitated. He would have run if he could have gotten to the door, but with nowhere to go he knew he would be shot making an attempt. He slowly went into the room with the captain. The sergeant shut the door behind him. It's not known and will never be known what Irish told Karl. The only sound those in the other room heard was a loud scream, followed by a pistol shot. When they heard the shot they knew Irish was dead.

****

Freddy and Benoit looked at each other in horror. They wanted to try and escape, but they knew there was no way out. They were like birds in a cage with nowhere to run.

"Sergeant, come in and drag this body out, and get a mop and clean up the mess," called the captain. "And get those other bodies out of here too."

"Okay, sir, right away," the sergeant replied as he went inside with a mop and bucket. In a few minutes he came out dragging Irish's body. He ordered the other two soldiers to get rid of the three bodies.

"I'll deal with Frederick Frieda last," said Karl. 'Bring in the other man, Sergeant, but first open that damn window. It's as hot as hell in here now. And, on second thought, bring in this Frieda next."

The sergeant went to the desk, pulled a drawer completely out and put it on the top of the desk. He put his hand inside and took out a crank that opened the outside shutter. He then pushed the window all the way up, letting in air.

"That's better," said Karl, unbuttoning the top button of his tunic.

The sergeant came out and asked which one was Frieda.

"I'm Frieda," said Freddy.

"You go inside next," ordered the sergeant.

Freddy slowly went to the door, his heart in his boots, his eyes looking for any possible way to escape. He noticed the open window as he entered the room and then he looked into the deadliest eyes he had ever seen, the eyes of a man who had sent many to their death.

"Stand there. I want to get a better look at you because I haven't dealt with anyone like you before. Maybe you can tell me what I want to know," said the captain. Freddy looked at the cold blooded killer. His eyes were like steel as they glared into his face. His moustache moved with each word he spoke.

"So, you are Frederick Frieda of Hopedale, Labrador," said the killer.

Freddy was puzzled that the German officer knew his name. Then the captain held out his hand. Freddy was afraid to refuse to shake hands for fear of being shot immediately. Wanting to take his eyes away from the glare of the man he thought would kill him in an instant, Freddy looked down at the outstretched hand that snaked toward him. What he saw dazed him! There was a tattoo on the back of the hand, a cross about two inches long, marked in blue ink with a red streak through the middle, making it stand out. Under the wings of the cross there were two letters. On the left side was the letter A, and on the right was the letter M.

Freddy was shocked at what he saw. For a moment he thought about how every Sunday for years he'd sat with his parents under the cross in the Moravian church. Now he was shaking the hand of the man who could blow his head off with the gun he held in his hand, a hand with a cross tattooed on the back. What the A and the M stood for he didn't know, but he knew what the cross stood for. Is it possible this man thinks he is doing the will of God by killing people, he thought, and even has the nerve in front of God Almighty to shake hands before passing his death sentence? If that is so, thought Freddy, it has to be the worst deed ever done on earth.

"I did a lot of research last night and I found out all about you. You might as well come clean and admit to me you are Freddy Frieda from Hopedale, Labrador," the captain said in German.

"Yes, I'm from Hopedale, Labrador," said Freddy, also in German.

For a moment it seemed to Freddy that the captain wanted to tell him something, but hesitated.

"Why are you here in France? Are you a member of the Newfoundland army that is fighting us?" he asked.

"No," Freddy answered. "We came here to scout out a landing area close to the city of Antwerp, but instead we got caught up in a situation doing bridge repairs west of Lille. We are not spies as you suspect, sir."

"You don't think I believe you? I know you are a bunch of spies," Karl spat out the words.

"Bring in Benoit, he'll tell you the same. All we want is to get back to England," said Freddy. "We are not a fighting force, we are with the Royal Engineers." He knew Benoit was in the other room listening to every word he said.

The captain called the sergeant and told him to bring the last man in. He said he wanted to question the two prisoners together. In less than a minute Benoit was brought into the room. He told the same story as Freddy. Karl shouted that he didn't believe either of them.

"You are liars, you are spies for the British, you will serve the same fate as your other three buddies," he snarled. He rose from his desk and took out his revolver. "Okay Freddy, come with me. I'll deal with you first."

****

Karl Hausser knew he didn't have the heart to shoot Freddy Frieda. He thought about when they were young, running around the dirt roads in Hopedale, laughing and having fun. He thought about Freddy's mother whom he'd called Aunt Nancy, and his father whom he'd called Uncle Michael. In his mind he could see them in the Moravian church in Hopedale, all decked off on a Sunday morning with Aunt Nancy playing the horn. He also thought about his own parents and knew he couldn't shoot Freddy for their sake.

No, he thought, I'll send Freddy to a labour camp, the one in the Bavarian Alps. He should be safe there. I'll pretend to shoot him in order to get the other fellow to talk. Provided, that is, I have the time to deal with him.

Freddy went into the other room with the captain and closed the door as he was directed. He thought his time had come when he saw the revolver in the captain's hand. But the captain fired a shot at the ceiling and stamped his feet loudly, then said in a loud voice, "Take the body out and bury it somewhere."

He told the sergeant to get Freddy ready to go to a labour camp in the Bavarian Alps. Freddy stood there, unable to believe he was still alive. He thought he had awakened from a dream and was now walking out into the heavenly sunshine.

The sergeant reminded the captain he had to leave in a few minutes as his car was waiting to take him to the train station. "You're right," said Karl. "Hold the other prisoner till I return. If you have any trouble with him, shoot him." He started to walk out and then stopped. "Oh yes, get someone to clean the place and bury the bodies. I'll be back in a week. One more order for you, Sergeant. Make sure you tell everyone to make sure no harm comes to prisoner Frieda. He is very valuable." With those words, Karl left.

The sergeant came out and told the two soldiers that the prisoner was very valuable to the German Army. "The captain has left orders he is to be protected at all times, even on the train. We will have him shipped to Munich and then he can go on to the Bavarian Alps. We will go now and deliver him to the train station," he said and then stopped. "Oh, wait just a moment. I'll go back inside and fix up with that prisoner in the office. I'll shoot him if I have to. The captain will never know. Why bother having him locked up. It's only another problem."

The soldiers agreed, "Yes, get rid of him. We'll keep our mouths shut."

When the sergeant went into the office the window was still open and Benoit was gone. The sergeant breathed a sigh of relief that the captain had left and would never find out that the prisoner had escaped. He muttered angrily to himself as he pulled down the window without even looking out at the snow ten feet below. "Silly fool! Just how far does that idiot think he's going to get before he gets a bullet through the head? He hasn't got a hope in hell of getting away. Stupid idiot."

When the sergeant came out to the truck, Freddy was standing next to it with one of the soldiers. Freddy looked down at the ground as the sergeant told the soldier he had shot the prisoner. The sergeant then ordered the soldier to drive to the railway station.

"You did the proper thing shooting that spy, saves a lot of fooling around," said the soldier. He and the sergeant laughed. "Now, what are we going do with this prisoner we have here, Sergeant? We can't put him in the back by himself, he might jump out."

"We should have shot him, but we can't now. The captain wants him so he must be important. Let's put him in the front between us. Get in the front, get in the front," he yelled at Freddy in German.

Freddy made no move to go anywhere, still pretending he didn't understand. The sergeant yelled again in English, "Get in the front or I'll blow your brains out."

Freddy jumped into the front seat and moved close to the driver, there was very little room. The sergeant got in last and slammed the door shut. It was slow going. The city was in turmoil and they were stopped every few yards. The sergeant complained about the slow progress the third time they were stopped.

"We have to get to the train station to ship this prisoner to Munich, it's top priority," he said to the soldier who had waved them over.

"Sergeant, it's slow going this way," said the soldier. "It's best if you go out of the city on the main road and go east. You can enter the city on the east side and go to the train station from there. It will save you time, although it's the long way around."

"Okay, that's what we'll do," said the sergeant. As they drove along, the sergeant took a flask from the glove compartment. He took a drink and offered one to the driver.

"This is what keeps your nerve up in this God forsaken war," he said. "If you didn't have liquor to drink and prisoners to shoot you would go crazy." The sergeant spoke German, convinced that Freddy didn't understand him.

"What about the body of the one you shot in the office? We'll have to get it out of the captain's office and clean up the mess as soon as we can. The captain might come back sooner than we think," said the driver.

"Don't worry about it. I waited for the idiot to get out the window and away from the building before I shot him. I'm too smart to shoot him in the office. Why make a mess if you don't have to," the sergeant laughed.

As they drove along they continued to drink and laugh about all the prisoners they'd shot within the last year. Freddy listened and cringed as he wondered how they could be so cruel. When they got out of the city and started going east, their conversation switched to Freddy.

"I wonder why this prisoner is so important to the Army," the sergeant said. "We have to make sure we tell the officer in charge of the train to have him put in a safe place by himself, with a guard on the door at all times. I wonder who he is."

"He looks different from all the other Englishmen we've dealt with. Ask him who he is. You can speak English," said the driver.

"Where are you from? What country are you from?" the sergeant asked.

"Me?" said Freddy, acting stupid. He knew he had to answer; he had spoken to the sergeant earlier in English.

"Yes, you, what country are you from?" the sergeant repeated.

"Oh," said Freddy. "From Labrador."

"Lar-bar-door," said the sergeant.

"Yes. Lar-bar-door," said Freddy.

"Where is Lar-bar-door?" he asked.

"Close to the North Pole," said Freddy.

"What did he say, where does he come from?" the driver asked curiously.

"Said he was from the North Pole."

"That's why he looks different," said the driver, looking at Freddy.

"Maybe Germany is going to take over the North Pole," said the sergeant. "And maybe that's the reason the captain wants him guarded."

Freddy smiled to himself. "What fools," he thought.

CHAPTER 18

Benoit escapes

When Karl and Freddy walked out the door and the shot was fired, Benoit quickly made his move. He had no intentions of dying in this hole, of being led to the slaughter by a German soldier. If there was a way of escaping he was going to have to make his move now. He was going to take advantage of the opportunity offered.

Benoit stood up and rushed to the window and leaped out, landing in a pile of snow ten feet below. He jumped up and made for a fence and clambered over it. He landed at the side of the road and raced away with the speed of a bullet. He dashed down a back alley and kept moving as best he could.

Most houses had piles of rubble around them. He kept watching the chimneys for signs of smoke, if there was smoke there were people and they might be able to help him. He cut through another back alley and over more fences until he came to a street where there were fresh footprints. He followed along the fence for a few hundred yards. Across the street he saw a house with smoke rising from the chimney. He looked up and down the street before making an effort to cross. He saw several elderly people looking at him suspiciously. He climbed over a pile of rubble and knocked on the door of the house. He heard movement inside. He knocked again and this time he heard someone calling, "Who's there?"

"It's me, Benoit, open up," he said in the best French he knew.

There was a pause. He heard someone inside whispering and finally he saw the door open slowly a couple of inches then the chain on it drew tight.

"What do you want?" someone asked.

"I want to get off the street," he whispered. "I just escaped from the Germans. There's no one following me and I'm not armed."

Again he heard whispering, then a pause. The door opened and a voice invited him to come inside. He stepped in and the door slammed shut behind him. As his eyes adjusted to the darkness inside, he could see a man standing close by.

"You are French?" Benoit asked.

"Yes," said the man. "Are you sure you are not working for the German Army? If I thought you were I'd shoot you now."

"I just escaped from the worst ordeal a human has ever witnessed. Our men were shot and killed right before our eyes," Benoit's voice shook as he spoke. 'I want to get in touch with someone from the underground."

The man told Benoit to come into the kitchen. A woman and two small children sat at a table under a window that was half open, letting the light in. A kettle was boiling on the stove. However, all attention was on the stranger who had come through the back door. Benoit said if the children weren't there he would tell in detail what he had experienced that morning.

"My God, where will all this end?" he wept. The woman came and tried to console him with an embrace. He told them he was from Newfoundland. They didn't know where it was so he said it was an island near Canada, a colony of Great Britain.

"Ah, oh yes. We know Quebec is in Canada and we understand colony," said the woman. She looked to be about thirty, the man was much older. Benoit figured he was sixty and learned he was her father. Her husband had been the victim of an artillery attack. He had been killed instantly about six months before. The artillery attack had also destroyed the family shop, located in the next building. Fortunately, they had managed to salvage some provisions from the shop.

"We have been hiding here for more than six months through the cold winter. Getting wood for the stove has been our greatest challenge. We don't know how long this war will continue, but our food supply is beginning to get low," the man said.

Benoit said he hadn't eaten for two days. He said he wanted to get in touch with the French underground and then try to get back to his unit. He said he didn't know where his regiment was located.

"I can put you in touch with the resistance in a few days," the man said. "One of the members comes here whenever he's in the city. I think he is fond of someone here." He winked and grinned at his daughter. "You can stay here with us until he gets back."

Benoit thought about how just a few minutes ago his life had been in great danger; now he was being sheltered by civilized people. The man put on his coat and went out back searching for firewood. When he left, Benoit started a conversation with the young woman. He told her his name was Peter Benoit.

"My name is Madeline and I am from Normandy," she told him. "I came here as a school teacher and met my husband and we got married. After that, I sent for my father and he came to live with us. My mother passed away when I was a little girl. When the Germans invaded we thought it would be over in a short time. We never thought they would level the city. We are lucky this place is standing. My children never go outside. We would go back to Normandy if it was safe to travel, but we are afraid."

After a meal of brown bread and sausage, Benoit asked if he could lie down somewhere. She led him to a room under the stairs that had a neatly made bed. After lighting a candle she said this is where he would sleep while he was there.

"I'm so happy your family took me in, Madeline. You're an angel." Benoit touched her cheek then put his arm around her and held her tight for a minute. He kissed her.

"You'd better go. See you tonight," he said.

"Okay," she whispered, then left.

****

Benoit had three nights with Madeline. During the day, he played cards with her father and games of checkers with the children. At noon on the third day a man came by and told them he was a member of the same underground unit as Pierre, the man who visited Madeline periodically.

"I have bad news," said the man. "Pierre was killed this morning. It happened not far from the city when the Germans bombed the railway station. I am sorry to be the bearer of such bad news."

Madeline and the children began to cry, it was a sad day for them. Madeline's father introduced the visitor to Benoit, who told him his story.

He told him how he and the others got to Antwerp, and how they were captured about thirty miles west of the city, and then he told of the interrogation by the German captain.

"I escaped the interrogation officer after he shot four of our team," Benoit shuddered as he thought about what had happened. "He shot three men, just gunned them down, and then he went in the next room and shot our team leader. I heard the shot and heard his body fall to the floor. Then, I escaped through a window in the office. I jumped down about three stories and landed in a snow bank and then I ran across the city through back alleys."

"What do you intend to do now?" asked the man. Benoit shook his head. "We may be able to help you, we have connections around the countryside. I'll bring your case to our chief, and get back to you with an answer. Don't do anything foolish. Stay here and don't go outside. Be ready to move at a moment's notice. We'll contact you."

Benoit assured him he would stay inside. He then wrote a coded message and asked the man to give it to his chief. He said the chief would know where to send it. The man tucked the note in his sock and left. Benoit spent two more nights with Madeline. She begged him to stay.

"The war will be over soon, then we can go to our home in Normandy. Papa still has a large farm. We can live there and raise the girls," she pleaded.

"I'm a soldier, I'm expected to return back to my unit at the first opportunity," he said.

Madeline became very emotional. "You said you loved me, Peter. If that's true you won't leave me. How can you even think of leaving me?"

As darkness closed in on the third day a knock came on the door. It was the same man who had been there two days earlier. "Let's go, Benoit. Right away," he ordered.

Benoit quickly put on the jacket Madeline had given him. He kissed and hugged the two children, thanked the old man and shook his hand, then he kissed Madeline and hugged her as she burst into tears.

"You'll come back to us again, Peter. We'll be waiting for you when the war is over," she said, as tears streamed down her face. Benoit promised her he would return as he hurried out the door.

Benoit was taken to an area on the east side of the city. It was a trek of about thirty minutes to get there and he saw it was not as heavily bombed as Madeline's neighbourhood. His guide took him to a house not far from the railway station. When Benoit entered he saw a dozen people sitting at a table eating supper. Passwords were exchanged so that Benoit was certain he was in the presence of members of the French underground. He was introduced to the leader, a man named Adrien, then asked to join them for supper. When everyone had finished eating Adrien tapped his spoon on the table.

"I would like to have your attention please," he said loudly. "We have Peter Benoit with us. He is a member of the British intelligence, London branch. He will give us their findings about the German build-up in the Somme area."

Benoit gave the group a full rundown on the build-up of German troops in the Somme area and how the German Army was entrenched along the high ground overlooking Beaumont Hamel.

"Our opinion is that the British would rather carry out an offensive in the Somme area than near the Belgium border," he said. "We think they are wrong and we told them so. As it stands now the German forces have all the advantages, they are entrenched on high ground and have their heavy guns in place covering an area with a twenty mile front."

Adrien nodded. "I agree with your assessment," he said. "There's no doubt if the offensive took place near the Belgium border it would certainly split the German Army. This might even neutralize their planned operation in the Somme area."

Benoit agreed. After the discussion, he said he would like to send a message to the War Office in London informing them of the deaths of his four comrades, and also requesting permission to join his own regiment. He gave the names of the four men killed at Lille, including Frederick Frieda, and requested a return back to the Newfoundland Regiment.

****

Private Peter Benoit was smuggled to the English Channel coast around the first of May 1916, and taken across to Dover. He was immediately assigned to another undercover operation in France. He tried on two occasions to reunite with Madeline at Lille but was unable to do so due to the heavy German presence in the area. A month later he did get to Lille and went to the street where she lived. He was shocked to see the house was no longer there. Heavy fighting had destroyed it. He sadly wondered if she had escaped with her children and father and gone back to Normandy. Benoit would never find out. On July 1, 1916, he was wounded in battle at Beaumont Hamel. He died a few days later.

CHAPTER 19
Bad news at home

Nancy Frieda was washing clothes on her bridge, using a washboard propped up on the side of a wooden washtub. It was a bright sunny morning; the snow was beginning to melt. She paused to look at the field of Arctic ice blocking the harbour and decided this was a good morning to hitch the dogs and go for a load of firewood.

While she was thinking about what she should do, she saw the Moravian minister walking down the snow-packed road toward her house. He had a serious appearance. She waved her hand; he didn't respond. She was sure he saw her. She wiped her hands in her apron, straightened up, and waited.

As he got closer she greeted him, "Good morning, Reverend," she said in as pleasant a voice as she could muster.

"Nancy, I need to talk to you, let's go inside," he said.

She knew he had bad news for her.

"It's Freddy. Reverend, has something dreadful happened to Freddy?" she asked in a frightened voice.

"Come inside, my child," he said. She followed him in and stood near the table. He began by saying, "I'm afraid I have bad news, Nancy. I received a pink message for you from the war department. I am so sorry, Nancy. Freddy was killed in action in France. The war department has confirmed it."

Nancy covered her face with her apron, put her head on the table and wept. In a few minutes the minister's wife arrived. She put her arms around Nancy, "I'm so sorry," she said, as her eyes filled with tears. "We all loved Freddy. He was a wonderful boy. A son you should be proud of."

When people saw the wife of the Moravian minister heading towards Nancy Frieda's home they knew something was terribly wrong. As the news of Freddy's death spread through the little settlement, everyone began flocking to Nancy's house. No one had any details on what had happened. The only thing known was that the message said Freddy had died on the battlefield in France. That was it!

Everyone wept: men, women and children. It was said even the husky dogs howled in lament over Freddy that morning. As the morning wore on and the impact of the sad news began to sink in, they thought about his girlfriend, Emily, in St. Anthony and wondered if she had been informed.

Emily's Aunt Rachel, who lived near Nancy, asked the minister if anyone had contacted Emily. If not, she said, it would have to be done by someone here in Hopedale and it might as well be her.

"We'll send her a wireless, a pink message, informing her of Freddy's death," said the minister.

"I know it will break her heart. She was going to marry Freddy as soon as he returned from the war. Now it's too late, he's gone forever." Rachel sounded totally shocked. She couldn't believe Freddy was dead.

"I am going to open the church. I want as many people as possible to come and pray, it will help," the minister said.

Nancy knew she would have to control herself for the sake of her other two children. But she wondered how she was going to find the strength to cope with the loss of her beloved boy.

Every day in St. Anthony, the war news was posted at the wireless office. Dr. Grenfell had insisted this be done before he left for overseas because there were a lot of young men from St. Anthony and the surrounding areas fighting in the war, particularly in the army. Thomas (Tom) Boyd, the young wireless operator, heard the dots and dashes indicating a message was about to be received by the St. Anthony wireless station. He put on the head phones and began writing.

To Emily Bromfield c/o Charley Bromfield. Stop.

With sadness we inform you. Stop. Frederick Frieda was killed in action on the battlefield in France. Stop. He gave his life for his King and Country.

War Office.

"Another pink message," he said as he typed it out. "Freddy Frieda was the young man from Hopedale who goes out with Charley Bromfield's daughter. I'll have to get the runner to take this message to the Anglican minister. He's the only one who can deal with this."

Tom asked the messenger boy to go and ask the Anglican minister to come to the wireless office. He said to tell him it was important; he had to deliver a pink message. The minister arrived in a hurry and Tom discussed the contents of the message with him.

"I can remember Frederick Frieda when he was here late last fall, came from Labrador on the *Strathcona* with Dr. Grenfell. He was a fine young man. He and Emily planned to get married when he returned," said the minister.

"She used to work at the hospital laundry, but I think her father made her quit and go housekeeping for him. The messenger boy likely knows," said Tom. "I'll ask him to go with you and show you the house. And then he can drop by my house and ask my wife Nellie to come as well. Nellie is good friends with Emily and the poor girl is going to need someone with her. Her father is out on the barrens with the reindeer herd. It's best not to leave her alone. I'm going to send word to Dr. Little and let him know about Freddy's death too. He may come to visit her as well."

The minister and the messenger went to Tom Boyd's home and broke the news to Nellie. Tears rolled down her face as she put on her coat. Nellie knew how much Emily loved Freddy; when she was with Nellie, Freddy was all she talked about. Nellie knew Emily was going to be broken-hearted when she heard the awful news.

Emily was in the kitchen of her father's house sweeping the floor when she saw the minister coming down the road with Nellie and the messenger boy.

"Oh my God," she said to herself. "They have bad news, something is wrong with Freddy. I know something is wrong." Emily put aside her broom and went to the door. The look on Nellie's face told her something terrible had happened.

"You have bad news," she said as she walked to the table and sat down.

Nellie saw the sorrow in her friend's eyes. She went to her and put her arms around her and said, "It's about Freddy."

Emily put her hands to her face and started to cry. "Don't tell me, Nellie, please, don't tell me," she pleaded.

There was silence and then the minister spoke.

"Yes, my dear, it's true that we have bad news. Freddy was killed on the battlefield in France two days ago. I have a message here for you. It came in this morning from the War Office."

It looked for a moment as if Emily would faint; her body shook like a leaf.

"I'm finished, Nellie, I'm finished," she moaned.

There was not much anyone could say in this moment of grief. Nellie kept her arms tight around Emily as the minister said, "Be strong, my dear. We'll pray for you. Things will be okay."

Nellie helped Emily to the couch and asked the minister to go and get Dr. Little so that he could give Emily something to calm her. He left immediately, headed for the hospital.

****

It was a sad day for the people of St. Anthony as the news about the death of Freddy Frieda went from house to house. Many people from St. Anthony and the surrounding area had relatives, sons and husbands and brothers, who had gone overseas to fight in the war. This news made them even more fearful and worried.

Freddy, who had spent two weeks in St. Anthony before going overseas, was from the North Coast of Labrador, but he was accepted as one of their own, especially as Emily's father, Charley Bromfield, lived in the town. Two men were sent to the barrens, a full day's walk away, to get Charley. In the meantime, Nellie and Tom had Emily come and stay with them.

Dr. Little sent a telegram to Dr. Grenfell advising him about Freddy. However, the telegram was returned. Dr. Grenfell was at a field hospital in the Somme area and could not be contacted. Nellie tried her best to comfort Emily but it was very difficult. Emily blamed herself for Freddy going overseas.

"I'm the one who signed his army papers," she sobbed over and over. "Dr. Grenfell had me witness them. I feel guilty. If I could see him once more, I'd ask him to forgive me, but now it's too late, he's gone."

"Don't talk like that, Emily. No one forced Freddy to go. He volunteered. You just signed a piece of paper. If you hadn't, someone else would have," said Nellie.

"Maybe so," Emily said as tears poured down her face. A couple of days later Charley arrived back home with Jimmy Patey, his dog team driver.

CHAPTER 20
On the train

When Freddy said he was from Labrador, the sergeant asked if he'd ever seen a polar bear.

"A polar bear, yes, we use them to haul firewood. Back home we always keep three; two for hauling wood and one for meat, part of living," lied Freddy.

The driver wanted to know what the prisoner was saying.

"He eats polar bears and uses them to haul wood," said the sergeant.

The driver stared at Freddy; he nearly went off the road.

"Unbelievable," he said. "That must be the reason the captain wants him protected, he's a novelty for Germany."

The sergeant and the driver began laughing. Freddy was silent as he pretended he didn't understand them. What fools! he said to himself.

When they arrived at the train station in Lille, the sergeant told Freddy they would have to put him in handcuffs.

"Just so you can't escape. We will take them when you get on the train," the sergeant said and then paused. "What did you say your name was?" he asked in English.

Freddy thought for a second, maybe this was his chance to get out of the grip of the killer captain; if he wasn't registered anywhere by his proper name, the captain wouldn't be able to track him down when he wanted him again.

"My name is Thomas Tedleyhooktuck" said Freddy. He had never heard such a name before but wanted it to sound like a name from the north.

The sergeant asked him three more times. Finally, after trying to get his tongue around the name, he wrote down Tom Thompson.

"So from now on you are Tom Thompson. Don't forget it, Tom." The sergeant told the driver to make sure the papers on the captain's desk that contained the prisoners' names were destroyed. "That way the captain won't have a record. We'll put the blame on the janitor, say the janitor burned them."

The word captain made Freddy cringe, all he could see was blood and brains. And of course the tattoo on the back of the hand of that monster as he held his hand out. He would remember that for the rest of his life.

Then he thought about Benoit and wondered if the sergeant had really shot him or if he had managed to escape. The window was open and he had been left alone for about ten minutes. Benoit was no fool and he could have been through the window and gone, out of sight in ten minutes.

Maybe he had escaped. But, on the other hand, the sergeant had bragged how he shot him in the yard below the window. There was no way Freddy could know what had happened.

Still handcuffed, Freddy was put aboard a railway car. He was put in a compartment and the handcuffs were removed. The soldier who'd driven the truck managed to get across that he would get him food. The soldier returned with a loaf of bread and some cheese and fruit.

Freddy thanked him in German. "I leave, leave, go," the driver said. "Okay, okay," said Freddy.

Freddy heard the lock on the compartment click. Before he finished eating some of his food, he heard a commotion outside in the hallway and heard someone saying in German, "This is the room, this is the room."

The door opened and the light was switched on. A German soldier stepped into the compartment. He didn't notice Freddy at first. "Bring them in, this is the room they have to stay in," he said. Another soldier shoved two men into the compartment. The first soldier looked over his shoulder and saw Freddy. Startled, he shouted, "What are you doing here?"

"I'm a prisoner on my way to Munich. I was brought here by an army captain and his staff," Freddy lied.

"You can't stay here. I have two prisoners to stay in here, you have to get out," he roared.

Freddy shrugged. "Why can't the three of us stay here. There's room, we can bunk together."

The soldier looked at the older of the two men and he nodded. The other soldier threw in a bag and a pack sack. The soldiers left, slamming and locking the door of the compartment behind them. Freddy looked at the older man and held out his hand.

"Call me Tommy," he said, speaking German.

The older man shook Freddy's hand. "I'm Simon and this is Jacques. He's my son."

"How are you, Jacques?" Freddy looked at the younger man.

"Jacques doesn't speak German, only me," said Simon. "We are French, from Lille. We were arrested at our factory and brought here to catch this train. We have no idea where we are heading," said Simon.

"Do you speak English?"

"Yes, we both do," said Simon.

From then the three men communicated in English. Freddy had to be very careful not to give away his real name or give the slightest clue who he was or what his business was. He said he was from Greenland and had come as a goodwill ambassador to France where he got caught up in a raid by the German Army. He said he was being sent to Berlin for further examination.

"Oh," said Simon. "We are being sent to Berlin too as far as I know. We are in the cooperage business. We make wooden barrels that are used to transport dry fish and glassware. However, the German Army is using our barrels to transport explosives; they say it's the best method. They want us to build a factory in Berlin, my son and I."

"Why are you traveling as prisoners?" asked Freddy.

"We refused to go with them so they arrested us. I fear the Germans are taking over the world. I am afraid they are going to shoot my son if we don't obey them."

"I don't know what they need me for in Berlin. Do they have a prison camp there?" asked Freddy.

"I don't know, although I've been to Berlin several times. In fact, my wife and I have traveled throughout Germany many times on holidays."

"Have you been to the Bavarian Alps?" asked Freddy.

"Yes, it's a very beautiful place. I have always felt that Germany is beautiful, however with the war raging, nothing in Germany now is beautiful," said Simon.

Just then, they heard a volley of rifle shots outside the train.

"Those damn Germans, they shoot anyone or anything that stands in their way. They are savages," Jacques exploded.

"If we want to stay alive all we have to do is keep our mouths shut and be quiet. There's nothing we can do about it. We're not going to fight the German Army, or at least I'm not," said Freddy.

Simon looked sternly at his son. "That is what I have been telling Jacques. If he wants to stay alive and get back home he has to keep quiet and do as he is told. He has no other choice."

"Back home we have a saying, 'If you don't go by the rules, tie a rock around your neck and jump over the wharf,'" said Freddy.

"Young man, you have a lot of knowledge," said Simon.

"No," said Freddy, as the train started moving. "Not a grain. To be here, I don't have a single grain of knowledge."

CHAPTER 21
To Lans

The train whistle blew several times as it picked up speed. Not long after it got rolling, Simon asked Jacques to get some food from the pack sack. Jacques took out a fruit cake that was wrapped in a cloth with paper around it. He broke the cake in pieces and shared it around.

Later that evening someone called from outside. "Tom Thompson, is Tom Thompson in this room?" a voice asked in German.

"Yes, I'm Tom Thompson," answered Freddy, also in German.

"You're to leave this train in about an hour. I will come and get you and you'll be transferred to another train for Munich. Be ready at a moment's notice."

"I'll be ready," said Freddy.

"Munich and not Berlin," said Simon. "Did you know that Munich is the capital of Bavaria, and is called the gateway to the Bavarian Alps?"

"You must be a very important prisoner if you are going to the Bavarian Alps," said Jacques.

"They think I'm important," said Freddy, as he prepared himself for the exit.

"Here, put your food in this pack sack," Simon said, adding half the fruit cake too. He also threw in his razor and soap without Freddy noticing. "Here you go, Tommy, it's yours now. May God bless you."

Freddy shook hands with Simon and Jacques and said thank you as he gave them both a hug.

"If we never meet again, look after yourselves. Lots of good luck to both of you," Freddy said. Tears welled up in Simon's eyes.

A few minutes later Freddy was taken from the compartment. He never saw the two Frenchmen again.

****

Things were a lot different in Munich.

The panic was not so great, although it was a busy place and there were hundreds of prisoners heading for places they knew not where.

Freddy was told to fall in line with a long line of prisoners going aboard another train. It looked as though half the prisoners were women, young and old. Most of them were speaking French, or other languages that Freddy could not understand. There were German soldiers all around with rifles guarding them. He was standing behind a woman who looked to be about thirty years old. She carried a large bag over one shoulder.

"Excusez-moi," she said, when she bumped into him.

"Do you speak English?" he asked her.

"Yes, English is my second language," she said.

"Do you know where we are headed, what city we are going to?" asked Freddy.

"We are going to a factory somewhere," she said.

"I don't know where I am supposed to be going. I was told I was going to the Bavarian Alps, to a prisoner of war camp," said Freddy.

"God help you if you are going there, I've heard of that place," she said.

Those were not very encouraging words to Freddy. He thought he would rather go to a working prison camp, at least they would have to feed him to keep him alive. He figured he would stand a better chance there.

"Maybe I should stick close to you. When you go on the train I'll follow you. When we get on the train we'll stay together," said Freddy.

She looked at him with gratitude in her face then reached for his hand and held it tightly in hers.

"That would be wonderful," she said. 'It is very frightening being on your own. Monsieur, my name is Olivie. I'm originally from Paris."

"My name is Tommy. Don't ask me where I'm from," he said.

As they arrived at the train Olivie handed her bag to Freddy. Someone in the railway car reached for her and pulled her up. Freddy handed her the bag then quickly mounted the step behind her. Olivie clung to his arm.

"I'll tell anyone who asks that you are my husband," she said. Freddy agreed.

He and Olivie got seats together. Freddy sat across from a woman wearing a long coat who looked to be about forty. She had a touch of grey hair and looked very sad and alone.

The train bumped along all night. Olivie told anyone she spoke to that Freddy was her husband. She whispered to Freddy that she was twenty-one and had been married for two years. She said she had tried to make herself look older because the German soldiers were capturing younger women and using them for their own pleasure and she wanted to make sure she wasn't one of them.

"If we say we are husband and wife we may be working together in the same factory," she said, as she squeezed his arm. "We could request to be together and live together. I am prepared to do anything to stay out of the hands of the German soldiers. Sleeping with you won't be a problem for me if I can find some comfort."

Freddy hesitated, not sure what to say. "If we go along with this scheme we have to decide now before someone comes questioning us," he finally said.

"Okay," she said. "What is your family name?"

Freddy had no intention of telling her his real name. He would go with the name he was given at Lille.

"Thompson," he said. 'I'm Tom Thompson."

"You're Tommy Thompson," she said.

"Yes, and now you'll have to be Olivie Thompson. Don't forget."

"I won't forget," she said. I'm Madame Thompson. No, that's not right. I am Mrs. Thompson. Olivie Thompson. And you are Tommy Thompson, my husband. I hope our plan works."

"Yes, I hope so too," he said.

As the train moved along through the night, Freddy asked the woman across from him if she could speak English. She nodded yes.

"Do you know where we are going?" he asked her.

"We were told before we got on the train that we are heading to work in an ammunitions factory next to a labour camp somewhere in the Bavarian Alps. But this evening someone else said it was Innsbruck, Austria," she said.

"Do you know what sort of work we'll be doing there?" Olivie asked.

The woman shook her head. She told them her name was Jacqueline, but she was called Jackie. She said she was French. Her husband was a soldier who was missing in action.

As daylight came the train started blowing its whistle and slowing down at every crossing. Sometimes it even stopped. It was early morning when they came to a complete stop. Freddy looked out and saw a sign that said Innsbruck.

"Everyone out," yelled someone from the outside.

Freddy helped the two women off the train. Other prisoners helped those who were staggering and needed help. No one was left behind. Olivie held onto Freddy for dear life as the two of them moved along in a long line of prisoners. Jackie, who had no luggage just the clothes on her back, stayed close to them. German soldiers holding guns kept a close eye on everyone.

****

Several people were walking along the line of prisoners looking at them and selecting those they would like for workers. Freddy noticed a man and a woman walking along the line accompanied by a German guard. As they got nearer, Freddy told Olivie and Jackie to be quiet.

"I'll do the talking if they ask us questions" he said. They agreed.

When the man and woman came by, Freddy spoke to them in German. "Excuse me, are you looking for workers?" he politely asked.

The German guard looked at Freddy but didn't say anything.

The man said, "Yes, we need a dozen or more people to work on a farm in the mountains. Do you have any experience with farming?"

"No sir, we come from a fishing village. We have small vegetable gardens for our own use but we know very little about farming as such. However, we are willing to work and we will learn how to farm," Freddy said. "My name is Tommy Thompson. And this is my wife Olivie and her mother Jackie."

The German guard and the couple put their heads together and had a brief conversation and then the guard asked Freddy and the two women to step out of the line.

Freddy heard the guard telling the couple that he and the two women looked like good workers, and he said as they were a family unit they would probably get along well together. The couple agreed.

After a few minutes more talking to the guard, the man and woman came back and told Freddy and the two women to come to their truck. As they waited by the truck, nine other people, all middle-aged men, came and joined them. Before they got in the truck, the man introduced himself and the woman with him.

"We are Julian and Monica Myer," he said. "We are from a small farming village called Lans, located not far from here. We grow root vegetables, corn and hops. We also farm sheep and goats, five hundred of them, and we brew beer. The road to Lans is a bumpy one but we should have no problems getting home and we will drive very slowly. There's one thing I want to tell you. You are not going to a slave labour camp. You'll have no problems with us, we'll treat you well."

That was a blessing for all to hear.

Julian had Jackie sit in the front of the truck with him and Monica. Everyone else sat in the back. After a bumpy ride they arrived at the farm. It was a beautiful place. The fields in the nearby valleys were beginning to turn green but the mountains in the background were snow-capped. When they arrived at the farm gate an old man met them and let them in. After they got down from the truck they were taken to a large room in the main building.

"We have bunkhouses for the men, and one for the women. We have twenty-five men working here now and eleven women. Your group will bring the total to fifty-one workers. We intend to put you planting. You'll need a few days to learn how it's done, after that you'll be okay." Julian paused. "I'll be paying you all for your labour. We'll talk about that later. You'll be fed the same food as us, three healthy meals a day and a lunch at night. Food will be available at all times."

After everyone had eaten lunch, Julian took Freddy into another room and told him that he and his wife and mother-in-law would be living in a house not far away from the main farm.

"It's near the foothills. It's our old home, where I grew up," he said. "It's vacant now, but it's the same as when we left it. It's where we grow root vegetables on about four hectares of prime land. We also keep sheep there and a few goats. You will enjoy it there."

Freddy was pleased. At least he would be away from the war. However, he had no idea how he was going to handle the wife and mother-in-law situation.

CHAPTER 22
On the farm

The truck stopped at an old farmhouse surrounded by large oak trees and a field of green spring grass. The mountains towering in the background were something to behold. Freddy had never seen anything so magnificent. Julian opened the gate to the yard that surrounded the house and walked to the front door.

Julian beamed when he opened the door and stepped inside. "This is where I was born and grew up," he said proudly. "There hasn't been anyone living here for close to three years. When Germany and Austria started recruiting soldiers and workers for the war they were planning, everyone, including our workers, ran to the mountains before they arrived. When our workers left, we had to close this part of the farm until last year when a few of them came back. We didn't let anyone live in this house for fear of damages, but we have decided to let the three of you use it as you seem like reliable people. There are four bedrooms in this house. Only two have beds in them, but that's all you will need, one for you and your wife and the other for her mother."

Freddy expressed his gratitude to Julian and assured him of their full cooperation.

"Whatever we can possibly do to satisfy you it will be done," he said. "We are prisoners of war, not criminals. We will do our utmost to take care of everything on this farm. We won't leave without telling you first unless we are forced out by the enemy."

"Thank you, Tommy," said Julian.

Freddy felt like telling him his real name, but his army training kept him quiet. On the drive over, Julian had asked Freddy what language the women spoke. When Freddy said French and English but not German, Julian suggested they all converse in English. He said he and Monica had learned English in school and would love the opportunity to practice it. Freddy said that was a wonderful idea.

"What is the water situation, do you have a well?" he now asked Julian.

"Yes, there's one close to the house but it needs to be cleaned out," Julian replied. "It hasn't been used for a couple of years. Not far from the house is a brook. I'll show you where the pump is and how to hook it up. Not far downstream is a deep hole where you can bathe. Later today, I'll bring the sheep and three goats. The goats will need milking every day. You'll have your own milk supply. I'll also bring you flour to make bread and whatever else is necessary."

Freddy hardly knew what to say. Within the last week he had gone from the edge of hell to the gates of heaven. Would it last?

As Julian left to return to the main farm, Freddy and Olivie and Jackie stood and gazed at the truck heading down the dusty road.

"I'm lost for words to describe what's happening to us," said Freddy.

"Yes, we are too," said Jackie, as she began crying.

"I'll never let this man down as long as I'm here," Freddy vowed.

"Me neither," said Olivie.

The three went into the one-storey house and inspected the interior. The walls were plain wood, well put together and painted green. The ceiling was wood with a lamp hanging from the rafters. There was a large stove and a brick chimney.

A sign next to the stove said, "Please remove the outside cap before lighting fire." Freddy was glad he could read German. Jackie pulled down the oven door and peeked inside. "Lovely," she said.

"Well," said Freddy, "I guess my first task will be to remove the chimney cap, and then we can get a fire going and get rid of the dampness. I saw a ladder I can use near the side of the house."

"I'll help you, I'll hold the ladder," said Olivie.

Freddy took the cap off the chimney to allow the smoke to flow freely. He came back down and lit the fire and then went to a stream not far away to get a bucket of water.

"The same as back home," he told Olivie. For a moment he forgot about the war as he stared at the snow-capped mountains. He told Jackie that he and Olivie would take a look around the farm and she said she would boil the kettle and make tea while they were gone.

"You said you wanted to talk to me about something," said Olivie as she and Freddy walked along.

"Yes, I wanted to talk to you about the man and wife plan we were discussing. Do you think it's right?" he asked.

"I know it's not right," said Olivie. "But both of us said we would do it to protect ourselves from the German soldiers. I've heard people say they sometimes leave women alone if the husband is present. That's why I agreed to the plan in the first place."

"It's a cover for me too. I don't think we would be here on this farm now if we hadn't said we were married and that Jackie was your mother."

"You're right about that. I might have been sent to a labour camp with a bunch of men and ended up being passed from one to another all night long," Olivie said as she looked down at the ground.

Freddy thought for a moment then said, "Maybe we can change our plans. It seems we'll be safe here. We could stop pretending, at least tell Jackie the truth."

"Listen to me, Tommy, or whatever your name is, the war isn't over yet," Olivie said, sounding angry. "We are in a foreign country occupied by the German Army. We don't know who Julian is. In fact, we don't even know who Jackie is. She could be connected with German intelligence for all we know. She could be someone trying to find out who you are. You don't know for sure who I am. There is one thing I know for sure, Tommy. You are no ordinary foot soldier and I don't want to know what your business is or where you came from. Jackie and I are grateful you took us away from the gangs and the labour camp. We owe you that."

Freddy thought about what she was saying as they walked across the field. She was holding his hand tighter than ever. The wind blew across his face as he looked back toward the house and saw it was out of sight. He stopped and put his arms around Olivie and kissed her. He saw tears on her face. It was the first time he had showed her any affection.

"You can tell me your first name," she said, "I know it's not Tommy. If you tell me your first name I'll tell you a secret."

"Call me Freddy and vow you will never tell anyone," he said finally.

"Freddy," Olivie rolled his name around her tongue. "And now I will tell you I'm not married. I never was. I am single and I work as a clerk in a shop. The Germans came to the shop and took me. They sent me away on the train and that's where I met you. I'd say my parents are worried sick by this time wondering what happened to me and where I am. My father is crippled, and I am the only source of income for him and mama. Now I'm here with you. You have been so kind to me and Jackie. I think both of us are a little in love with you."

"I hope it stays that way," Freddy smiled. "We could be happy here if Julian does what he said. I should be able to hide out here for some time, unless I'm forced to run."

"If you run, you have to take me with you."

Freddy looked at her mischievously. "Now you have told me you are not a married woman do we still go on as man and wife. What I mean by that is do we share the one bed? Do we sleep together?"

"It's too late to change that now," said Olivie. "We still have Jackie and Julian and Monica to worry about. And anyway, I can always turn to the wall," she said with a smile, and then added, "but I don't intend to."

Freddy didn't comment.

When they reached the end of the field he held her and kissed her again. By the time Freddy and Olivie arrived back at the house Julian was there with the supplies and three milking goats.

Freddy had seen goats on the Isle of Man, but had never come in contact with them. He and Julian lifted the goats from the truck and took them to the barn. Julian told the three of them that the goats were usually milked in the morning. He said he would show them how to do it.

"Don't bother," said Jackie. "I've milked dozens. I'm an expert."

Julian had a supply of hay for the animals.

"You can relax until tomorrow and get the place in living order," he said. "I'll be here in the morning to show you how to plant seeds and potato eyes. I'll also bring a load of sheep manure to fertilize the seeds."

Freddy knew he was going to be very busy. There was so much to be done. He would talk to the women to see what jobs they preferred doing. Being a farmer was a new experience for him. "Unbelievable," he said out loud.

Freddy found oil for the lamps in the barn. He brought water and chopped enough wood for several days. He was an expert at chopping wood. He also went to the outhouse and made sure it was in order. When the outside work was done he went inside. The women had the house dusted and in top shape. It felt like a home; it was a home, a good one.

He sat at the table and surveyed his surroundings. He could not believe what was happening to him. Three days ago someone was holding a gun to his head and he had watched his friends get shot and killed. For some unknown reason he was allowed to live and meet up with two women and come to this farm. He stared out through the window and wondered why as tears ran down his face. The women saw his tears and came over and put their arms around him and wept with him.

"I was thinking about four friends who were with me. It breaks my heart, the way they died, the way they were murdered, that's the only way to describe it," said Freddy.

"Please don't tell us about it. We have heard and seen enough and we are in this wonderful place now. So far, it's heaven," said Olivie.

"It is heaven for us," Jackie agreed. "I only wish my husband could be here too. But I know he is dead. There's no doubt about it. He fought in a terrible battle. I was told there were no prisoners taken and he did not answer the roll call. He must be dead."

"You have to have proof before you say he is dead. He may show up one day," said Freddy.

"The problem now is that we won't be getting any news about the war, about what's happening on the battlefront," said Jackie.

"I don't want to hear anything about it until I'm an old old woman and then it won't matter anymore," said Olivie.

"I don't want to hear anything either," said Jackie. "And now I think we should change the subject and talk about our dinner. I do believe it's ready."

"I'm happy to say that we three prisoners are blessed so far. We can only thank the Blessed Master," said Freddy.

"We are more than blessed," said Jackie. "And we should surely give thanks."

The three had a wonderful meal of cooked vegetables and beef. It was a meal fit for a king. After supper, Freddy said, "I'm going outside to make sure the barn doors are closed. And I want to look at the mountains again to see what they look like in the twilight."

"I'm going with you," said Olivie.

"No, you have to stay here and don't even look at the way I'm going. I'm going to a deep hole in the river to have a bath. All I need is a towel," he said.

Later in the evening, the three of them sat near the stove and even though they'd said they didn't want to talk about the war they found themselves engaging in a conversation about why it had happened. It was a trying time for them, especially when they didn't know what was going on at the present time.

"Maybe Julian will have news for us from time to time. I wouldn't have the nerve to ask him, though, because Austria is on the side of Germany. I know that for a fact," said Freddy. "Austria is one of Germany's main Allies. Their army is fighting the war against us."

"Did Julian say who Monica was? Is she his wife?" asked Olivie. "I would think she is his wife. They seem to be very close."

'No," said Jackie. "She is not his wife. He told me she's his sister."

"Whoever they are they appear to be fine people," said Freddy.

Freddy wondered if Jackie knew what was going on. She went along with the plan that she was Olivie's mother, and stuck with it when they started working for Julian and Monica. Did she know Olivie and Freddy were not married? Freddy wasn't sure. He hadn't seen any sign indicating she knew the difference.

As Freddy surveyed the kitchen later that night, he saw two loaves of freshly made bread on the table. There was also a block of cheese and one of butter. The smell of home was everywhere.

****

Although Freddy was working hard, the first week at the farm was like heaven to him. All the seeds he and Olivie and Jackie had sown were showing above ground and growing rapidly.

Julian and Jackie became very friendly. One morning, Julian brought her a lovely dress and shoes and invited her to go out that evening somewhere in the hills. Jackie became very excited and couldn't wait.

"I'm speechless, lost for words," she said, her eyes beaming with delight.

"I'll pick you up around six-thirty. Is there anything you need?" he asked.

"No, I'm fine, thank you," she said.

"Okay, don't forget, six-thirty," he said as he left.

She stood in the yard waving to him. As Freddy and Olivie watched from the kitchen window they saw a happy Jackie.

"What will Monica say about this?" whispered Olivie.

"Jackie said Monica is his sister. Do you still think she's his wife?" asked Freddy.

"I don't know. They just seem like a couple," said Olivie.

"Maybe he is really single," said Freddy. "We don't know, do we? Anyway, whatever the case it's really none of our business."

"I'm happy for Jackie, though," said Olivie."This is making her happy."

Jackie spent the rest of the evening preparing herself for the night out. When she was ready, Freddy told her he had never seen a more beautiful woman.

As Julian promised, he was at the gate in his best clothes at exactly six-thirty.

He came inside, smiling, "Where is my girl?" he asked.

Freddy laughed. "You had better watch out. She is so beautiful that someone may take her away from you."

When Julian saw Jackie he stared at her for a minute, stunned at her beauty. He said he felt privileged to be taking her out for the evening.

"We have a forty-five minute drive to get to the next town so we may not be back until past midnight. Don't worry about us, and don't wait up. Your mother will be in good hands," Julian assured Olivie.

She smiled. "I always worry about Mama, even when she's just going to the market," she said.

"I know I'm in good hands, Olivie, don't worry," Jackie said as she and Julian headed out the door.

CHAPTER 23
Gustav Meyer

The war raged through Europe during the spring of 1916. The Newfoundland Regiment was fighting the German Army from trenches in France. The Somme became the battleground that will forever be remembered by people in Newfoundland and Labrador. Men were being killed daily. In June, the Newfoundland Regiment was entrenching themselves at Beaumont Hamel, preparing for one of the worst battles of World War 1.

****

Freddy talked about the war with Jackie and Olivie every day, and wondered what his chances of escape would be if he decided to make a run for it.

"If you go and get caught you won't be brought back here," said Jackie. "You'll end up in a prisoner of war camp or get shot on sight. That's usually what happens to escapees. There are army reserves watching everywhere, according to Julian They especially watch the prisoners on these farms."

"I don't feel justified living like this, sleeping with a lovely young woman every night and eating the best of food served up by a beautiful cook," Freddy smiled.

"You are fine here," Olivie said forcefully. "You escaped death once. You might not be as lucky the next time. You said God allowed you to live for some reason. Don't you believe him? Why commit suicide now?"

"I still have a part to play in the war, at least something keeps telling me that," said Freddy. "I should be out there fighting."

"Wait and see what happens," said Jackie. "If you should be fighting then things will fall into place. But, it's like I've told you many times, you are a prisoner of war. The Germans could come for you tomorrow. They could come for Olivie and me too. We don't know what will happen."

"I know what you are saying is true, but it looks as though I'm hiding from duty, afraid to get involved," said Freddy.

Olivie reached out and patted his hand. "You have been involved in great risks and that is why you are a prisoner," she said.

Freddy knew there was no use trying to explain his feelings to the two women. They were afraid he would leave them. They saw him as their protector. Maybe, he thought, protecting Olivie and Jackie was why he'd been allowed to escape the bullets of the German captain.

Jackie said Julian and Monica were coming over in the afternoon and Freddy suggested they invite them to supper. In late afternoon Julian and Monica arrived and accepted the invitation to stay for supper.

Just after Julian arrived he asked Freddy and the two women to sit down for a talk. Speaking in as good English as he could he told them how pleased he was with their work.

"You have done better on this farm than any other workers we've had in years past," said Julian. "We are amazed with all the seed you have planted in such a short time, and the way you have looked after the crops. It's the first of July and the potatoes are ready to come out of the ground, this puts our vegetables the first on the market. It means we'll get rid of them quickly."

"Tommy has been the push in getting the work done," said Jackie. "He's been in the fields from daylight till dark, eating his meals there six days a week in all weather."

"We have all worked in the fields," said Freddy. "These two women are the best I've ever seen. They are both hard workers and it is a pleasure to work with them."

"You have all earned some money and when the crops are sold I'll be paying you," said Julian. "In the meantime, we'll start harvesting the potato crop tomorrow. I'll send a couple of men to help you."

"No, we don't need anyone, we can do it ourselves," said Jackie.

Julian smiled when he heard Jackie's words.

After supper, he and Jackie went for a stroll around the farm. They said they were going to look at the sheep in the field at the back of the farm.

"I think Julian is in love with Jackie," Monica said after they left. "Julian is my brother and I've never seen him so content. I hope he doesn't get disappointed because when the war is over she could be returning to France. She has a husband, I think, although she says he got killed. However, she has no proof yet of his death."

"Jackie will never leave this place unless she is forced out, husband or not. I don't think she's ever had it as good," said Freddy, laughing.

"Tell me what you are laughing about?" Olivie demanded.

"We were just talking about Julian's love affair with Jackie," Monica paused and added, "Jackie could have a war baby before it's over."

Neither Freddy nor Olivie said anything.

Later that evening, after Julian and Monica had left, Freddy mentioned again that he should try and escape.

"If you do, you may get shot," said Jackie. "And I'm expecting the war to be over soon, according to the news Julian was telling me."

"What news?" he asked.

"He said there was a major battle between the British and the Germans at the Somme yesterday. There were many lives lost but it ended as a stalemate."

****

The July 1, 1916, battle of Beaumont Hamel had been fought while Freddy was in captivity. For the British Army, July 1 was the bloodiest day of World War One. They suffered almost 60,000 casualties. German dead or wounded totaled 8,000. By the time the battle ended, little remained of the 801 men of the Newfoundland Regiment. Casualties numbered more than 700, one third of which were fatal. Only 68 escaped serious injury.

****

At midnight on July 10, Freddy was awakened by the sound of explosions. He jumped out of bed and looked out the window. In the distance he could see the reflections of fire in the sky. Explosions were booming, lighting up the countryside.

"I think fighting has broken out around Innsbruck," he said.

Olivie and Jackie got out of bed and looked at what was happening.

"There's no doubt something is happening. It's not lightening, it's not stormy out," said Jackie.

"No, it looks like an attack on Innsbruck, or somewhere nearby," said Freddy.

"What can we do? Should we run to the mountains?" Olivie sounded anxious.

"No, there's not much sense doing that. We'll have to wait and see what happens. Let's see what Julian and Monica are going to do," said Jackie.

"I'm going outside. Do you want to come too?" Freddy said to the women.

As soon as the three of them went outside they heard more explosions and what seemed to be the sound of heavy machinery moving in the vicinity of Innsbruck. There was also the sound of gunfire.

"I wonder if they'll head this way. If we see them coming, we'll head across the fields and try to get away," said Freddy.

"If that's the case we should prepare ourselves," said Jackie.

"Yes, that's a good idea. Best to be ready at a moment's notice," said Freddy.

They put on their boots and coats and packed some food, ready to run and hide at the first sign of danger. Freddy went to the barn and made sure the animals were in their pens and the barn doors were securely closed. The explosions kept up for an hour and then everything was quiet.

"You go to bed. I'll stay on watch. If I see anything move I'll call you," Freddy told the women.

"I don't feel like going to bed. I'm worried about Julian and Monica. We don't know what's going on out there," said Jackie.

"We don't know what to do so all we can do is wait. I am sure Julian will come to let us know what is happening as soon as he can," said Freddy.

Shortly after daylight, Julian was spotted in the distance coming their way. They could see the dust from his truck. When he arrived, the look on his face told them there was bad news. He said the Serbian Army had blown up his brewery and hit the bunkhouse with a mortar shell. Four of his workers had been killed and three more had been injured.

"They were all French prisoners of war who arrived when you did," Julian sounded despondent. "I don't know what else can happen. This war is terrible."

Jackie patted his shoulder and tried to comfort him. "I'll make you some breakfast," she said. "It must have been a long horrible night for you. After you eat you must lie down and get some rest."

Julian looked at her with gratitude in his face.

"When I selected the three of you to come work here it was the best thing I have ever done. You've been my family this summer," he said. "Monica and I talk about you all the time even though you are prisoners. I know very little about any of you and I understand you not revealing your true identity because we Austrians are supposed to be on the side of the Germans – but I must tell you that I hate them." Julian looked fierce as he spoke.

After eating his breakfast, Julian lay down and went to sleep. It was close to noon when he got up. He felt refreshed, but his mind was still in turmoil.

"I won't be able to rebuild the brewery now and I don't know if I ever will," he said, sounding dejected. "I just don't have the money."

"You can have the money you were going to pay me, if it will help you. I don't need it. I'm a prisoner anyway," said Freddy.

The two women also said they would give Julian their money. Julian thanked them for the kind offer but told them their money wouldn't put a dent in the cost of rebuilding the brewery. He said he'd have to try and get a loan when the war was over.

"My main concern now is trying to live out the war," he said. "We don't know how much longer it will last. Nothing or no one is safe anymore."

"We can only continue on," said Jackie. "We live from hour to hour."

"There's one thing I can do in order to protect Tommy," said Julian.

Freddy put his head to one side as he looked at Julian and listened intently. "I have you listed as a prisoner named Thomas Thompson," Julian continued. "That's the name I was given at the train station. I could register you as one of the prisoners killed in last night's raid. Those poor unfortunates are being buried today, but I haven't prepared the paperwork yet."

"How will I get away with saying who I am if the Germans come here and want to know?" asked Freddy.

"If anyone comes here and asks who you are tell them you are my brother, my younger brother, and you have one sister, Monica. I'll fill her in on everything. You will continue to say Olivie is your wife and Jackie is your mother-in-law, that way no one can track you down," said Julian.

'I will need a new name too," said Freddy.

"Yes," said Julian. "We will name you Gustav. Yes, that's it, Gustav Myer. We'll call you Gus from now on."

The two woman laughed, then Jackie asked, "How many names do you have now, Gus?" She knew now he was Freddy/Tommy. Freddy had told her his real first name. It didn't seem fair to keep her in the dark.

"We'll only call you Gus when we think someone is around," said Julian. "But, in the meantime, stay out of sight as much as possible."

"Okay, next question," said Freddy.

"Yes, what is it?" asked Julian.

"Let's say a German officer comes looking for Tommy Thompson and you tell him he was killed and buried. And then you tell him I'm your brother and he will surely notice there's no resemblance whatsoever, no more than chalk and cheese. What explanation will you have?"

"I am not sure," said Julian.

"It's not a problem. Just tell them I'm from your father's second marriage. He married a woman from Northern Norway, a Laplander, and I'm your half-brother," said Freddy.

"Good idea. I won't forget that part," said Julian.

"One more question, what was your father's name?"

"Detlef. Detlef Myer."

"Oh Julian, I've asked you to tell enough lies for now. I hope God will forgive me," said Freddy.

"Hey Gus, remember there's a war on," said Jackie with a saucy grin.

"Okay," said Freddy. "Julian, go ahead and put a cross on one of the graves and print my name on it. If anyone comes looking for Thomas Thompson tell them I was one of the prisoners killed in the artillery attack. Take them to the grave and show them my cross and then they'll write me off. Also, make sure you do your paperwork and say I was killed in the attack."

It was a good plan, they all agreed on that. Freddy winked at Julian then and said, "Olivie and I are going out to the field to have a look at the sheep, we'll be back in a couple of hours." He knew Julian wanted an hour or two with Jackie and in his opinion he well deserved it.

CHAPTER 24
Karl to Berlin

Karl Hausser left the compound at Lille after interrogating Freddy and his comrades, he was happy to get away from the bloodshed. He knew he had not accomplished anything with the information acquired from the five prisoners. However, he was satisfied he had eliminated any threat they intended to make against the German Army. Out of the five, only one prisoner remained now! Freddy was going to a prison camp somewhere in the Bavarian Alps. Karl figured sometime later he would track him down and tell him who he was. It would be quite a surprise.

Karl sat on the train enroute to Berlin and thought about his father and wondered why he was so upset with the Kaiser and the great battles he was winning for the Fatherland.

As Karl sat looking out the train window he couldn't help feeling proud of himself. He was just twenty-three and a captain. There was no doubt he could climb to the top in a short time, especially if Germany won the war. All he needed was a boost from someone who had influence with the government or at Army High Command.

The train chugged its way through Luxenbourg and over the border into Germany. From the window, Karl could see that the German Army had swept through the area on a mop-up operation. Vehicles and equipment filled the ditches. Dead horses lay rotting along the sides of the roads, their stench filling the air.

When he arrived at the train station in Berlin, Karl got a cab to his parents' house. He quietly opened the kitchen door and peeked in. His mother was sitting at the kitchen table reading a magazine.

"Oh my," she said, startled when she looked up and saw Karl in the doorway. "Karl, my Karl, is home from the war." She ran to him and kissed and hugged him and started crying. "You should have sent a message telling me when you were arriving. I would have had supper ready for you."

"I'm not interested in eating, Mutter. I want to know how Vater is. You said he was very sick."

"Yes, your father is not well. He's in bed."

"Has he been in bed all day?" he asked.

She lowered her voice and whispered, "Your father has been in bed for almost a month. He gets out only to use the bathroom, and I have to help him then. There are times when I have to feed him with a spoon. He is quite helpless."

"Has the doctor seen him?" he inquired.

"Yes. The doctor has been here a few times to see him. He's treating him for a heart condition and bleeding from the bowel," she said.

"You should have let me know earlier. I would have come home," said Karl.

"I wanted him to send you word about his illness but he refused. All he's been talking about is the war and the poor people of Hopedale, Labrador, and how they are being dragged into the war to be killed for nothing. He's very upset about it. And, dear Karl, I must tell you that right now he might not even know you. During the last few days it seems like his mind is deteriorating." Maria put her hands to her face and wept quietly.

Karl sat down. He stared at the black shiny woodstove and the steaming kettle on the back burner. This house was where he had spent his early years, his best years, but now it was a darker time, a much less happy time. He thought about Freddy Frieda and wondered what had happened to him, where he'd ended up, what prison camp he was in. Thoughts of Freddy tormented him. He wished he had never come in contact with him in Lille. Then he heard the words of his father before he left home the last time telling him to leave the army.

"Go in the bedroom, Karl, see if your father knows you," his mother's voice broke into his thoughts. "You may have to shake him to wake him."

His father was lying on his side, his face to the wall. Karl saw sadly that he was a shadow of what he had been the last time he was home.

"Vater," he said softly. "Can you hear me? This is Karl. I just came home."

His father made no response. Karl shook his shoulder and called to him again, "Vater, this is Karl," he said a little louder.

Albert stirred. He opened his eyes and turned his face toward his son, immediately recognizing him. "Karl, it's you, Karl isn't it?" he said.

"Yes, Vater, it's me. I heard you weren't well and I came home to see you."

His father held out his hand.

"Karl, my beloved son," he said, "hold my hand for a moment. I think I'm about to go on my journey to a better world." Albert held Karl's hand and then paused to take a number of deep breaths before he continued. "But how can I go into paradise when my only son is involved in this senseless war? I greatly fear that God may not take me in. I think he may be angry with the German nation."

Karl wasn't expecting to hear those words. His father had always been a kind generous man, full of humour and faith. Now, thought Karl, he is very bitter towards me and the Kaiser and what we are doing. I guess he doesn't understand why we are fighting our enemies.

"Vater, don't worry about the war." Karl patted his father's hand. "Very soon now you will be feeling better and be up and having supper with Mutter and me."

"The next table I sit at will be God's table, if he will let me," Albert looked into his son's eyes. "But, Karl, I still can't help fearing that God might not take me in." With those words he turned his face to the wall. It was the last time Karl talked to his father.

Karl stayed a few days more. His mother told him if his father died she would spend the rest of her days in a home in Germany that was operated by the Moravian Mission. She said too she longed to see Hopedale again, even if it was only in her dreams. After a day or so, Karl finally had a discussion with his mother about Freddy Frieda.

"Mutter, I came across Freddy Frieda of Hopedale," he said. "Do you remember him? His parents were Aunt Nancy and Uncle Michael. Freddy and I were close friends, almost like brothers. We used to go to the off-shore islands in the summer when his father fished cod. Do you remember?"

"Yes, Karl. I remember Freddy quite well. Where did you see him? Did you visit Labrador?"

"No, I met him when he was a prisoner in Lille, France," Karl said smoothly. "The army has since sent him to a prison camp in the Bavarian Alps."

"Whatever you do, don't tell your father about this," his mother warned. "He has been very worried about the people in Labrador who have come over here to fight in the war ever since he had a letter from one of our missionaries." His mother paused and then as if she had given herself a mental shake she continued, "Freddy Frieda. Little Freddy Frieda. Did you know I used to call him my boy? Did Freddy know you? Did you ask him about his family and how they are?"

"No Mutter, I didn't make myself known to him. We shipped him off to a nice place to spend the rest of the war, a place where he won't have to fight on the battlefields. He will be fine there," said Karl, lying to his mother.

"Karl, will you do something for me?" His mother looked at him sternly then added, "Promise?"

"I promise, Mutter, if it can be done," he vowed.

"I want you to find Freddy and ask him how his mother is. I would like you to send greetings to her from your father and me, and tell her we'll meet again someday. Tell her too you will make sure not a hair on Freddy's head is hurt."

Karl vowed on the last breath of his beloved father that he would keep his promise to his mother. He thought it wouldn't be hard to do. His mother stood up then and went over to his father's desk. She opened a drawer and took out a small book.

"This is for you," she said as she brought it over and put it in Karl's hand. "It's your testament and I want you to have it. Your father and I gave it to you for your tenth birthday, when you were a boy in Hopedale. I want you to have it now. Never go anywhere without it. Keep it with you at all times for my sake. If you do, nothing will happen to you. You will be safe."

Albert Hausser died that night, a broken-hearted and very unhappy man. After he was committed to the ground by an old Moravian minister, Karl headed back to Lille to resume his duties.

But he didn't forget he had a promise to his mother that he had to fulfill: Find Freddy Frieda.

CHAPTER 25
The hunt for Freddy Frieda

The train stopped at the station on the outskirts of Lille, France. Captain Karl Hausser got off. He was met by his sergeant and a driver. Both saluted him.

As they drove along the sergeant said the French underground was attacking everything that moved outside the city. Karl told both men his father had died while he was home and they offered condolences. Karl went on to ask about the two prisoners he had left with them before he went home.

"Did you put Frederick Frieda on the train?" he asked.

The sergeant paused for a moment then said, "I don't know anything about a prisoner named Frederick Frieda. You handed me over a prisoner, remember, the short fellow, he told us his name was Thomas ahhh, just a minute till I get my notebook."

The sergeant pulled out his notebook and thumbed through the pages.

"Oh yes, here it is," he said. "Thomas Thompson, put on the train for Munich 4:50 p.m. April 27/1916."

"Good God, Sergeant, do you know what you're saying?" bellowed Karl.

"I know exactly what I'm saying, Captain."

Karl bellowed again. "We never interrogated a prisoner called Thomas Thompson. The prisoner I handed over to you was Frederick Frieda. Before I left for home, remember? I left another prisoner in my office and brought Frieda out and turned him over to you."

"Yes, I remember it quite well,'" said the sergeant. "But you didn't tell us his name and we didn't have time to go back and search for it in your office. We had to put him on the train. He told us his name was Thomas Thompson. I asked him where he was from. He said Northern Greenland, near the North Pole."

"Did you register him with the purser on the train? Where did you tell him Thompson was going?" Karl was upset and angry. He was afraid of losing track of Freddy.

"I told him the purser he was a very important prisoner and was on his way to a prisoner of war camp in the Bavarian Alps, the one near Innsbruck," the sergeant answered. "I also told him to arrange an escort when the train arrived at Munich and have him transferred to the train going to Innsbruck. What happened from there I don't know."

Karl held his temper in check. "We have to track him down. The War Department wants him back," he said.

"That shouldn't be a problem," the sergeant spoke calmly. "If he reached the prison camp under the name Thomas Thompson all we have to do is travel there and get him."

Karl asked, "What happened to the other prisoner, the one I left in my office? I told you to hold him until I got back. Where is he now?"

"Do you remember when I opened the window for you in the office that morning?" asked the sergeant. "Well, when I returned to the office the prisoner wasn't there. I knew right away he'd gone through the window. I ran over and looked down and saw that he was almost to the fence. I immediately drew my revolver and put three shots in him. I killed him dead. We collected the body with the other three and had them dumped in the pit."

"Well, at least you did something right," said Karl. "However, as for Frederick Frieda, we have to get him back. It's important."

"All you have to do is find a reason to go get him, Captain. But remember, Austria is a very dangerous place those days. There's talk of a rebellion against us in some parts of the country," said the sergeant.

"I know, I know. It doesn't look good in the east. Russia is massing three armies on the Eastern Front, a million men they say, and if this is true we might have to go there and fight. However, if we are successful around the Somme area and can make inroads toward the English Channel we may have to stay in Lille and help hold the line." Karl sat without saying anything for a while and then he shrugged his shoulders and said, "And now, as it happens, I have been given new orders and what that means is that we may not be able to search for Freddy Frieda for some time."

CHAPTER 26
Happy news

It was the beginning of August. Julian came to the farm to spend the weekend with Jackie. It was Sunday evening and they went for a ride in the truck, out to the main farm. Freddy and Olivie stayed at home and took care of things. They knew Julian and Jackie wanted to be alone.

"They are really and truly in love," Freddy told Olivie. "If the war was over I am sure they would never separate again."

"Jackie told me Julian is the only man she's ever really loved. She will never leave him," said Olivie. "And it's quite obvious how he feels about her."

"Her husband may show up. What then?" asked Freddy.

"She still won't leave him. I am sure of that," said Olivie. "And I think Monica will be fine with whatever decision Julian makes. Monica is very fond of Jackie, the same as I am."

"I think Jackie is a wonderful woman too," said Freddy. "But she is a married woman and her husband could still be alive. She hasn't heard anything official about his death."

"According to her, he's dead."

"We'll see," said Freddy.

As the sun was setting, they saw Julian's truck returning with a cloud of dust in its wake. Freddy looked alarmed.

"Julian is in a hurry to get back. I think something is wrong," he said.

The truck swerved into the yard and Julian jumped out, waving for Freddy to come over. Jackie got out and came to stand besides Julian.

"My God, Freddy," Julian was gasping for breath. "Five German soldiers came to the house looking for you. One was a high ranking officer, a captain, who said he was looking for a man named Thomas Thompson or maybe Freddy, ahhh something, I forget the name now. Anyway, I wrote it down at home. He wanted you, and he demanded to see our records."

Julian paused to catch his breath. "I was lucky I did what you told me. I wrote in the records you had been killed in the artillery attack a while back. When the captain didn't believe me I took him to the grave and showed him your name on the cross, Thomas Thompson. And then he went crazy and attacked the sergeant, punching him in the face and saying he was to blame. The poor sergeant never struck back."

"What happened after that?" asked Freddy.

"The captain said something about his mother but I didn't catch what it was. I was too much taken up by the look on his face. It seemed as if he was going to explode."

"Was he a tall man with a big mustache and black eyebrows?" asked Freddy.

"Yes, his mustache curled on each side of his face and he was young. I'd say not more than twenty-five," said Julian. "As he rushed out, I heard him shouting that they had to get the hell back to Innsbruck and saying he felt like shooting the sergeant right then. He was in a very bad mood."

"Do you really think he believed you? Or was he putting on a show?" asked Freddy.

"When they left they were heading away from the farm, high-tailing it for Innsbruck. The thing that convinced me he believed my explanation was when he got so angry he punched the sergeant in the mouth," said Julian.

"I have to be sure he wasn't bluffing. He's a very crafty man. I will stay hidden until late tonight and then I will sneak back," said Freddy. He looked at Julian and a grin crept across his face. "Maybe you should stay here for the night. I think Jackie just might take you in."

"I'll take him in," said Jackie, looking fondly at Julian."That's not a problem."

Julian's close encounter with the German captain made Freddy nervous and brought back terrifying memories of the killings of Irish and the Dutchmen in Lille.

One night he dreamt he was back in Lille being interrogated by the captain. He could see the tattoo on his right hand as clear as day. Olivie had to shake him hard to get him awake. He was bathed in sweat.

"Freddy, you are going to have to tell me what's bothering you. You are having nightmares," said Olivie.

Freddy said nothing.

But one night he started yelling and screaming in his sleep and then he began calling out for Emily. Olivie asked who Emily was.

"Emily is the girl I promised to marry if I returned home after the war. She promised to stay true to me until I returned, and she will," said Freddy.

"Do you really think she will stay true to you while you are away from her?" she asked.

"Yes. I'm sure she loves me," said Freddy.

"Do you love her?"

"I loved her," said Freddy.

Olivie looked at Freddy and her face was sad.

"You have been here with me for months, living with me and sleeping with me as if I was your wife," she said. "You've told me a thousand times you loved me and I believed you. Now you say you are going to marry a girl named Emily when the war is over. Not once did I ever tie you up or handcuff you and drag you into bed. You came to bed with me because you wanted to. Don't you think Emily is doing the same thing with someone back home? She's only human too, you know."

Olivie's words bothered Freddy.

What she was saying might be true. He was tormented by the fact that every time he closed his eyes he could see Emily's beautiful face and hear her calling his name. Yet he loved Olivie too. She was so good to him. What was he to do?

"There is only one hope for us now, Freddy. One of us has to go. We have to separate," Olivie said as she began to cry.

"Don't cry, Olivie," said Freddy. "Don't worry. I'll never leave you, so dry your tears."

"Shall we continue as we have then, working hard together, eating and living together, and sleeping together as man and wife?" asked Olivie. "Or, do I sleep with Jackie and you sleep alone until I can see my way clear to leave?"

Freddy reached out and held both Olivie's hands in his. "Let's continue as we have until the war is over," he said, wishing with all his heart this conversation had never started. "After the war, we can decide what to do."

****

One day Julian and Monica came to show Freddy how to cut and make hay, using a scythe. The women helped spread the grass in the sun for drying, moving it around with hay forks. This was hard work but enjoyable.

Freddy wished Benoit was with them. He would have loved Monica's company.

When the hay was harvested they all moved to the main house in Lans where they helped with the hay harvest there. One morning, Freddy noticed a trumpet case on a dresser in the living room. He asked who owned it and if there was a trumpet in it. Julian said there was indeed a trumpet in the case and it had belonged to his and Monica's father. He said their father used to play it at the Lutheran Church they attended in Lans. Freddy asked if he could play.

Monica and Julian nodded yes and Freddy picked up the trumpet and began to play 'Amazing Grace.' The rest of them sat and listened, amazed at how well he could play. When he was finished, he asked them if they had heard the new hymn that was sweeping the Christian world, 'The Old Rugged Cross.' They said they regretted they had not and he played the tune for them.

"Tomorrow is Sunday, would you like to play it in church?" asked Julian.

"I don't think I should take that chance," said Freddy.

'He'll play for us only," Olivie said.

"Yes, I agree with Olivie," said Freddy. "When the war ends I'll play in your church. I promise you that. If I'm still here."

****

Most of the sheep were returned to the main farm during October. Several dozen were butchered and the mutton sold to the Austrian Army. All the vegetables were sold except some that were kept for their own use.

On the first of November it began snowing heavily.

Julian decided to close the small farm and bring everyone to the main farm for the winter.

He told Monica he intended to propose to Jackie, but Monica was against it. She said Jackie's husband might still be alive. She advised waiting until the end of the war to see what happened then.

"I don't disagree," said Julian. "But in the meantime Jackie and I are going to live together as man and wife. We love one another and want to be together."

"That's fine with me. But I hope Vater and Mutter don't return one of those nights. If so, all hell will break loose," said Monica, laughing.

"Vater and Mutter will never return," Julian said after a long pause. "It's up to you and I, Monica, to live our lives the best way we know how. In this terrible war we can only attempt to do what's right and I think we have done very well so far. The three people we selected from many hundreds have turned out to be the best family we've had since our parents passed away eight years ago."

Julian paused again and Monica knew there was something more he had to tell her. She waited, not saying anything. "I have something very important to tell you," he said finally.

Monica could see excitement in her brother's eyes. "What is it, Julian?" she whispered, as if someone was listening. "Are we going to have an increase in our lamb population? Or perhaps in our family population?"

Julian laughed. No one could fool his sister.

"You are going to be an aunt before spring. Jackie is going to have a baby. I am going to be a father," he said, and his joy was evident in his voice.

Monica couldn't help smiling at her brother's delight. "I can see this news makes you happy, Julian."

"Yes, very happy," he said.

CHAPTER 27
Julian conscripted

Christmas time was about to arrive in the Myer household. The animals were in barns for the winter. Julian had all his supplies stored in the cellar. Although he'd lost his brewery in the artillery blast he'd still had a very good year. The farm that Freddy and the women operated had boosted profits.

Freddy grinned when Julian told him the good news. "Now that we're trained as farmers we're experts in making butter, cream and growing vegetables," he said. "We're also excellent at making hay. I grew up as a fisherman but if I die tomorrow I'll die a farmer. No one would ever believe it back home."

"And on top of all the things we've learned, I'm going to have a baby," said Jackie. "Or, I should say, Julian and I are going to have a baby."

This was news to Freddy, although he wasn't at all surprised to hear it. He was all smiles.

"Congratulations," he said, "at least there's something good coming out of this awful war."

Olivie gave Jackie and Julian a kiss on the cheek. Monica just smiled.

Christmas was a joyous time.

But things were about to change.

Around the middle of January, Julian saw soldiers approaching the house. He told Freddy to hide in the cellar. He and the women waited for the soldiers to arrive. Julian was nervous. "Remember what I told you, Jackie, you are my wife and Olivie is your sister," he said. "You came from Paris. Don't let anyone change the story."

Julian welcomed the soldiers to his house. He was surprised to learn they were with the Austrian Army.

"My sister, my wife and my sister-in-law," he said as he introduced the women.

The officer in charge was polite but direct as he spoke to Julian.

"We are here on business, sir," he said briskly. "You have been recruited into the Austrian Army. The government is putting together a force to help win the war. We need a hundred thousand Austrian men to build up the armed forces."

Julian was shocked. He had never thought he would taken from his home and thrown in the army. He could not believe it was happening.

"I can't leave," he said. "My wife is pregnant and there is no one around for many miles if she needs help. We have over four hundred sheep here, who will feed them? And on top of that who will keep the stoves going this winter? Someone has to get wood." Julian pleaded his case but to no avail.

The officer had his orders and quickly got down to business.

"Almost all of the German Army has left Austria," he told Julian. "They have gone to the Eastern and Western fronts. The war is raging in France. The French Army is helped by the British. They'll push the Germans out of France within a year if we don't do our part. On the Eastern Front, the Russians are pushing towards Germany. We have to help, if not we will lose the war. Everyone has to do their part. That includes you. We need you now."

"Will you give me a few days to get things ready? At least let me get enough firewood so that everyone doesn't freeze to death," said Julian.

"We can give you twenty-four hours at the most. When the train pulls out of Innsbruck tomorrow afternoon we'll be on it, and whoever is going with us will be on it too," said the officer. "So at noon tomorrow you must be at the station. If not, you'll be arrested and taken by force. There will be no place for you to hide."

It was heartbreaking news for everyone. However, there was no choice. Julian was going in the Austrian Army to help fight the war whether he liked it or not.

The officer said he would send a truck to get Julian at 11 a.m. the following morning. He said Julian would be kept in the army until April 30. He would be released then because his crops were important to the country.

Julian felt a sense of relief. He would be away for the winter and back in the spring. After the soldiers left Julian thought about his options.

"If I run away to the mountains I may have to pay the price after the war is over for refusing to defend my country," he said out loud. "If I join and go on the battlefield I may never return. And I can't forget that they can also return and burn the house down and level everything, I have heard about the army doing that to people who refuse to join up."

He finally decided he had no choice but to do as the officer said, and hope he was telling the truth about releasing him in the spring.

Freddy didn't believe a word the officer said.

"I have never seen an officer who tells the truth when it comes to the battlefield," he said. "He can't, especially if things are not going the way they should be. If you go into the army you will not get released until the war is over, even if it takes ten years. But, if you intend to go, we have to get to work and do the most important things before they come here to get you tomorrow."

Julian nodded.

"I'll show you everything that has to be done, and Monica can help too," he said. "She knows the way we operate. It's fortunate you are here. Having you here will take a great burden off me while I'm gone."

"I hope they don't come and take me," said Freddy. "If they find out who I am I won't be around long. That officer would have me shot on sight."

"I doubt if you'll see any more German soldiers coming through here. I would say they are out of Austria for the remainder of the war," said Julian.

Freddy looked thoughtful.

"Maybe I should try to get back to England. I might be able to travel through Austria as a civilian right now," he said.

"Please don't try and escape. You might get yourself killed," said Julian. "Please please stay and run the farm. It's too much for the women by themselves. A man has to be around to do the heavy work. Don't forget, I will be back in early May. I would so much appreciate your help."

Shortly before eleven the next morning a truck came plowing through the snow. Julian climbed in with his duffle bag and the three women waved goodbye. They kept waving until the truck was out of sight.

CHAPTER 28
Birth of a baby

Freddy didn't know what to do when Olivie told him Jackie was in labour.

"What do we do now? Do you know anything about it? What does Monica know?" he asked. "I don't know anything about having a baby."

"We are going to take Jackie to the midwife in Innsbruck," said Monica matter of factly. "If we go to get the midwife to bring her here the baby could be born before anyone gets back. The best thing to do is take Jackie to town."

It was the last week of April. All the snow had disappeared and the roads were muddy. Monica drove the truck and Jackie was packed in between her and Olivie.

The truck left for Innsbruck and Freddy sat alone in the kitchen and waited. He thought about Julian and wondered where he was at this moment. If he could only tell him he was about to become a father. Freddy also thought about his own situation. He had to get out of Austria and back to his Regiment. He had spent long enough hiding in the hills of Austria. My fellow soldiers are dying on the battlefield and here am I. What can I do? I didn't enlist to do this. Where can I go? What can I do?

Jackie's baby was born just before midnight on April 26. It was a healthy boy. Jackie named him Julian Frederick Myer.

****

Olivie decided she would stay on in Innsbruck for as long as Jackie was there. The midwife said she would be glad to have her around to help with the chores.

The morning after the birth, Monica left to return to the farm. Freddy was happy to see her. He whooped with delight when Monica said Jackie had a baby boy and he said he felt honoured that Jackie had named her baby after him as well as Julian.

Monica cooked a roast of mutton for dinner. After they finished eating Freddy went outside. It was beginning to snow heavily. He came in and said it was likely they were going to be stuck at the farm for a few days.

"I would say you and I are stuck here for a week, Freddy," Monica said, after going out to have a look for herself. "But we are fine. We have plenty of food for ourselves and for the animals. And Jackie and the baby are safe in Innsbruck and being looked after by Olivie."

After the dishes had been washed and dried Freddy put them away while Monica swept the floor and tidied up the place.

"Did Julian ever show you the flute our father used to play in the school concerts?" she asked, as she hung her apron on a hook behind the kitchen door.

"No, he never mentioned it. Do you still have it?"

'It's in the old trunk. Come, I will show it to you. Take the lamp and follow me. It's in the back room."

Freddy followed her, holding the lamp. The back room hadn't been used for some time. It smelled stale and musty. Monica opened a large trunk and rummaged through it. In the bottom she found the case containing the flute. It was still wrapped in its velvet cloth. She passed the flute to Freddy and they returned to the warm kitchen.

"Our father used to play the flute at weddings and engagement parties. He said the music brought the lovers good luck," said Monica. "Do you play?"

"Let me try," said Freddy. The flute seemed as if it was brand new. He blew into it. The sound was wonderful. "I'll play you the tunes I used to play on the trumpet when I was in the Moravian band."

Freddy started playing tunes that Monica had never heard before. When he played several old waltz tunes she longed to get up and dance. He played until close to midnight. When he finished, she told him she would get them a cup of tea.

Freddy went outside to check the weather. He opened the door, intending to go to the outhouse, but the force of the wind and snow met him. He dashed to the outhouse and back as fast as he could. He reported to Monica that there was a blizzard in progress.

"I don't like the sound of the wind," said Monica. "I'm not happy when there's a storm on. This house creaks like an old ship in a gale that's ready to crash on the rocks whenever there's a storm. It frightens me."

Monica made tea and toasted bread with jam and cheese. She attended to Freddy as if he were a prince. The two of them sat opposite each other at the kitchen table and chatted about Jackie and her baby. Monica said the baby had Julian's eyes and nose. As they sat and talked in the dull flickering lamplight with the wind roaring outside, Freddy could feel her legs under the table close to his. He noticed she made no attempt to move them.

"I like the wind blowing and the house creaking," he said. "It reminds me of the fishing shack we lived in when we fished at Turnivik Islands. Dad used to say 'think about how lucky you are, there's no brick chimney to fall on you from the strong wind.' But Mom was uneasy. She wouldn't go to bed unless Dad was with her while the storm was on."

"The wind frightens me and especially when I'm worried," Monica said. Then she added, "I'm worried sick these days about Julian. It gets worse and worse."

"You have to keep your courage up," said Freddy. "Worry doesn't help." Tears came to Monica's eyes. She put her hands to her face and started sobbing.

"Monica, you don't have to cry. Julian will come barging in any day now. The officer told him he would let him return before the time comes to put the crops in the ground," said Freddy, as if it was true. "Anyway, I'm going to bed now. But before I do, I had better make sure the outside door is secure and the windows are locked."

Freddy went to the room behind the stove and got into bed. He could hear the wind beating on the window and was happy he had a roof over his head. An oil night lamp was turned down low on the kitchen table. It gave off a soft glow that Freddy could see through the half-open door. He was drifting off to sleep when he saw a shadow moving on the wall.

"Freddy, are you awake?" whispered Monica.

"I am. What are you doing up?"

"I am afraid to stay in bed," she said. "The storm is making the house creak. It's scary."

"Go back to bed. Everything will be okay," he said.

She came to his bedroom door in her nightgown. With her hair hanging loose around her shoulders she looked like a young girl in the dim light.

"Monica," Freddy said softly as he pulled back the covers on his bed. "If you are afraid to sleep in your room by yourself you can get into bed with me. There's room enough for the two of us."

Monica literally leaped into the bed with Freddy as the wind and snow continued to beat wildly on the windowpanes. She wasn't afraid anymore. If truth be told, she was never afraid. The only fear she had was of being refused. But she need not have worried. Freddy was fast becoming a ladies' man.

CHAPTER 29
Sad news

The storm kept up for three days. It was a spring storm that halted all travel around the central region of Austria. The heavy snow and high winds meant Freddy and Monica had a hard time getting out to feed the sheep and milk the goats. On the third day it began to rain, and the rain kept up for twenty-four hours.

"I have lived here all my life and I have never seen a storm like this, with so much snow and rain at this time of the year," said Monica.

"We are doing okay. The sheep are being fed, we have lots of food, and lots of firewood. Jackie and Olivie and the baby are being well looked after. And you sleep with me at night because you are afraid to go to bed alone. I believe we're all okay," said Freddy.

Monica smiled.

"I guess we do have it okay, or at least I do," she said

"Why do you think you have it better than me?" asked Freddy.

"You are my prisoner, my prisoner of war," she said with a laugh.

Freddy felt guilty when he thought of Olivie. But in the meantime he was enjoying the attention being lavished on him by Monica.

"As soon as the weather clears and the water runs off, we have to take the milk to market. We have about thirty gallons. The cream and butter has to go to market too," said Monica.

"Olivie and Jackie and the baby will be coming home as soon as we can get them. They're probably restless by now," said Freddy.

"We'll try to go to town tomorrow. If the road is too bad for the truck we'll go with the horse and sleigh. We can get Jackie and Olivie and the baby after we bring our goods to market," said Monica.

By the next day the weather was suitable for travel. Freddy

loaded the dairy products into the truck and he and Monica headed for town. It was a muddy ride but they made the trip without any trouble. After delivering their products they bought groceries and then they drove to the midwife's home. Monica saw a difference in the baby in the week since she'd seen him. She cried and said how much he looked like Julian. Jackie wanted to know if they had heard from Julian.

"No, we haven't," answered Monica. "We have been isolated in one of the worst storms I have ever seen."

"Yes, they said the storm was bad here too," said Jackie.

"Have you heard any war news?" asked Freddy.

The midwife spoke up. "Yes," she said. "The Austrian army has been fighting side by side with the German army. They are fighting the Russians, I think, with a great loss of life on both sides. We heard yesterday they are retreating to Innsbruck. If that's the case the German Army will take control of the city again." The midwife looked at Monica, "If they are coming this way you had better lie low, especially with all of the livestock you have."

Monica nodded and smiled at the midwife.

"We brought you two legs of freshly killed mutton," she said. "We also have milk, cream and butter as payment for taking care of Julian's wife and child and his sister-in-law."

The midwife was overjoyed. It was more than she had expected. She thanked Monica wholeheartedly.

When they got back to the farm in Lans, Freddy told Monica he wanted to go back to the old farm and plant the ground.

"I want to be ready to put the seed in the ground during the first week in May," he said. "It will give us an early crop. That way we'll get a better price on the market, the same as last year."

****

Two days later, they saw a truck coming up the road to the farm. Monica stepped outside with Jackie and Olivie and Freddy and they watched the truck approaching. It was not a military vehicle. The truck drove into the yard and Reverend Jens, the Lutheran minister, got out.

“My dear Monica,” he said as he went to her and took her hand. “I have a message for you. “Let’s go inside where I can talk to you.”

The minister led Monica inside. Freddy put his arm around Jackie and they followed them in. Olivie brought up the rear. Freddy knew even before the minister spoke that the news he was bringing would break all of their hearts.

“I’m very very sorry to inform you that your brother has been killed in action,” said the minister.

On hearing his words, Jackie slumped to the floor in a faint; Monica swayed in her chair but managed to stay upright.

Olivie put her arms around Monica as Freddy picked Jackie up and sat her in a chair.

“Reverend Jens,” he said, “This lady is Julian’s wife and the mother of his newly born son.”

“Oh my dear, I am so sorry for you and your son,” said the minister. He addressed his next words to Jackie and Monica. “Julian was involved in fighting near the Belgian border. Over a thousand of our men lost their lives in the same battle.”

Reverend Jens stopped and bowed his head. “My dears, I am so very sorry to bring you this sad news. Julian was a fine man. He will be greatly missed by everyone in Lans.”

Monica and Jackie put her arms around each other and wept together. Freddy and Olivie said nothing as they watched sadly. The minister looked at them and asked if they were relatives. Freddy answered, “We are close friends and employees.”

Reverend Jens nodded and his face grew even sadder as he said, “I’ve got ten more of those messages to deliver today. This war is tearing the hearts and souls out of our people.”

“I’ll pray for you, Reverend,” said Freddy.

“That’s something different,” said the minister. “Usually someone is asking me to pray for them.”

“Where is your parish?” asked Freddy.

“In and around Lans. Although I travel to Innsbruck on occasions, my church is in Lans.”

“Do you ever come in contact with the Moravians?” asked Freddy.

"Yes, we are in constant contact with them," he replied. "They have a large congregation in Austria and throughout Germany. They are like us, all dead opposed to this awful war."

Reverend Jens prayed with everyone before he left.

Freddy followed him out. When they were outside he asked if he could speak in confidence.

"Yes, my son," the minister replied. "You can ask or tell me anything you like. My lips are sealed."

"I am a prisoner, brought here by the German Army," Freddy confessed. "It's important that I get back to England as soon as possible. I have been watching for a way of escape, I don't know anything about Austria or Germany or the route I should take to get out of here. If I visited you at Lans someday would you be able to help me? Could you tell me the best way out?"

"Yes. I can and will help you," said Reverend Jens. 'But if I were you I would not make any move until November. By then the German Army should be out of Austria. America has come into the war and they are fighting the Germans on the Western Front. The Russians are advancing rapidly into Germany on the Eastern Front. According to the newspaper, the Allies are driving the Germans out of France and Belgium. We are hoping the war will be over by spring."

After Reverend Jens left, Olivie made tea for Jackie and Monica.

Freddy wanted to put his arms around Monica and hold her. But he couldn't do that with Olivie there. Freddy found himself in a situation where he had no control and he didn't like the feeling. Putting on his coat he went out and took a long walk around the farm. As he went through the fields he knew it was too big for him to plant on his own. He decided to tell Monica they should move to the smaller farm.

Freddy's mind was in turmoil. He had three women and a baby to care for and he didn't want to hurt any of them. Then he thought about Emily back in St. Anthony, the one he was supposed to marry, and he wondered where it would all end.

Monica agreed with Freddy that the best option for the coming season was to move to the smaller farm.

Monica had fallen in love with Freddy, but she knew Olivie stood in her way. She didn't want Olivie to get hurt. She didn't want anyone to get hurt. But there seemed to be no easy way out of the situation without someone getting hurt. For the first time in her life, Monica felt defeated.

CHAPTER 30
Olivie

Everyone was worried about the spring planting. How would it go without Julian's usual input? It was a relief to find that everything went better than expected.

While the others were busy out in the fields, Jackie cared for the baby and did the chores around the house. She milked the goats, made butter and cream, and did all the cooking. She also cared for the more than one hundred and fifty lambs that were born in the early spring. Jackie was a busy woman.

One afternoon around the middle of July two trucks pulled off the main road and headed towards the farm. Freddy and Monica were out in the fields when they saw the trucks approaching.

"Military vehicles," said Freddy. "It has to be the army. Do you think it's the German Army?"

"I'm not sure, but I'd say it is," said Monica. "I'll go and check. You stay here."

"Okay, I'll keep watch. If you need me, signal." Freddy sat near a hedge, partly hidden, as a flock of sheep grazed nearby. He saw the convoy pull into the yard just before Monica arrived.

Monica saw soldiers milling around the house and barn. A couple of them were looking over the fields.

When she arrived at the house, she heard someone screaming. She hurried inside and saw two soldiers holding Olivie by the arms and dragging her towards the door.

"Help me, Monica. Please help me," Olivie implored. "Don't let them take me."

"What are you doing with that woman?" Monica shouted. "Let her go."

"We are taking her with us," one of the soldiers replied.

"You're not taking her. You can't. She is three months pregnant," Monica said, hoping they would have sympathy and release Olivie.

"You'll have to tell that to the lieutenant. He ordered that she be taken," the soldier was indifferent.

"Where is the lieutenant?"

"He's outside," the soldier pointed.

The lieutenant was a big man with a drooping mustache and fiery eyes, ready to blast anyone at the drop of a hat.

Monica tried to speak to him calmly,

"You are taking a very sick girl, Lieutenant," she said. "She is three months pregnant and is having complications."

"Pregnant, my eye. She looks okay to me. She is going with us. We need a cook. It's either her or the one with the baby," he said, pointing to Jackie.

Monica felt her heart pounding like a drum as she began to plead with the lieutenant.

"Olivie is very young and we are taking care of her. Please leave us alone. We're only poor farmers trying to survive."

She couldn't stop her voice from rising in anger as she continued.

"You took my brother a couple of months ago. He was this woman's husband," she pointed at Jackie. "He was killed leaving a baby boy he never got to see. A baby boy who will never see his father. Haven't we suffered enough already."

The lieutenant's eyes flashed in anger.

"Don't talk to me anymore, you witch," he said, then punched Monica in the face and knocked her down.

Taking out his revolver he waved it at Jackie and shouted that he had full authority to take any person, male or female, in order to fight the war. Jackie hung her head and said nothing.

Monica lay on the ground, half-dazed. When she regained her senses the trucks were leaving the yard. Olivie was sitting in the front seat of the lead truck next to the lieutenant. He was laughing and enjoying the ordeal. Olivie was crying. Jackie helped Monica to her feet. She was dizzy and blood was running from her nose.

"My God, my God, what can we do?" cried Monica, as she put her hand to her throbbing jaw. "Olivie. Poor Olivie. They have taken her and they will probably kill her. But what can we do? We don't have anyone to turn to."

She was silent for a moment and then she said furiously, "If I had a gun, I would have shot that ugly beast. I wish I could have killed him."

"Maybe they'll let Olivie go after tonight," said Jackie. She stood holding her baby and crying as she stared at the trucks moving towards the distant town of Innsbruck.

"No, she is too clean and decent." Monica practically spat the words out. "The lieutenant will keep her as long as he wants her then he'll have her shot. They do it all the time."

"Tommy will go crazy when he finds out about Olivie," said Jackie.

****

Olivie's detention was like a death blow to Freddy. The impact was as devastating as when they received the news about Julian's death. Freddy sat on the couch with Monica and Jackie as they held hands and wept. None of them could believe what had happened in such a short time.

"I should have come to the house when you did, Monica. It's all my fault," said Freddy. "I should have been here to save Olivie."

"If you had been here and interfered they would have shot you. They are demons," said Monica.

"What can I do now to get her back?" asked Freddy.

"You can't fight the German Army. All we can do is hope," said Monica.

Freddy knew she was right. He also knew he had to get out of Austria.

****

The summer was gone, the crops were harvested and sold. Monica had a good harvest. It was the first of September, a touch of frost was in the air.

At the supper table, Freddy told the women he wanted to talk to them later in the evening. Jackie was apprehensive. Freddy had been acting strange ever since Olivie's detention. He said he felt like a failure because he hadn't been there to save her. And he didn't know what he could do now.

After the dishes were put away, Freddy played the flute for a while. When he finished playing he informed them he was leaving. He said he had to try and get back to his Regiment as soon as possible. He said not only was he a failure because he hadn't been able to save Olivie, he was also a failure as a soldier. He was despondent.

"You can't go. We won't let you. I'm responsible for you. You are a prisoner here, Tommy Thompson," Monica said.

"Tommy Thompson is dead and buried. Remember?" said Freddy.

"What will we do without you? There are so many things we can't do without your help," said Monica. "We need you here."

"I'll be leaving within a week," Freddy said firmly. "We'll start doing the most important things that need doing before I go."

"Almost every job here on the farm calls for a man. We can't manage without you. Please don't go," Monica pleaded.

"Surely you must realize that I have to try and escape to return to my duties as a soldier. If not, I will be classed as a deserter," Freddy said.

"We know that. But don't you forget you are a prisoner here. You were captured and brought here by the Germans in order to work on this farm." Monica sounded angry. "We have done our best to cover up for you, to protect your identity, to make it as comfortable as possible for you."

"You're right, Monica, and I am more than thankful for that. But I have to get back to my unit. I have to try to find my way across Germany to the English Channel. It's important that I get back."

"I don't think you are interested in getting back to your unit, Tommy. I think you are setting out to find Olivie. You haven't been the same man since she left. She has been on your mind night and day," said Jackie.

"If you're going looking for Olivie you'll be playing with fire," Monica said. "If the lieutenant has Olivie it will take the defeat of Germany to get her back. Prisoners like her have armed guards protecting them around the clock. Those soldiers shoot first and ask questions later."

"I want to get Olivie back more than anything in the world but I agree that there is little one man can do against an army." Freddy looked at both women as he spoke. "And it is true that Olivie is on my mind all the time. But Monica, if they had taken you instead of her it would have been the same. I care as much about you as I do about Olivie."

"But I'm not pregnant like Olivie," Monica blurted. "And I can't blame you for trying to find her because they'll treat her like an animal, especially when they are drunk."

Freddy stared at Monica and then at Jackie.

"Monica, do you realize what you're saying?" he was almost shouting.

"Yes, ask Jackie," Monica looked uncomfortable. "She knows all about it."

Freddy turned to Jackie. She looked away, trying to hide what she knew.

"Jackie," he demanded, "do you have something to tell me that I don't know?"

"Yes, Tommy, I do," Jackie looked him in the eye. "Olivie told me she was pregnant. She was going to tell you soon."

Freddy was dumbfounded.

"Good God in heaven. I can't believe it. Olivie was having my baby and didn't tell me. And now Olivie has been taken away and I have no way to help her, no way to bring her back."

Freddy put his head down on the table and wept. Jackie and Monica put their arms around him and wept with him. They felt the same sorrow as he did over the disappearance of Olivie.

CHAPTER 31
Reverend Jens

It was late October. The weather was starting to get cold. Frost was in the air.

Freddy was finding it hard to sleep. Every time he closed his eyes he saw Olivie. If she had been with him in the field that day the soldiers would not have seen her. She would not have been taken.

He pictured Olivie screaming as she was abused by her captors. He saw her crying for rescue. The awful pictures filled his dreams and he would wake in tears, afraid to close his eyes again.

Freddy spent much of his time cutting wood and hauling it to the farm with the horse. He had enough wood packed into the shed for about two years. Monica took care of the livestock and milked the goats. Every week he would accompany Monica to Innsbruck to sell goat milk, butter, cream, and mutton.

"I would like to give Reverend Jens a leg of lamb," he said to Monica one day.

The next day Freddy dressed the meat for the minister.

On the way back from Innsbruck, they stopped in Lans and while Monica did some business Freddy delivered the leg of lamb. He went to the house next to the Lutheran Church and knocked at the back door. Reverend Jens recognized him and invited him in.

"You're the farmer from the hills," he said.

"Yes, I am, Reverend. I've come to bring you a leg of lamb, if you'll accept it."

"Thank you, my son. It will be a blessing in our home. Food is not so plentiful these days but it seems that God always helps supply our needs," he said.

Freddy brought in the lamb and placed it on the kitchen table. He said it was actually a gift from Monica Myer.

"Give my family's thanks to Miss Myer. God will bless and protect her," he said.

A woman with grey hair in a bun came into the room and the minister said, "I would like for you to meet my wife, Amalie."

The woman smiled at Freddy and expressed heartfelt thanks for the lamb. She said she would cook it that night. She invited Freddy to dinner but he said he and Monica had to get back to the farm.

"Would you like to talk to me in my office?" the minister asked.

"Yes, please," said Freddy.

They went in and closed the door. Reverend Jens asked Freddy to sit down. He began by saying, "As you know, Austria is an ally of Germany. However, the church is not, and whatever is said behind those closed doors stays here. You can trust me."

"Thank you," said Freddy.

The minister listened quietly as Freddy told his story.

"I am a prisoner of war brought to this area by the German Army," he said. "I slipped away from them and have been here for over a year and a half, running and hiding from soldiers searching for me. I want to get back to England and join my Regiment. I got captured in France and was shipped to Austria to a prisoner of war camp near Innsbruck. But I was lucky enough to end up on a farm here and I don't know how to get back to England without going through Germany. This is what I want to discuss with you. Are there any other routes?"

"Yes," said the minister. "You could go south through Slovenia to the Adriatic Sea or you could go through Italy, southwest to Verona, then east to Venice. I think the Venice route would be the best. I have a map that shows what I am talking about. If you go to Venice, go and see Father Bellini and tell him I sent you. But be aware the war is still active in Italy."

They studied the map for a few minutes more and then Reverend Jens folded it neatly and gave it to Freddy.

"When you're alone you'll be able to study it closer, it will give you a better idea of where to go," he said.

Freddy thanked him and put the map inside his shirt. He would keep it hidden.

"I'd like to ask you something, Reverend," said Freddy. "Is it possible for me to get a message to my army unit telling them I'm in captivity here in Austria. You know, tell them my whereabouts."

The minister thought for a moment then said, "I don't know of any resistance organization inside Austria and the media here are frightened to do anything. For me to get involved in contacting the British would be like putting a noose around the neck of the church. The German Army is entrenched at Innsbruck. They could fire a shell from there and destroy this church with one artillery blast, even while we're sleeping."

Freddy saw the minister was nervous.

"I understand, Reverend," he said. 'War is hell."

"If anyone is sick or hungry, we would do anything to help them. However, to get involved in the war is impossible," said the minister. Freddy told him again that he understood.

Reverend Jens left the room and came back with a stack of newspapers that he passed to Freddy. He said Freddy could read all about the war, especially about the war in France.

****

Monica was in a good mood.

"They gave me a good price for all our goods. They also paid me for the vegetables we delivered earlier this fall, and they paid me for our deliveries today," she said.

"That's wonderful," Freddy said as he patted her hand.

"We'll make another trip in a few days and bring Jackie and the baby. It will be a break for her," Monica said.

"Good idea."

"Was Reverend Jens happy with the lamb you brought him?" she asked.

"Yes, I told him it was a gift from you. He said thanks from both him and his wife."

"You didn't have to do that. It was your idea," she said.

"Reverend Jens gave me this bundle of newspapers that I'm anxious to read. He said the papers have lots of news about the war."

"According to the store manager I was talking to, the Germans are taking quite a beating on the Western Front," said Monica. "The Allies have pushed them out of Belgium and out of most of France. Russians are killing thousands of German soldiers on the Eastern Front. If this keeps up the war could be over soon."

"I hope so, and then everything would go back to normal," he said.

"Nothing will ever be back to normal, Tommy."

"We can only hope it will be," he said.

"When the war ends you'll be gone." Monica looked sad. "The only way I will have you with me is if the war continues."

"I could return after I leave the army, marry you, and remain a farmer for the rest of my life. Just you and me," he said.

Monica said nothing as she leaned over and put her head on his shoulder.

****

Freddy seemed on edge when he returned from town.

When he wasn't working around the farm he spent much of his time reading the newspapers Reverend Jens had given him. Almost every night he'd play the flute and sing to baby Julian in Inuktitut. He didn't tell the women which language it was even though they begged him to.

Freddy made up his mind he would leave as soon as possible.

He first decided to go by way of Italy, and then he reconsidered. He read in the papers about the October battle at Caporetto. The Austrians had attacked the Italians near the town of Caporetto and the Italians were forced to retreat with heavy losses. With Allied assistance, the Italians managed to stop the German advance just short of Venice.

The fighting was still continuing in Italy and Freddy realized it might be too much for him to get through the country. As well, Italy and Germany controlled the Adriatic Sea. To get through Austria and Italy to secure a passage by ship through to the Mediterranean would be too great a gamble. For those reasons, he decided to avoid the Italian route.

There was only one way out, he decided, and, that was through Germany. While he pondered his options, he read that German troops were now executing prisoners rather than transporting them to labour camps. This was not good news. It would be like going on a suicide mission. What should he do? He finally figured he should postpone his plans for another month or two.

Around the tenth of December the weather turned nasty. Several snowstorms swept the area. At times it was too stormy to let the sheep out to the watering hole and Freddy had to haul barrels of water for them as well as for the house. The whole countryside was buried in snow. Freddy was kept busy, working hard from early morning till dark.

On Christmas Day, Freddy felt guilty as he sat by the warm kitchen stove with Julian in his arms. His mind was with his comrades, probably advancing under rifle fire, somewhere on the battlefields in France. But, it was Christmas Day. Jackie had a roast of lamb cooking in the oven. Monica brought out her father's flute and persuaded Freddy to play some Christmas carols as she and Jackie sang along and the baby gurgled happily. Freddy put his guilt aside. This should be an enjoyable day for everyone. He would think about what he should do tomorrow.

****

In February 1918, Germany was in a desperate situation. Austria was ready to withdraw support for the Kaiser. The allied forces were advancing on Germany from the west. The Americans had declared war on Germany and were pushing their way east through France.

But, in spite of everything, some German generals still had hope. Freddy read in one of his papers that the German Army was successful in driving the Russians from their territory and that Germany then transferred every available soldier to the Western Front.

"Maybe all those German troops who took two days and nights to pass by the farm a few days ago were heading to the Western Front. You probably saw them," Freddy said to Reverend Jens the next time he visited him.

"Yes, they were all heading for the train station at Innsbruck," said the minister.

"I guess my chances of getting through Germany now are next to nothing," said Freddy.

"You'll stay where you are until spring if you know what's best for you," said the minister.

"I guess so, Reverend," said Freddy.

"It looks as though Germany is going to win the war," Reverend Jens told Freddy. "There's only one way it can be stopped now and that's by the Americans. It appears the Americans have better weapons, but we'll have to wait and see."

CHAPTER 32
1918

Karl Hausser wasn't with the Interrogation Corps during the final years of the war. His father's dying words led him to transfer to the German Navy. After the battle of the Somme, he became an intelligence officer with the Submarine Corps. He was promoted to a commander and became the head of communications for the submarine command at Ostend.

In 1915, the sinking of the British passenger liner, *Lusitania*, with the loss of many American lives, led to the United States putting pressure on Germany to eliminate unrestricted submarine warfare. But in 1917 the Germans once again resorted to unrestricted submarine warfare, convinced that was the only way to defeat Britain. In April of 1918, the British attempted to block the German submarine bases at Ostend and Zeebrugge in Belgium. They succeeded in Zeebrugge by sinking three old British cruisers in the harbour, but failed at Ostend.

Karl was transferred to naval planning in Berlin for the last two years of the war. He was among those who reviewed plans to have a submarine base along the North Labrador Coast. However, the German agents involved in the process got caught with the plans in New York and this resulted in the idea getting shelved. Karl tried to get his superiors to revive the plans, but it was too late in the war to attempt such a venture.

****

It was mid-summer of 1918.

In Russia, there had been major changes.

In 1917, the February revolution had resulted in the March 17 toppling of Nicholas 11, the last emperor of Russia. The Boleshevik party imprisoned the royal family and seized power in a military coup on November 7. On November 20, the new government offered Germany an Armistice. On December 15, an Armistice was signed between Russia and Germany and fighting ceased on the Eastern Front.

In July of 1918, Czar Nicholas and his wife Alexandra, and their five children, a son and four daughters, along with the family's medical doctor, the Emperor's footman, the Empress's maid and the family cook, were all killed by the Bolesheviks. News of the execution would shock the world when it was found out.

In the spring of 1918, German General Erich Ludendorff ordered a massive German attack on the Western Front. With 500,000 troops from the Eastern Front added to Germany's strength, the general was confident of success. The offensive began on March 21. In five hours the Germans fired one million artillery shells at the British lines. By the end of the first day, 21,000 British soldiers had been taken prisoner. The German attack was the biggest break-through in three years of warfare on the Western Front.

The first few days of the attack were such a success that March 24th was declared a national holiday in Germany.

But between March and April, Germany suffered 230,000 casualties. By June 1918, the German Army was seriously weakened by the number of casualties it had suffered.

The last offensive took place on July 15.

The Germans advanced one mile into land held by the Allies but suffered huge losses. The French then hit back on the Marne and a massive counterattack took place. Between March and July, Germany lost one million men.

Freddy read the news in the papers supplied to him by Reverend Jens and knew he couldn't hold out any longer.

The harvest was over. Monica had a bumper crop. The farm was running smoothly. When the crops were sold she shared the money collected with Freddy and Jackie, a gesture they very much appreciated. Monica was hoping Freddy was madly in love with her and would never leave her again. But that was not the case.

Reverend Jens said that when he was in Innsbruck he'd noticed the number of German troops seemed to be dwindling. He told Freddy he drove by the railway station to make sure it was not controlled by German troops. He saw no soldiers. It was an encouraging sign.

Freddy figured his best escape route would be through Austria and Italy, then east to Venice. He still had the map and the name of the clergyman at Venice that Reverend Jens had given him.

He knew it would be next to impossible to get to the English Channel by going through Germany with half a million troops massed along the Western Front. The Adriatic Sea would be his best hope.

CHAPTER 33
Fighting ending

It was five a.m. on September 2, 1918, when Freddy got out of bed. This was his big day. This was the day he would escape. He had his mind made up and nothing was going to change it. He was escaping from a place he described as paradise and had no idea where he was going to end up.

"If I wasn't in the army I would never leave here," he said many times.

But then he would remind himself that he wasn't a farmer. He was still a soldier who was supposed to be fighting in a war. Although he was a prisoner, there were no steel bars or barbed wire. Now there was an opportunity for him to escape. His consciousness caused him to make the move.

After he fed the goats and put them in the pens to be milked, he checked the sheep. When he returned after the morning chores Jackie had a hearty breakfast ready for him. Monica was at the barn. She was busy milking the goats. Jackie asked if he was going to Innsbruck. He said he was as soon as he had loaded everything they intended to sell. Jackie said she might come with him and bring the baby. She said she really felt she needed a break. She said she'd been thinking about Julian a lot and missing him terribly.

"What do you plan to do when the war is over," asked Freddy. "Will you return to France?"

"I don't know. I may not have anything to go back to. The German Army has destroyed France, especially the area I come from," she said.

"Suppose your husband is still alive and comes looking for you. What will you do, would you go back with him?"

"No. I want to stay here and raise Julian's son," said Jackie.

Freddy didn't speak for a few minutes and then he said, "I'm a soldier. If the war ended now I would be gone tomorrow. I have to, it's my duty. I know I must go. My duty as a soldier comes first. Whether I will come back is something I have been pondering over and over in my mind for months. I'm not a farmer. My people are not farmers. We are fishermen, trappers and hunters. I have enjoyed working here with all of you. We are like a family, and when we got the news that Julian was killed it was as if I had lost a brother. But when the Germans came and took Olivie it broke my heart. I hate the thought of leaving you and Monica and the baby. Little Julian is like my own son. I can't bear to think I might never see him or any of you again. Jackie, I will come back after the war after the war."

Freddy went outside and walked out into the field. The high mountains in the background seemed to loom higher than ever this morning. Their majestic splendour was something he would never forget even if he lived a hundred years. When he was returning to the house, he saw Monica coming to meet him. She looked as if she were dragging her feet.

"Good morning, Monica," he said. "Do you have the milk ready for the trip to town?"

She looked at Freddy with far away eyes. He knew she sensed something was up.

"I don't know how I feel this morning. I hardly slept at all last night. I have an uneasy feeling that you are going to leave us," she said.

"Monica, I have to leave," he said, as he put his arms around her and held her tight. He felt tears on her face. "I can't stay here forever. Now is the best time for me to leave. The harvest is over, the produce has been sold. You have enough firewood for two years, and enough money to keep you for a long time. I have to get back to my Regiment and try to do my part."

"Julian would never have left," Monica spoke through her tears. "He went only because he was forced to leave. You know that. He lost his life because some low down rotten dictator or a group of drunken generals forced him to engage in their game of greed and control. Now you are saying you have to get back to fight for some general who is trying to become famous by defeating another general. Fools like us are brainwashed to go along with their schemes. It's been happening from the beginning of time. This very land you see here has been fought over for a thousand years. The blood of innocent men and women has flowed and mixed with the soil throughout Austria and Germany. If the men who died could live it over they would have hid in the mountains or valleys instead of being butchered on foreign soil for some rich king or queen or some other lunatics. Who wants to get their name inscribed on the history books of time? Not one poor family around here has benefitted."

Freddy knew she was right, but what could he do?

"I'm a soldier. I took an oath to fight for the King," he said.

"Good God, man. Julian did the same." Monica was getting angry. "He took an oath to fight for the King, or the Kaiser, whoever the devil they are. He's now in an unmarked grave somewhere in western Germany. My father did the same. He came back home crippled in both legs, with pain enough it drove him into an early grave at age fifty-two. Every day Reverend Jens is going from town to town breaking the news to parents about their sons and daughters killed on the battlefield for their king. King of what? I know what. A king who signed a document with the German Kaiser to send our young men and women to be slaughtered like sheep. You are a prisoner, my prisoner. If I can keep you here until the war is over and release you as a healthy man then I have contributed something. I know you don't understand that. Maybe you'd rather be shooting at someone rather than helping us with our crops. I suppose it's the same with every soldier. They get brainwashed in basic training."

Freddy felt her body tremble. She was going to have to sit down. She could barely stand up. He helped her sit on a grassy knoll.

"You are not feeling well, Monica,' he said. "We should head for the house so you can have breakfast."

"I guess you're right. I am not feeling well," she said.

"And don't worry. I'll stay until the war is over, whatever it costs," he said.

"I won't let you leave," Monica said passionately. "If you do, I'll go to the German authorities and report you as an escaped prisoner. You could die an easier death in the prison camp at Innsbruck than be shot to death somewhere on the battlefield. When the war is over you can leave."

Monica slumped down in a faint as she finished talking. Freddy picked her up and carried her to the house.

The first thing he saw when he entered the kitchen was his packsack hung on the back of a chair. Jackie had brought it in from the barn where he'd hid it after he'd packed his things.

Jackie looked frightened.

"Is something wrong with Monica?" she asked.

"No, I think she fainted because she's hungry. She's okay now but I think you should get her a cup of tea." Jackie got the tea and handed it to Monica. She poured one for Freddy, and then put Monica's breakfast on the table in front of her.

Little Julian toddled over to Freddy. Freddy picked him up and hugged him. The baby looked so much like Julian it was remarkable.

"When I finish breakfast I will go to Innsbruck with you," said Monica. "There are a couple of new customers I have to see." She looked at Jackie. "We could be late getting back. Is there anything you need?"

"Perhaps some sugar?"

"I'll get some. And Jackie, while we're gone can you please unpack Tommy's bag. He's not going anywhere. He's still my prisoner."

Jackie laughed and said, "Yes, and so am I."

It was obvious that Monica would not let Freddy go to town alone again.

****

In late October, Freddy and Monica went to Innsbruck to deliver milk to the shops. The town was busy, especially around the train station. There was a lot of talk about the war. Some people were saying the war was coming to a close.

At the station there were hundreds of soldiers milling around. The decals on their uniforms indicated they were from different countries. Most were from Austria, although there were Hungarians, Turks and Slovaks mixed in with the crowd.

The troops were in a very demoralized state. They were dirty, ragged, unshaven and frail looking. Most looked half-starved. Monica saw an Austrian army officer sitting on a food container near a doorway and she asked him what was happening.

"We are retreating from Germany," he said. "The whole German Army and its Allies are on the run. It looks like the war will be over in a few days. It's the end of the fighting for us. All troops have been told to start heading back to their own countries. Germany is defeated. It's only a matter of time before surrender is signed. Western Germany is covered in blood, they haven't any ammunition left. There is nothing left to fight with. And I have to say I am glad there isn't," he joyfully stated.

"We should have never been involved in the war in the first place," Monica spoke angrily. "I lost my brother in this senseless war. I'd like to see Germany wiped off the map."

When Monica returned to the truck she told Freddy what the soldier had said.

"Austria is finished fighting in the war," she concluded. "It's over for Austria. Poor Julian is dead and what was it for." Monica began to cry.

Freddy suggested they drop in to see Reverend Jens before they left to return to the farm.

"Reverend, we have heard good news about the war," Monica said as soon as they arrived at the minister's house.

"Yes, so have I," he replied.

"We heard the war will soon be over," Monica continued. "The train station is crowded with troops returning home from the Western Front."

"This morning I had a visit from one of our army padres who just returned from the Front," said Reverend Jens. "He said there had been a heavy loss of lives on both sides with Germany taking the greatest losses. He called what happened a massive slaughter of young men. He said our armies ran out of ammunition and supplies. It must have been awful."

"When do you think the war will be over? Have you any idea?" asked Monica.

"From what the padre said it can't last any longer than two weeks. But it won't be over until someone signs a surrender document. I wouldn't advise anyone to stick their nose out until then. It's still too dangerous," said the minister.

"As far as Austria is concerned it's over now, according to the officer I was talking to," said Monica. "He said soldiers were advised to return home."

"Thank God for that. If that's the case it will definitely soon be over," the minister said.

"When the war is over the first thing you'll have to do is release me as a prisoner," Freddy said to Monica as they drove back to the farm. "And then I'll notify my unit of my whereabouts and have them contact my family and wait for further instructions."

Monica knew the end of the war would mark the end of her relationship with the man she had grown to love. It would be a sad day for her when she and Freddy said goodbye.

Jackie whooped with delight when they told her the news about the war and how it might be over in a couple of weeks.

"I suppose I'll be all alone this winter," said Monica. "I'll release you both as prisoners the minute we find out about the war. You'll be free to go your way then."

"I won't be leaving unless you drive me away," said Jackie. "This is the only home I have now and it's the best one I've ever had. I want Julian to grow up in his father's home so I won't be leaving unless you make me."

Freddy closed his eyes. He pictured the hills of Hopedale.

"I will wait until the war is declared over before I decide on anything," he said finally.

A few days later, Freddy and Monica went to Innsbruck with a load of bagged potatoes. After they made their delivery they went to the train station in search of more news of the war. They saw the station was still crowded with returning soldiers. There were lots of wounded men among them. Some were carried on stretchers to waiting trucks headed for the hospital. Others were treated on the spot by medics or Red Cross personnel. Most of the regular soldiers resembled walking skeletons. Some wore uniforms that were in tatters.

A train station attendant informed them that the prisoner of war camp near Innsbruck was going to start releasing the prisoners in a day or two. Freddy asked what nationality the prisoners were. The attendant said they were mostly British, but he had heard there were Americans among them as well.

"Where will they be taking them from here?" asked Freddy.

"I would say they will be moved home by way of Italy. The railway to the Western Front is in bad shape, blown to bits. The Mediterranean will be the proper route," the attendant said.

"There's no doubt the war is over." Monica was jubilant. "With the prisoners being released we could be on the verge of a German surrender."

"All the fighting has stopped," the attendant said. "I was told that yesterday by a high ranking Austrian army officer who passed through here. He was the one giving orders to release the prisoners."

When they left the train station, Freddy and Monica decided to drop in and visit Reverend Jens to see what news he had about the war.

Before the truck had even stopped, the minister came out into the yard to greet them. He was smiling and waving. "Come on inside, come inside," he shouted.

"Reverend, you must have good news," said Freddy.

"Yes, I have good news. It's an answer to our prayers," he said enthusiastically. "Kaiser Wilhelm has announced the war is over. I haven't heard that personally, but Reverend Meck from Innsbruck was here last night and he says he heard it on the radio. He said nothing official has been signed yet, but a surrender document is expected to be signed in a few days. He said all the fighting has been halted."

When Monica and Freddy got back to the farm, Jackie was boiling milk in a large iron pot on the kitchen stove. She also had a roast of lamb and vegetables in the oven.

"What a lovely smell to greet two happy, hungry people with good news," shouted Freddy as he entered the door and gave Jackie a hug that made her yell.

"It has to be news about the war. Tell me about it before you do anything else or I'll go crazy," she demanded.

"The war is over," shouted Monica.

The impact on Jackie was such that she had to sit down on the closest chair.

"I can't believe it," she said.

She started crying as she thought about the devastation of her beloved France.

"Yes, I know. It's almost impossible to take it in. I can hardly believe it myself," said Freddy.

"When a surrender is signed, what do you intend to do?" Monica asked Jackie.

Jackie dried her eyes.

She looked at the baby who had managed to pull himself up and was now holding on to Freddy's knee and gazing up into his face.

"As long as you let me stay here, I'll not leave," Jackie said as she looked at Monica. "This is the only real home I've ever had."

Monica smiled.

"Jackie, you know that you and Julian are welcome here for as long as you want. I know Julian would want his son to grow up here," she said and then she looked at Jackie and Freddy and continued, "Tomorrow is the first of November. We should make sure we have extra hay for the animals. And we have a hundred sheep too many. Two hundred is enough to keep over the winter. We should butcher a hundred between now and Christmas. We will have no problem getting ten dollars a carcass and five dollars for the fleece. That's fifteen dollars for each animal. That's a lot of money."

"We have enough wood and oil to last until spring no matter how cold it gets. We have plenty of food too," said Freddy.

"Thanks to you," said Monica. "Without you we would not have been able to do it. I don't know what we'll do after you're gone."

"Let's not talk about that until I'm ready to leave," he said.

Freddy picked Julian up and held him in his arms as he joined hands with the two women he loved very much. With hands joined, they bowed their heads and gave thanks for a return to peace.

CHAPTER 34
War is over

On the afternoon of November 11, Freddy was at the brook, filling the water barrels. Just as he put the last barrel on the sleigh and called to the horse to giddy up he heard Monica calling him.

As he neared the yard he saw Reverend Jens' truck. As Freddy came in through the back door Monica said, "Tommy, the war is really over. A surrender has been signed. Germany and her Allies have surrendered. There is no more war in Europe."

Freddy looked at the minister and asked, "Reverend, do you have any proof the war is over. Or is this just a rumour?"

"No, it's not a rumour. I heard the radio broadcast several times. I also had a visit from the mayor. He said they're planning a celebration tomorrow."

"This is the day the whole world was longing for. Thank God we've lived to see it," said Freddy.

After the minister left, Freddy sat at the kitchen table with little Julian in his arms. He knew what Reverend Jens had said was true. The war was truly over!

Monica and Jackie sat and wept when they realized what the news meant.

They were weeping for the past, but knew there would be tears for the future too.

"I suppose we're going to have to face the future as best we can," said Monica.

Freddy was silent.

"I guess we'll start to piece our lives together now," said Jackie.

"I guess so, if it's possible," said Monica.

Freddy knew the women wanted to know what his plans were.

They knew he was a soldier from a foreign country that had fought against Germany and its Allies. But, although he had been with them for almost two years, he had not told them where he was from or what his duties were in the army.

As Freddy looked at the two women who had suffered so much during the five years of war through no fault of their own he felt great sympathy for them.

He was different. He had volunteered to come and fight in the European conflict. However, he never thought he would spend most of his time as a farmer. That was something beyond his wildest dreams. But it too was through no fault of his. If he hadn't been sent to Innsbruck he might have escaped and returned to his Regiment.

But as it happened he ended up in Lans raising sheep and growing potatoes. Imagine, he thought, a British spy from the North Coast of Labrador turned into a farmer.

"Monica and Jackie," he said, "now that the war is over I don't want you to call me Tommy again. My name is Frederick Frieda, but everyone calls me Freddy. Freddy Frieda. I told a German sergeant my name was Tommy Thompson and that's the name I had when I met you. I gave the sergeant a false name because I wanted to get out of the clutches of a savage captain and I succeeded in doing that. Monica, meeting you and Julian changed my life. You both were so good to me and to my dying day I will never forget Julian. He was the only real brother I ever had. When Olivie was taken it broke my heart. I still can't think about her. I am not a very emotional guy, but every time I'm alone I shed tears for her and for Julian."

Freddy was quiet for a few minutes and then continued, "I have never killed anyone. Although I was trained how to kill people in different ways I never had to do it. I was trained as a spy because I could speak the German language. I never thought I would spend most of my time on a farm in Austria. But now I have to contact my Regiment and take orders from them. They will tell me what to do. If they tell me to stay on this farm for the rest of my life, I'll stay. If they tell me to leave tomorrow, I'll be gone."

The two women put their arms around Freddy. They knew what the answer would be. He would soon be leaving.

****

Freddy told the women he would wait for a few days before he decided what to do.

"Everything is in total chaos right now, especially with prisoners trying to let their families know they are still alive," he said.

"It may take a month before you get out of here. I hope it takes a year," said Jackie.

"It's not a good time of the year for you to leave. Certainly, no time will be good for you to leave us. Neither of us wants you to go." Monica paused and then asked, "After you leave, when should we expect to hear from you?"

"I'll write you as soon as I'm able," Freddy answered. "I won't be staying in the army after I get back to my country. I only volunteered to serve in the war."

"I suppose the first thing you want to do is get in touch with your family. Does anyone know where you are?" asked Monica.

"No, not even the people in England who sent me to Belgium. For sure the Germans who sent me to prison didn't report where I am. According to Julian, the captain who sent me here was satisfied I was killed. No one knows where I am."

"You might as well stay here with us," said Monica. "We can run the farm together and make a good living. The people in England will never know you survived the war. To hell with the army."

Freddy knew he could not stay in Austria for the rest of his life. Labrador was his home. He had no intention of exchanging potato fields for the rich fishing grounds of the Turnivik Islands. Corralled woolly sheep would never take the place of the caribou trotting on the barren mountain ground of the Kogaluk. He loved Monica and Jackie and baby Julian. And his heart broke whenever he thought of Olivie. However, Emily was the girl he had promised to marry and nothing was going to stop him from going to her. He would make it back to Labrador even if he had to crawl.

In mid-December, Freddy went to Lans and sent a telegram to the War Office in London, telling them who he was and saying he had been released as a prisoner of war. Am waiting your instructions. Frederick Frieda, member of the Newfoundland Regiment, service

#4012, he ended his message. His return address was Reverend Jens, Lutheran Church, Lans, Austria.

He was told by the wireless operator that there were several hundred prisoners working on farms around the Innsbruck area. The operator said they were mostly British and every day they were showing up at the office trying to reach their commanding officers. Freddy was surprised. He'd figured all prisoners were in camps except for him.

Christmas rolled around and there was no reply to his message. Freddy wasn't sure if the telegram had gotten through to the War Office in London. He began to make plans to head out on his own.

During the first week in January, 1919, he finally received a message from the War Office in London.

It read: *Delighted to know you are alive. Have contacted your Regiment at St. John's, Newfoundland. They will be notifying your relatives. Please confirm your identity again.*

Freddy replied with proper identification.

After the War Office received the mid-December telegram from Freddy they contacted the Newfoundland Regiment seeking information on Frederick Frieda #4012. They were told Frieda had been killed in action around the city of Lille during the winter of 1916. The War Office then sent the Regiment a copy of Freddy's telegram and requested a reply.

The Regiment did a further check and produced a file in which they found a written statement from Private Peter Benoit indicating Frederick Frieda had been shot and killed by a German interrogation captain in Lille. With Freddy's death confirmed, the Regiment notified his relatives. The clerk pulled a file on Private Peter Benoit and discovered he had been killed in France in 1916.

A captain from the Newfoundland Regiment was dispatched to the War Office to discuss the Frieda case. It was decided to have Freddy confirm his identity again before proceeding further.

After Freddy replied, confirming his identity for the second time, the captain wired him, instructing him to wait for further instructions.

Freddy was happy he had made contact with his Regiment. He knew he would soon be on his way, maybe by the first week in February.

CHAPTER 35
More news of Freddy

World War One began on July 28, 1914, with the declaration of war by Austria-Hungary on Serbia. Hostilities between the Central Powers, consisting of Germany, Austria-Hungary, Turkey and Bulgaria, and the Allies, Great Britain, France, Russia, Italy and the United States, continued until the signing of the Armistice on November 11, 1918, a period of four years, three months and fourteen days.

Dr. Grenfell returned to St. John's immediately after the Armistice was signed. He knew he would have to leave for the Northern Peninsula before freeze up, not later than the twentieth of December. After that date the mail boats would be finished running until the spring.

When Grenfell and several other war veterans arrived by coastal boat at St. Anthony, it was a day of celebration. All flags were flying. Everyone was at the dock to meet them. Welcome speeches were made. Hymns were sung and the 'Ode to Newfoundland,' the Colony's anthem, rang through the hills.

After the arrivals were greeted and the handshakes, hugs and kisses were over, Dr. Grenfell was pleasantly surprised at the sight of a dozen of his reindeer all decorated and standing on the dock along with Charley Bromfield and his herdsmen. Charley and the herdsmen and the reindeer followed Dr. Grenfell all the way to the hospital gate. After the crowd left, Grenfell started chatting with Charley.

"I would like to have a meeting with you this evening, if it's possible," said Grenfell.

"Yes, after supper would be fine."

"Good," said Grenfell, then added, "By the way, I didn't see Jimmy Patey. Is he still with us, still with the reindeer herd?"

"Oh yes. He's out with the rest of the herd," Charley answered. "By the way, Jimmy got married since you left. He married my daughter Emily. They have a daughter of their own now, they named her Emma."

Grenfell did not look pleased. He stared at Charley and said, "So she couldn't wait for young Freddy Frieda to come back. But I suppose you can't blame her."

Charley was miffed. "Dr. Grenfell, haven't you heard? Freddy was killed somewhere in France. After we received the news that Freddy was killed Emily almost died. She cried for weeks. We were happy when she started going out with Jimmy. I'm not sure if she is over the news about Freddy yet. She may never get over it."

****

Jimmy Patey, a herdsmen for Grenfell's reindeer, says he fell in love with Emily the first time he met her: "I tried my best to get her to go out with me but she wouldn't, although she spent a lot of time in the country with me and her father, Charley Bromfield. Emily had promised to marry a young fellow Freddy Frieda from Hopedale who had gone to Europe during the First World War. One day we received word that Freddy had been killed in a battle somewhere in France. It was an awful shock for all of us. Finally, like everything, the news of young Freddy's death started to fade away. I spent most of my time with Charley, practically living with him and Emily at their home. It seemed whenever I looked, Emily was there. She depended on me for everything, wood for the stove, water for the house and going to the store. She was as good as me with a team of reindeer and we went everywhere together. Finally she let me start dating her. After three or four months we were married. Six months after we were married we had a baby girl. We named her Emma. When Dr. Grenfell returned from the war I became his personal dog team driver."

****

Grenfell was shocked when Charley told him about Freddy's death. He was also angry because he had never been notified.

"This is terrible news. Tragic news," he said. "I'm the one who recruited Freddy. I feel responsible for his death."

"It's funny someone didn't notify you. Everyone here knew about it," said Charley.

"How are his family in Hopedale coping?" asked Grenfell.

"As best they can," said Charley. "They accepted Freddy's death as him doing his part for his country."

Grenfell hung his head. There was nothing more to say.

****

It was close to the end of January before the army confirmed that Frederick Frieda, service #4012 of the Newfoundland Regiment, was alive and had been released as a prisoner of war in Austria.

Plans were put in place to get Freddy back to England.

Regimental headquarters in St. John's were informed he was alive and asked to notify his family that he was alive and well. The officer in St. John's opened the file on Frederick Frieda.

In the file it was stated that in case of his death, they were to notify Nancy Frieda (mother), Hopedale, Labrador, also Emily Bromfield (girlfriend), St. Anthony, Newfoundland. When the office received the news that Freddy had been killed in France almost two years earlier they had notified his mother and Emily of his death. Now, they would have to notify them that he was alive.

The officer smiled at the staff members who had gathered to hear the good news about Freddy. "This is wonderful news," he said. "No doubt there will be a celebration on the North Coast of Labrador tonight, and in St. Anthony his girlfriend will likely go crazy."

****

It was dark enough to light the lamp when a knock came on Nancy Frieda's door.

"Whoever is knocking come on in," said Nancy, who was hanging up dog harnesses behind the stove. She had been hauling firewood with the dog team all afternoon. Her daughter, Blanche, was setting the table for supper.

The door opened and the Moravian minister entered. He started brushing the snow off his boots with his woolen mitts.

"I know you're not lost and you're not drove out. You have to be on business," Nancy said.

"Yes, I'm here on business. I have a telegram for you, and it's good news," he said.

"Good news is alright for a change. I've heard a lot of bad news in my day, so a bit of good news could go a long way," Nancy said in a less than enthusiastic manner.

"Sit down, Nancy, and listen very carefully," he said.

She sat on a chair with her arms on the table. Her shirt sleeves were partly rolled up. The minister pulled out a chair and sat down. He took an envelope from his pocket. "This telegram is for you, Nancy," he said. "I'll read it to you."

To Mrs. Nancy Frieda, Hopedale Labrador. Stop. We are happy to inform you that your son Frederick Frieda has been found alive and well at a prisoner of war camp in Austria. Stop. Arrangements are being made to have him return home travel permitting. Stop. We will keep you informed. Signed, Newfoundland Regiment, St. John's.

The news hit Nancy almost as badly as when she was told Freddy had been killed. She fell forward on the table and began crying uncontrollably.

Blanche heard what the minister had read and shouted, "Oh my, oh my good God, Reverend, did you say Freddy was still alive? Is that what you said?"

"Yes, my dear, that's what the telegram said," he said.

"Mom, Mom, is it true?" Blanche grabbed her mother by the arm and pulled her head up.

Tears were streaming down Nancy's face. "I believe it, Blanche, I believe it," she said. "I've never stopped praying for Freddy every day and every night since that dreadful day we received the news he was killed. I knew he would be back. I knew he wasn't dead."

The two women turned and put their arms around the minister who was by now crying. He knew a cry for joy brought the biggest tears.

"Blanche, call out next door and tell Aunt Rachel to come quickly. We have to tell her the news," said Nancy.

Blanche dashed to the door and screamed for Aunt Rachel. Rachel heard the loud scream and knew something had happened at Nancy's house. She left without closing her door and rushed next door.

"What's the matter, Nancy? For God's sake what's wrong?" she shouted. And then she saw the Moravian minister standing in the kitchen with tears running down his face. "What's the matter?" she yelled, her hands clenched in fists.

"Freddy has been found alive. They've found Freddy alive in a prison camp. He's not dead," said Blanche.

"Is this true? Do you know what you're saying," demanded Rachel.

"Yes," said the minister. "I have the telegram here. I'll read it to you." He read the telegram aloud to Rachel and Sarah, who had just arrived home. The news that Freddy was alive was almost unbelievable, even to the minister.

"Do you think it's really true? Who signed it? Who is it from," asked Sarah, wanting to make certain that what she was hearing was real and true.

"It's from the Newfoundland Regiment in St. John's. The Newfoundland Regiment, that's the regiment Freddy joined," the minister said.

It was now twilight and the stars were beginning to appear in the western sky. The rays from the sinking sun cast an orange glow over the small northern village of Hopedale. The news that their native son, whom they thought had been killed and buried in the war almost three years ago, had been found alive and was coming home quickly spread. It took only a few minutes for the news that Freddy was alive to reach every household in Hopedale.

****

During the early evening, people started gathering at Nancy's. It was a joyous time for everyone. Rachel Bromfield finally returned to her home and lit the oil lamp. She'd had to leave Nancy's house. It was filling up with people who had heard the news about Freddy and getting too crowded for her.

Rachel had cried with joy and clapped her hands when she heard about Freddy, but she also felt a tinge of sadness when she thought about Emily. Her thoughts went back to the days when Emily was getting married, five months after receiving the news that Freddy had been killed.

Rachel had traveled to St. Anthony to attend her wedding. The groom, Jimmy Patey, a friend of their family, was a good person who loved Emily. But Rachel favoured Freddy over Jimmy, probably because he was a Labrador native. Or, maybe it was because Freddy was so much like her own child. Rachel had no children of her own. She loved Freddy and she loved Emily, who called her mom because Rachel had raised her from the time she was an infant of two months. A day or so before the wedding, Rachel had time to have a private discussion with Emily.

"I'm proud of the man you are marrying, my dear," she said. "I know he'll love you and look after you."

"I love him too, Mom. I would never marry him if I didn't," said Emily.

"I know and I'm happy for you. Your father thinks Jimmy is the best man in the world and he should know because they're together all the time," said Rachel.

"Yes, they're gone most of the time with the reindeer herd. But that's all right. I don't need a man around all the time," Emily laughed.

Rachel paused for a minute then said, "I have to tell you the truth, Emily. I liked Freddy more. Freddy was a different man, carefree and fearless. Remember when he would take me on his back and run up and down the road, with me screaming and everyone laughing. He was great fun."

"I think about Freddy every day," Emily said as tears came to her eyes. "My heart is still broken. I think it's a wound that will never heal even if I live to be a hundred."

"I still have the feeling Freddy will come back home some day. I've dreamed about him returning to Hopedale a thousand times," said Rachel.

"There are times when I sit and cry for hours, especially when I think about how I co-signed the papers for him to go into the army. It's the thing I most regret doing in my life," Emily said sadly. 'I was asked to co-sign the papers and I couldn't refuse."

"I never knew that. But he would have gone in the army anyway. His mind was made up." They were quiet for a few minutes and then Rachel said, "Emily, if Freddy returned home today would you still marry Jimmy?"

"Yes, Mom, I would," Emily said firmly. "I have to marry Jimmy. I'm going to have his baby. I'm two months along now."

Rachel put her arms around Emily and held her close. "Don't worry, my child," she said to the young woman she thought of as her daughter. "Freddy will never return. I've never yet had a dream that came true."

CHAPTER 36
Sports Day

It was Sports Day and the town of St. Anthony was getting ready for the dog team races. Everyone was in a festive mood. Dr. Grenfell was the guest of honour. He was preparing a speech in his office on this bitterly cold day. He would go to the school first and present his speech then proceed to the harbour ice where the teams would line up. At 10 a.m. just as he was about to leave for the school Tom Boyd, the wireless operator, came into his office.

"I have a telegram for you, Dr. Grenfell," he said.

"Thanks, Thomas. Put it in the 'in' basket. I'll see to it later this afternoon when the races are finished. I'm about to leave now."

"Dr. Grenfell," Tom said as he put the envelope on the desk. "This is from the War Department. It's important. It requires your immediate attention."

Grenfell pushed aside the note pad he was writing on and quickly opened the envelope. His eyes scanned the telegram and then he laid it flat on the table and stared at Tom.

"Imagine that. It's unbelievable. I can only say thank God something good has happened," he whispered.

In telling this story, Tom Boyd says that tears ran down Grenfell's face after he read the telegram. Tom says he guesses he's the only man who ever saw Dr. Grenfell cry.

Tom knew what was on the telegram when he gave it to Grenfell.

"I was just as shocked as you are when I received it," he said now. "It's great news."

Grenfell regained his composure and dried his eyes with a tissue.

"Thomas, don't tell anyone about this," he said. "I will announce it at the school when I give my speech. It will be a great announcement."

"I have another telegram here for Emily Patey. You know her. She was Emily Broomfield who married Jimmy Patey. Her message is much like yours," said Tom.

Grenfell thought for a moment then replied, "Delay giving it to her for about an hour and let me announce it at the school first."

"I am going to get Nellie to go with me to see Emily. She can handle things like this better than me. By the time I get home and discuss this with her and we walk to Emily's house it will be close to an hour," said Tom.

"Thanks, Thomas," Grenfell said as he picked up his notepad. He placed the telegram in it and left for the school. He had received wonderful news.

****

Emily saw Tom and Nellie Boyd coming towards her house. She remembered sorrowfully how they came to see her almost three years earlier with the dreadful news that Freddy had been killed on the battlefield.

She wondered why they were coming to her now.

Her heart was in her throat as Tom tapped on the door. She stood near the woodstove and told him and Nellie to come in.

"You're not strangers here," she said. "Come on in."

"I haven't got bad news for you, Emily. This time it's good news," Tom said. "We have a telegram for you. Do you want me to read it?"

"Yes, please go ahead."

"You had better sit down," said Nellie.

"You read the telegram, Nellie," said Tom, as he opened it and handed it to her.

"Okay," said Nellie, clearing her throat.

To Miss Emily Bromfield. Stop. We would like to inform you that Frederick Frieda has been found alive in Austria. Stop. Will keep you informed when he is arriving in Newfoundland. Stop. The War Office. Newfoundland Regiment. St. John's.

Emily almost fell off her chair. Tom had to steady her as she buried her face in her hands and wept like a child.

"I suppose I'm finished. My life will come to an end," she sobbed as she wiped her eyes with the hem of her apron. "I should have known before I gave myself to Jimmy that someday Freddy would return. I don't think I'll ever know another peaceful day."

Nellie put her arms around her. "Remember what you told us? You said you felt responsible for Freddy's death because you co-signed his army papers. And you said if you could see him once more to ask his forgiveness you would be okay. You will get that chance when he comes home. I will personally see to it."

"I guess you're right, Nellie," she said.

"Don't feel sad, Emily," said Tom. "It's not your fault that Freddy was out of the picture when you married Jimmy. And, another thing, you married one of the best men you could find anywhere in Newfoundland. Everything will work out okay. You have Emma and Jimmy who both love you, a roof over your head and food on your table. What more could you ask for? Let everything take its course. And now I have to get back to the office. Nellie will stay with you."

"Thank you for bringing me the news," said Emily.

****

The school at St. Anthony was standing room only. In fact, only half of the people could get inside. Visitors from the nearby communities were there to take in the Sports Day events. There were great prizes to be won. And, of course, people were there to see and hear Dr. Grenfell. He was now a war hero!

Dr. Grenfell entered the building amid the roar of the people and a resounding three cheers. He shook hands with the sports day committee and started his speech. He began by thanking everyone for having him as guest speaker.

"When I arrived back home from the war six weeks ago and was walking to the hospital I received news that broke my heart," he began. "I was told the sad news that young Freddy Frieda from Labrador had been killed on the battlefield of France, not far from where I operated a field hospital. Today, I received more news that lifted my spirit higher than the clouds. I can only say the prayers of many people have been answered." Grenfell paused for a moment and then said, "Moments before I left my office to come here, Thomas Boyd handed me a telegram. I will read it to you." He reached into his pocket.

Dr. Wilfred Grenfell was an orator. He had given speeches at Carnegie Hall, in the White House in Washington, in the halls of Buckingham Palace, and to the household of the King of Norway. People who heard him speak never forgot it. Now he opened the telegram and read aloud:

To Doctor Wilfred Grenfell: It is with great pleasure that we inform you that Frederick Frieda has been found alive as a prisoner in Austria. We are making arrangements for his return to Britain. Will keep you informed. War Office. Newfoundland Regiment, St. John's.

The people went mad with joy. They shouted and clapped. For a few minutes they forgot it was Sports Day. Young and old alike, everyone was talking about Freddy Frieda coming home.

CHAPTER 37
To St. Anthony

The winter of 1919 was a cold one in Austria. There was also lots of snow. Freddy and Monica were kept very busy with the livestock. It was too cold to allow the animals out into the yard. Feed and water had to be hauled to the barns.

With the threat of retaliation lifted Freddy started asking more questions about the rail lines, especially the railway going west across Germany. He wanted to find the best route back to England.

Freddy and Monica went to Lans with the horse and sleigh loaded with products to sell. Freddy went to see Reverend Jens while Monica made the sale. He asked the minister about the war prisoners leaving for their respective countries.

"All the prisoners from around here are going home by way of Italy," said the minister.

"I suppose that's the way I'll be traveling when I get the word to move. I'm packed and ready," Freddy told him.

"I suppose whoever is in charge has to do it right. They don't want to overcrowd the trains," said the minister. "Freddy, are you aware that during the war hundreds of prisoners died when they were trying to escape from farms?"

"No, I didn't know. I guess I was lucky I ended up with such a good family or I might have met the same fate," said Freddy.

"The way it was around here, everyone suspected everyone else, especially if they were a stranger. They shot first and asked questions later. You know how it is in a war. Yes, I'd say you were a lucky person."

"I'm very anxious to get moving now. If you receive a message for me I would appreciate you notifying me as soon as you can," said Freddy.

"I certainly will," said the minister.

"If I get orders to go, would you be able to drive me to the train station in Innsbruck?"

"I would be more than happy to do that," said Reverend Jens.

Freddy was about to leave when the minister held up his hand.

"Monica says you play the flute really well. If you're still around on Sunday, I'd like for you to play it during the morning service. We would enjoy it very much," he said.

****

It was the last Sunday in January, 1919, when Freddy walked into the Lutheran church in Lans with Julian in his arms. He was followed by Monica and Jackie. Everyone there knew Monica. Her family was well known around the area. The church was full of people. Freddy and his group sat in the second seat from the front. Freddy felt very much at home sitting in the church. It reminded him of when he used to attend the Moravian church in Hopedale, back when he played in the church band.

After Reverend Jens opened the service, the congregation sang a German hymn with no musical accompaniment. The minister then said, "My friends, this morning we have a special treat. I have the pleasure of having Mr. Frieda here. He's going to play the flute for us. He'll be playing a new hymn called 'The old Rugged Cross.'"

The following morning, Reverend Jens arrived at the farm with a telegram for Freddy.

Freddy opened the telegram. It read: *From the War Office in London to Corporal Frederick Frieda #4012. Stop. W/O Gillard will be at train station Innsbruck, Tuesday noon. Stop. Be ready to board train. Stop. He'll have travel arrangements confirmed for you. Stop. Reply.*

Freddy gave his reply to the minister: *Received telegram. Stop. Will be at station Tuesday noon. Frederick Frieda.*

Freddy was finally leaving. This was the last day he would spend under the clear blue sky of Austria.

The last night at the farm was poignant.

Freddy played the flute and Monica and Jackie sang songs that all had a tinge of sorrow and loss. Freddy slept with Monica the last night he was in Austria.

At 5 a.m. he was out of bed, attending to the livestock as if he was staying forever.

Monica milked the goats and gave them water. At 8 a.m. Jackie had breakfast prepared as always. They were a family, each with their own duties.

As 9 a.m. rolled around it was time to say goodbye to Jackie and Julian.

Jackie wept when she saw Freddy was ready to leave. Little Julian wasn't aware his Papa, as he called Freddy, was leaving Austria, never to return. Freddy took out the flute and played 'God be with you till we meet again' and then he kissed Jackie and Julian. Jackie was holding Julian as Freddy put his arms around both of them and hugged them for the last time. Freddy and Jackie had tears in their eyes when they said their final goodbye.

As Freddy walked out the door he turned around and looked at the farmhouse for the last time. Monica, who was sitting on the sleigh waiting for him to get aboard, heard him say "War is the devil" as he brushed away tears.

Monica and Freddy had little to say to each other as they travelled the road to Lans. When they arrived, they went directly to Reverend Jens.

"I hope he is able to get his truck started. It's very cold," said Freddy.

"It doesn't matter to me," said Monica. "I hope he never gets it going and then you'll have to come back home with me."

"We should leave for Innsbruck immediately," said the minister as soon as they came into the house.

"I'm ready when you are," said Freddy.

Freddy was dreading the moment he had to say goodbye to Monica. She was the best friend he'd ever known. She was both a friend and a lover. Monica was very special. He might never meet anyone like her again.

He put his arms around her and held her close.

"Monica, I want you to know that I have spent the best days of my life with you," he said as he kissed her. "Now I'm leaving and I don't know when I'll be back, or if I'll ever be back."

"Don't talk that way, Freddy." Monica looked close to tears

"I hope you understand why I have to leave."

"Freddy, tell me the truth. Do you intend to come back?"

He put his hand under her chin and tilted her head so they were looking into each other's eyes.

"I don't know," he said. "Answering that is like trying to predict your future. However, I'm going to ask you something right now. You don't have to give me an answer if you don't want to."

"I'll try to answer," she said. "What is it, Freddy?"

"If I return, will you marry me?"

Freddy surprised himself. He hadn't known he was going to say those words until they came out of his mouth.

"Freddy," Monica said as she looked lovingly at him, "I'll marry you right now if you say the word. Reverend Jens can perform the ceremony. But if you don't want to do it now, and I can understand that too, when you get to wherever you're going if you need money to return, just send me a telegram." She then gave him an envelope filled with money. "This is the money we promised you for the work you did," she said.

"Monica, I told you not to do this. You may need the money before the winter is over so please take it back." Freddy tried to pass the envelope back to her.

"It's yours. You've earned it," she said.

With a lot of persuasion, Freddy was finally forced to accept the money. They embraced again, holding each other tightly for a long time. Monica began to cry. Freddy had tears in his eyes as he kissed her lips gently and said goodbye.

****

Reverend Jens' truck plowed through drifting snow that was more than a foot deep in places as it headed for Innsbruck.

The station was crowded with people. Freddy saw someone holding a sign saying, 'British prisoners of war this way.' He walked over and was directed to W/O Gillard. He was a big man, very rough looking, and sporting an admirable mustache.

"You finally showed up, Corporal Frieda," he said. "They tell me you were missing in action for almost two years."

"Yes sir. I was held on a farm out in the countryside. I couldn't relay word to anyone. I believe I may have turned into a goat."

Gillard laughed, then said, "So, you're from North America. From Labrador, I believe."

"Yes sir. Hopedale, Labrador."

"Very good. You were one of the lucky ones because you were sent to a family farm. Many of the prisoners who were sent to the prison camps did not survive."

"I was treated very well by the people I worked for," said Freddy.

Their conversation was interrupted by the arrival of the train.

"You'll be going to Italy first, to Venice," said Gillard. "Then you'll board a passenger liner for England. I have your tickets here. I also have a new ID card for you."

"Who do I report too when I get to Venice?" Freddy asked.

"When you arrive at the station you'll see a sign near the main entrance saying 'British personnel.' Go there, they'll tell you what you have to do."

"Are you going on this train, sir?" Freddy asked.

"No. I'm here to oversee the transfer of British and Commonwealth prisoners. I may be here for another month. The medical people are trying to get the sick prisoners well enough to travel." Gillard paused and then continued, "You're lucky, you're in good shape. The members of your Regiment were not as fortunate as you. They lost over six hundred men in one battle at Beaumont Hamel. It was probably the greatest battle of the war."

Freddy couldn't answer. This was devastating news. He feared the other news he might hear about the Regiment before he arrived in England.

"Corporal, keep your pack-sack on your back, your duffle bag over your shoulder and your tickets in a safe place. If you do that you'll make it okay. All the best," Gillard said.

Freddy stood to attention and then he thanked him and walked away.

****

The train to Venice was uneventful.

It seemed the Italians weren't concerned about who entered their country. All they were concerned about was that the war was ended. They were trying to return to a normal life. They waved the train on through without even coming aboard to check for security.

Freddy was amazed at how beautiful Venice was. He gaped in wonder at the winding canals and saw with shock how badly the city had been damaged by aerial attacks. A particularly severe raid had taken place on February 27, 1918.

In the harbour, ships were waiting to take people to different countries. He saw a hospital ship moored to a dock not far from where the train stopped. A sergeant walked through the train and said everyone had to go aboard the hospital ship for a medical check. Those who passed the medical would go on a transport ship which would leaving for England the next day.

Freddy had no problem with his medical.

Late in the evening he went aboard the transport ship. Most everyone was happy to be aboard the ship. They had a comfortable bed to lie on and food to eat. But Freddy's thoughts were back at the farm with Monica and Jackie and little Julian. He wondered what they were talking about as they sat around the kitchen table bathed in soft light from the oil lamp. How was the farm doing? How were they managing? Did they miss him? He wondered too about Olivie and prayed to God that she had survived. He was afraid to think about the baby she'd been carrying. Thoughts of Olivie and the baby were so painful he could barely endure them. He had to put them aside or else he would lose his mind.

Now, he was on his way to Emily, the girl he'd promised to marry after the war. "Yes," he said to himself, "I'll go back to St. Anthony, marry Emily, return to Hopedale and live with her forever." He kept his mind focused on Emily in order to distract him from visions of his loved ones in Austria. Not once did it enter his mind that Emily might not be waiting for him.

The ship was delayed by weather several days enroute through the Mediterranean Sea. This idle time gave Freddy time to find out news about what had happened during the war. He tried to get information about his Regiment and what had happened at Beaumont Hamel. No one could tell him anything. Almost everyone aboard the ship had been in prison camps during the war. Some had tried to escape but were caught and severely beaten.

A storm was brewing as they prepared to leave the Gibraltar Strait. The captain decided to go into the Spanish port of Cadiz to wait out the storm. They were there three days before they left.

Four days later, they entered the British seaport of Dover. Freddy knew that Dover was the place where the first German bomb had fallen on British soil on Christmas Eve 1914.

Everyone disembarked in Dover and they were taken to an army camp just outside the city. They stayed there for two weeks.

In the first couple of days Freddy was surprised to be given back his Newfoundland Regiment uniform. While he was at the army camp, Freddy was questioned about all his activities during the war.

He was shocked to be told that Benoit had survived by jumping from the office window and was successful in reaching the French underground. He had even made it back across the English Channel.

His mind went back to the German sergeant aboard the truck on the way to the train station in Lille. The sergeant had bragged about how he had shot and killed Benoit after he jumped through the window. He'd talked about it to the driver, not knowing Freddy could understand German. Maybe Benoit had survived the war. He would find out when he arrived in St. John's.

****

Freddy and his fellow soldiers were sent by train to Liverpool where they boarded the troop ship *S.S. Corsican* to take them across the Atlantic to St. John, New Brunswick.

After a ten day sea voyage, the ship arrived in St. John. Freddy and seventy others then boarded a train for North Sydney. From there, they would cross the Cabot Strait to Port aux Basques. It was April tenth.

They travelled across the Cabot Strait on the *Prospero* and when it arrived in Port aux Basques and everyone came ashore they thanked God they were back on Newfoundland soil. But Freddy would not be satisfied until he touched the shores of Labrador. Most of all, he longed to get to St. Anthony to see Emily. He thought about her more and more every day. He was sure she would be waiting for him.

It took four days for the train to cross from Port aux Basques to St. John's. By the time it arrived in the city, more than half of the veterans aboard had left the train to return to their homes. It was something to witness! There were welcoming parties at all the different stations. Wounded soldiers were helped off the train by joyful relatives. Tears flowed like water as families reunited.

When the train arrived in St. John's, Sir Charles Alexander Harris, the Welshman who'd been appointed Governor of Newfoundland in 1917, was at the station to welcome the remaining veterans. To Freddy, this was a moving experience. The Governor shook his hand and people hugged and kissed him as if he were their own. He knew he would have to wait a month or longer before joining a coastal steamer going north to St. Anthony. There was no other way except by boat. It was now the 20th of April.

Freddy went to the bank with his Austrian money and had it exchanged into Newfoundland currency. It came to three hundred and seven dollars. He also received a lump sum payment from the army. It was one hundred and forty-three dollars. This gave him the grand total of four hundred and fifty dollars. He considered himself to be a rich man.

Freddy was put up at the Crosbie Hotel on Duckworth Street where he could stay until he caught the boat for St. Anthony.

When he visited the Newfoundland Regiment office the sergeant in charge told him there was no record of him being promoted to a corporal while in Europe. He was a private and would be discharged as one. Freddy wasn't concerned about rank. He only wanted to get out of the army and go north to St. Anthony and Hopedale.

While in St. John's, he sadly discovered that Peter Benoit had fought in the battle of Beaumont Hamel, had been wounded, and died a few days later at a field hospital in France. He read Benoit's report about his escape. And he also read Benoit's description of how his friend Freddy Frieda was among four men who were shot and killed by a German captain after being interrogated in Lille. He dismissed the report of his death as a mistake made by Benoit and thought no more of it. It never entered Freddy's mind that his family or anyone else had received word about his death during the winter of 1916.

****

During the first week in May, he received word that the *S.S. Kyle* would be making a trip to Corner Brook. The *Kyle*, which was also an icebreaker, had begun service on the Labrador coast in 1913. It was one of the Reid Newfoundland Company's so called Alphabet Fleet, ships all named after Scottish towns. The *Kyle* was loaded with freight for the Northern Peninsula. The people along the coast were on the verge of starvation, all food stocks were depleted due to the long harsh winter they had experienced.

The *Kyle* would not be going to Labrador. It would be making the trip up the Northern Peninsula, through the Strait of Belle Isle and down the west coast to Corner Brook. That would be fine for Freddy. He would book a passage to St. Anthony, stay there until ice conditions improved, and then go to Hopedale on the first mail steamer heading to the North Coast of Labrador.

The Newfoundland Regiment booked a first class passage for him, shook his hand, wished him well, and told him he would officially be a civilian by the time he reached Hopedale.

After he walked up the gangway he turned and saluted the lieutenant who had accompanied him to the ship. "Thank you sir," he said, and went aboard. For the first time since leaving Austria, he felt relieved and happy.

Freddy was anxious to see Emily.

Although he knew he loved her, Monica and Jackie and Olivie were continually on his mind. He was torn between the women. As he lay in his bunk aboard the *Kyle* his thoughts were more in Austria than in Hopedale. "What should I do, should I return to Austria?" he asked himself a thousand times. Then Emily's face would float in front of his eyes and he knew he had to get to St. Anthony to be with her.

The *Kyle* battled ice floes as it plowed its way north, and kept in constant touch with the sealing ships that were in the heavy Arctic ice hunting seals. Although the ship hugged the shoreline as it dropped off freight and mail from port to port it still ran into heavy ice. Most of the harbours had not yet thawed out, and the ship had to butt its way in to discharge freight.

After the ship reached the Horse Islands on the eastern side of the Northern Peninsula, it had to divert and go to the aid of a sealing vessel in distress. This caused a day's delay.

It took two weeks to reach St. Anthony. Freddy enjoyed the trip. There were lots of passengers, including some other war veterans, to chat with. Everyone wanted to talk about the war.

Freddy thought about Dr. Grenfell and wondered if he had survived the war and returned to St. Anthony.

A couple of days before he arrived in St. Anthony, he decided to send him a telegram informing him he was arriving on the *Kyle*. He also sent a message to Emily. He expected to stay with her at her father's house while he waited for the coastal boat to begin making its run along the Labrador Coast. He didn't think it was necessary to let her know he was arriving on the *Kyle*.

Freddy was sitting in the smoking room on the *Kyle* when the purser walked through and loudly announced that the next port of call was St. Anthony.

Freddy was excited. He would soon be seeing Emily. He had been away for almost three years. It was Saturday afternoon, sunny and warm for this time of the year. He checked his tie, and made sure his uniform was perfect. He wanted to be at his best. He had his pack sack on his back and his duffle bag slung over his shoulder. He made sure his wallet was in his inside pocket.

Flags were flying and the dock was filled with people as the *Kyle* docked. Dr. Grenfell was at the head of the crowd that was there to welcome Freddy back. Freddy waved from the rail. He tried to see Emily among the crowd but couldn't. Where was she? She had to be there. The walkway was lowered and made ready for passengers to disembark. The purser arranged for Freddy to be the first one off.

When Freddy stepped onto the dock the crowd unfolded a large sign which read, "Welcome home, Freddy."

Dr. Grenfell shook his hand and welcomed him to St. Anthony, saying there was a dinner planned for him at the school and they would go there right away. Freddy shook hands with everyone, young and old. Everyone was happy to see him. He spotted Charley Bromfield among the crowd and rushed to him.

Charley cried when Freddy hugged him. "We heard you were killed in France," he said. "We never thought we would see you again."

"Killed in France? What are you saying, Uncle Charley?" Freddy asked.

There were too many people around to hear Charley's answer. People were reaching to shake Freddy's hand. He was shocked, to say the least, when he heard Charley say he had been killed in France. But he had no time to question him as he was swept away in the crowd. On the way to the school Dr. Grenfell briefly told him what had happened regarding the report that he had been killed at Lille, France.

"I didn't know about it either," Grenfell said. "When I returned after the war I was shocked to hear about you being killed in 1916. It wasn't until the end of January that we received the news you were alive, that you had been found at a prison camp in Austria. That's the reason all the people are here to see you. You are their hero."

Freddy put two and two together.

He remembered reading the report written by Benoit in St. John's which stated he had been shot by a German captain in Lille. Then he remembered the reason Benoit had made such a mistake. Benoit heard the pistol shot when the captain fired into the ceiling and pretended he had shot Freddy. It was then the captain took him outside and handed him over to the sergeant and told him to send him to a prison camp in the Bavarian Alps. The captain left after that. And then, when Benoit was left alone for a few minutes, he must have jumped through the open window and escaped. But why did the sergeant tell his driver he had shot Benoit in the back and watched him die? Maybe he was afraid the captain would find out Benoit had escaped and it was best to say he'd killed him. Freddy's mind went back to Lille and he again saw the tattoo on the back of the captain's hand. It was all he could do to stop from screaming.

CHAPTER 38
Home in Hopedale

At the school, Freddy told the people briefly what had happened at Lille and how he ended up on a prison farm in Austria.

"For some unknown reason God protected me. It's a mystery why I was spared when so many young men paid the supreme price. It had to be the prayers of the people from Hopedale and St. Anthony," he said.

Everyone cheered him and welcomed him back. Dr. Grenfell presented him with a Bible and a parka made from Grenfell cloth on behalf of the people of St. Anthony. Freddy thanked them sincerely. When the dinner was over and everyone had left, Dr. Grenfell and Freddy sat down for a chat.

"I have something very important to tell you," Dr. Grenfell said. "It probably will be the last thing you will want to hear. It's about Emily."

Freddy held his breath. He wondered fearfully if she had died.

Dr. Grenfell continued, "When she received the news you were killed in France, she fell to pieces. However, with time and help from her friends she recovered. She began to date Jimmy Patey. I believe you know him. He's a herdsman with Charley Bromfield, Emily's father. After several months Jimmy and Emily were married and they now have a little girl. I went to see them when I received message and I talked to her and Jimmy. They want you to visit them. Emily has something important to ask you."

Freddy was silent for several minutes and then he said, "Dr. Grenfell, while I was on the Isle of Man I trained to be prepared to try and accept the worst that could possibly happen. When you started to tell me the sad news and you said it was about Emily, I thought you were going to say she had died. That's not the case and I am relieved. To know she has married another man grieves me, but I know life must go on. My family is at Hopedale, I have to return to them."

"We were worried about you," said Grenfell. "We didn't know how you would react after you heard this news. And two things you have to remember. You have your health; many men are coming back from the war with arms and legs missing and will never work again. Second, you're like me. You have a deep love for Labrador; only men with deep compassion have that. It's more than the love for any woman, country or treasure. I spent my time helping others save lives during the war, but every spare moment I thought about my work back here."

"What will I do now, Doctor?" asked Freddy. "I have to wait here until ice conditions become favourable to get to the North Labrador Coast. It may take a month or more. Where will I go? Where will I stay?"

"I have a job for you if you'll accept it," said Grenfell. "When I left for the war three years ago our reindeer herd was over eighteen hundred strong," Grenfell began. "When I returned in December there were only one hundred and fifty animals remaining. People poached them and shot them at will. It made me angry because the Government promised to protect them. I got fed up with the whole project and sold them to the Canadian Government. I've employed William O'Neill to take them across the Strait of Belle Isle to Chateau Bay in Labrador and then he'll drive them to Fort Smith in the North West Territories. You can go with them if you want. The Canadian Government will pay you. If you don't want to go on the reindeer drive, you can help get the herd ready for the trip, and put them on a schooner to go to Chateau Bay. All told, it will take about a month. By then the ice should be moved off along the Labrador coast, and you can come with me on the *Strathcona*. In the meantime, you'll be staying at the Annex. There's a room for you there."

Freddy graciously accepted the offer and thanked him. He was much relieved.

****

Freddy went to work with William McNeill helping with the reindeer and preparing them for the journey to the North West Territories.

It is to be noted that the reindeer drive by William McNeill in 1919 was the longest drive of any herd of animals taken anywhere in the world. The trip started by boat across the Strait of Belle Isle to Chateau Bay, then went across Labrador and Quebec to Hudson Bay, all the way around Hudson Bay to Thompson, Manitoba. Then it traveled west to Fort Smith in the North West Territories. It took five years to make the drive. After William McNeill arrived in Fort Smith, he saw what was happening to the buffalo in North America. The population was all but wiped out, and he devoted the rest of his life to protecting them. He founded Wood Buffalo Park and brought the buffalo populations back from extinction.

Freddy worked with Jimmy Patey, Emily's husband. This wasn't intentional but the person in charge needed Jimmy to operate the boat used to transport people to the bottom of Hare Bay and take the reindeer to the St. Anthony area, where they would be loaded on two schooners for shipment to Labrador.

Jimmy invited Freddy to his house.

Emily was sitting in a rocking chair with Emma in her arms when Freddy opened the door. She looked at him in surprise. He stood and stared at her. She had changed, she looked older. The sorrow she had endured had left its mark on her. He walked to her and gave her a hug.

"How are you, Emily?" he said. "I missed you a whole lot when I first left, but I suppose it's like everything. A person forgets and moves on with his or her life. I'm happy you married a good man. Jimmy and I are friends."

For a moment she was silent. He looked more mature than when she had last seen him, but he was the same Freddy Frieda.

She lowered her head and hugged Emma.

Freddy saw tears trickle down her face.

Jimmy took Emma and went into the next room.

When she was alone with Freddy, Emily started to weep. "I missed you so much, Freddy, when you went away," she said through her tears. "I almost died. When the news came that you had been killed it broke my heart. I spent weeks crying. I didn't expect to ever see you again. Dad took me out on the land with him, herding the reindeer. We stayed in a tent and that's where I met Jimmy. If I hadn't met him I'm sure I would have died of grief. Not long afterwards he asked me to marry him. I refused. But then I discovered I was pregnant and I had no other choice. Dad agreed for me to marry Jimmy. He used to say 'Freddy will never return again. He's gone forever. You go ahead and marry Jimmy. He'll take care of you.'"

"You did the proper thing," said Freddy. "It was all my fault. I should never have left. Now you're married. You have a good man, a child and a home. I have nothing. Perhaps I'll go back to Hopedale and live with Mom. I have to support her. I suppose I'll go fishing out on the Turnivik Islands again during the summer and trap animals in the winter. There's not much more I can do back there. In fact I don't know how to do much more than that."

"I suppose I'll spend the rest of my days here in St. Anthony, looking after Dad and Jimmy and Emma and longing to go back home to Hopedale. That's what I get for being too hasty. I should have waited for you a little longer."

"Emily, you have your family now. Hopedale is just where you grew up. If you want to be happy here with Jimmy and your daughter it's all up to you."

"I loved you. I don't know if I will ever love anyone else that much," she said.

"Emily, I was madly in love with you when I left. I told you so and I meant it. But war changed things," said Freddy. "I was a captive on a farm in Austria with two women prisoners. The farm was owned by a single man and his sister. I got involved with one of the prisoners. She was very beautiful and I fell in love with her. The Germans took her and it broke my heart. I then got involved with Monica, one of the owners of the farm. When the war ended I had to say goodbye to her and I know I will never see her again. I had my hopes built on having you. I never knew anything about the rumour that I had been killed or that you had married. If I had known that I would have stayed in St. John's until ice conditions became favourable to go to Hopedale. If you had waited for me I would have married you. But just remember, I am not the white knight you think

I am. Jimmy is a better man than me. Dr. Grenfell and your father are very fond of him. You are a lucky girl and you should not forget that."

When Freddy was about to leave, Emily asked him if he would forgive her for signing the papers that resulted in sending him to war. He tried to tell her she was not to blame for anything. It was not her fault he went overseas in World War 1.

"I would have gone regardless," he said. "But, if it will set your mind at ease, I'll forgive you a thousand times over."

"Will you kiss me before you go, Freddy?" she asked.

"Yes, I'll kiss you goodbye," he said.

****

It was around the first of June before the Arctic ice started to clear out and the *Strathcona* finally started on its hospital run along the North Labrador Coast. When it did, Freddy was on board.

During the trip, Freddy told Dr. Grenfell about his ordeal in Lille and how the German captain had shot his men in cold blood. He said it was something he would carry to his grave.

"I suppose I'll hate Germany and everyone there for the rest of my life, and I will especially hate the German captain with a tattoo on the back of his right hand."

"I know it hurts, Freddy," Dr. Grenfell spoke soothingly. "Being a doctor on the battlefield one gets to see it all, and the horror is unimaginable. But now the war is over and we have to get on with our lives. There's no doubt the average German citizen will tell you the Kaiser was wrong."

"Austria was on the side of the Germans, but the people were different, none of them seemed to want war," said Freddy. "I seriously thought about staying in Austria. It's a wonderful country. I was involved with the girl who owned the farm I was held captive on. She is a beautiful person. Her brother was killed on the Western Front ten months before I left. She is a very successful farmer. Her parents died three years ago."

"Maybe you should return to her," said Grenfell. "Being a farmer would probably be better than fishing and trapping. You wouldn't have Arctic ice to deal with."

"But Labrador is my home," said Freddy. "As we get closer to Hopedale the blood in my veins seems to flow better. It's like I have giant arms around me, keeping me safe. I can't wait to lie on the ground and look up and see the Northern Lights dancing in the sky."

Grenfell knew the feeling. He too loved Labrador.

"If you go back fishing you could face a lot of problems," he said to Freddy. "You'll need new boats, nets, and the rest of the fishing gear. Your boat and wharf and sheds are likely gone, pushed out into the ocean by the ice. It's going to be costly to get back into fishing. It could be a struggle to get started."

"I have enough money to buy what I need, Doctor," Freddy said. "Before I left Austria I was given a sum of money from the profits of the farm I was working on. That money will help me get back fishing."

"You're a lucky man, Freddy. But take my advice and keep it to yourself. If people hear about your being given money they'll start rumours and hold it against you," Grenfell advised.

Freddy agreed. "My lips are sealed," he said.

After two weeks dodging ice floes and treating patients in every little village, the *Strathcona* finally arrived in Hopedale. It was still cold and everyone was wearing heavy coats. Freddy was dressed in his uniform. This was his last day in the army as he had finally arrived in Hopedale.

He'd sent his mother a message saying he was arriving on the *Strathcona*. Everyone knew he was coming and the entire community was on the wharf to greet him. That included the Moravian minister who was now a stranger to Freddy. The minister who had been there before he went to war had been taken to a prison camp in Mount Pearl, near St. John's, and when the war ended he returned to Germany.

Nancy Frieda was eager to see her son. She didn't know what to expect. She wondered if she would recognize him.

Everyone in the village waited quietly on the wharf as the crew on the *Strathcona* tied up the vessel. The gangway was lowered and secured. Dr. Grenfell appeared on deck and waved to the people. They waved back, but not one person spoke. Grenfell came down the gangway onto the wharf and spoke to no one.

Then Freddy stepped out onto the deck. He had his packsack on and his kit bag was slung on his shoulder. He looked toward the hills then walked down the gangway. Everyone was silent. They were surprised he could walk. Nancy stood watching him as tears ran down her face. Dr. Grenfell held her arm. She looked as though she would faint.

Grenfell raised his voice and spoke loudly as he gestured towards Freddy. "People of Hopedale," he said. "Here is your native son Freddy Frieda."

The crowd broke into cheers and Nancy leaped into her son's arms. It was a moment Dr. Grenfell forever remembered.

Freddy shook hands with everyone on the wharf except the Moravian minister. He intentionally avoided him. Most didn't notice it. However, Dr. Grenfell did.

Freddy thanked Dr. Grenfell and offered to pay him for his hospitality. Grenfell wouldn't hear of it.

"I've enjoyed every minute with you. As one soldier to another, keep the flag to the top of the pole," Grenfell said, then added. "I'll be back here in two days. We'll get together then."

He and Freddy shook hands as the crew cast off the lines and the *Strathcona* moved away from the dock.

CHAPTER 39
Letter from Lans

After the welcoming ceremony was over and all the tears had been dried, Freddy took inventory of the damage nature had done to his fishing gear during the three years he was away. Some planks in his boat needed replacing and most of the salmon nets were rotten. But he would be able to replace what was necessary and be ready for the fishing season. There were only two of his original dogs left. Four had to be put down due to injuries. The first thing Freddy after he arrived was go hunting seals for a couple of days.

After a week, Freddy started to settle into the normal way of life in Hopedale. Most of the snow around the town was gone, but the barren country was still snow covered. Night after night he would sit for hours and ponder his time in the army, especially the time he'd spent on the farm. Monica was continually on his mind. He wondered how she was managing, especially with sowing the seed, attending to the birth of the lambs, milking the goats, and taking the milk, cream and butter to market. He felt guilty for leaving her.

"Maybe I should go back. I have enough money for my passage back," he would say to himself. But then memories of his mother and sisters in Labrador would flood his mind and he knew he couldn't leave.

Two years after he came home, he received a pink telegram from Jimmy Patey in St. Anthony.

It read: *Sorry to inform you Emily passed away in childbirth last night. She was twenty-six. Funeral services for her and the baby will be held Saturday. Stop. Jimmy.*

Freddy settled into life in Hopedale. He fished for salmon during the spring, and cod during the summer on the Turnivik Islands. He would move there each spring when the ice floes permitted and return again Hopedale in August after he sold his catch. During the winter he travelled to his cabin twenty-five miles in the country and went trapping. It was a life he loved.

When he was twenty-eight, he met Mary Solomon, an eighteen-year-old clerk at the Hudson Bay store. He courted her a few months and then they were married. Freddy loved her more than any other girl he had ever met.

Freddy and Mary had three children, two sons and a daughter, and they lived a happy life together.

Many times he would tell Mary about the people he had lived with in Austria during the war. The stories became part of local folklore. Freddy wept as he told Mary about Olivie. He talked about Julian and Jackie and their baby and he told her about Monica. Mary listened and understood. She encouraged him to send a letter to Reverend Jens in Lans and ask him to forward it to Monica. Freddy was hesitant, but at last he sat down and wrote the letter.

Months later he and Mary had forgotten all about the letter. One day after the mail arrived on the coastal boat Freddy was shocked when someone came to his door with a letter. The return address was Lans, Austria.

The letter was from Monica and it was written in German.

Freddy read it aloud to Mary.

Monica said she had sold the small farm and focused on the one in Lans. She said the farm was doing well and so was she. Monica had married someone she had grown up with. They were happy but had no children. Jackie had married too. Her husband had been a friend of Julian's. He came back from the war and he and Jackie bought the small farm from Monica and were doing fine. Julian was doing well with his studies and planning to become a veterinarian.

And, the very best news of all was that Olivie had not died at the hands of the Germans. She had lost the baby she was carrying, but she and a group of others had somehow managed to escape and fled to Italy.

After the war she settled in Innsbruck and she was now happily married and a mother of two.

Freddy was very happy to get the letter from Monica, and while he intended to reply sometime in the future somehow he never got around to it.

CHAPTER 40

Hilter comes to power

It Captain Karl Hausser was now a commander in the German Navy. After the Treaty of Versailles came into effect at the end of World War 1, the Germans had their army reduced to 100,000 men, they were not allowed to have an air force, and their navy was permitted to have six battleships, six light cruisers, 12 torpedo boats and zero submarines.

The Germans had surrendered most of their fleet to the Allies, consisting of 10 battleships, 17 cruisers, 50 torpedo boats, and more than 100 submarines. This fleet, with the exception of the submarines, was interned at Scapa Flow, north of Scotland, in November 1918, with German captains and crew aboard.

In one last gesture of defiance, the Germans scuttled the ships that were interned at Scapa Flow on June 21, 1919.

During World War One, Germany lost almost two million men and Austria-Hungary more than one million. All told, the total deaths of all the nations that fought in the war is believed to be 8.5 million with a further 21 million wounded. Deaths among the civilian population caused indirectly by the war approximated 10 million.

Under the Treaty of Versailles, Germany lost much of its territory and was also required to pay billions in reparations to the Allies.

Immediately after the war, a German team was secretly put in place to determine the cause of the defeat and to determine how to build a more modern military machine that would reunite the country with territory lost as a result of Versailles.

The Germans thought they were unfairly treated by the Treaty of Versailles. Most were convinced they had not started World War One. It was instead the fault of the countries that had carved up Germany during former wars.

In 1933, when Adolf Hitler came to power, the German people were more than willing to support him. They thought he was sent from the gods to right the wrongs that Germany had suffered by having the country carved up by a self-appointed group at a meeting in Versailles, France, in 1919.

Hitler wasn't going to abide by that treaty and he had the German people behind him. After Hitler came to power he rejected the Treaty of Versailles, calling it a burning torch around the necks of the German people. His fiery speeches stirred the people to the brink of retaliation.

"We will take back what belongs to the Fatherland. We will again build our nation and our armed forces and make Germany great," he screamed in the ears of the world.

But the world didn't listen.

The Great Powers were concentrating more on the rising threat of Communism as Germany built its armed forces without any restrictions.

Hitler had some of the smartest military minds in the world building his military. They were people who had directed armies in previous wars and felt the need for smarter weaponry. Fast moving and more powerful ground vehicles, capable of moving large numbers of troops at lightning speed, were needed.

And Hitler had at his disposal naval experts who knew that the next conflict would be fought on a different scale: submarine and air warfare.

Hitler knew that submarine warfare would be the tool to bring Britain, France and their European Allies to their knees.

"Cut the supply lines to the Allies in Europe and you'll starve them into surrender," he told the screaming thousands. The Germans showed their approval with the Nazi salute.

Air power was also vital.

In 1935, Hitler ordered Hermann Goring to establish the German Air Force, the Luftwaffe, breaking the Treaty of Versailles ban on German military aviation. At the start of World War Two, the Luftwaffe was one of the most modern, powerful and experienced air forces in the world.

Hitler and his advisers knew Britain and France weren't capable of building bombers that would be superior to German ones. Their only way to counter attack a German onslaught was by using heavy bombers that would be built in North America and flown to Europe via the northern route. These large bombers would fly to Gander, Newfoundland, where they would be refueled, then fly along the North Labrador Coast, cross the Labrador Sea to Greenland and then on to Reykjavik, Iceland. After refueling in Iceland, they would go to Scotland and England where they would prepare for their bombing missions.

"We have to come up with a way to disrupt the delivery route of these bombers," said Hitler. "Something has to be put in place between Iceland and Newfoundland to disrupt the flow of aircraft to Britain."

Radar beacons were fast becoming the equipment of choice as a guiding system for long range aircraft. Hitler knew any bomber flying from Newfoundland to Iceland had better stay on course in order to refuel. The weather along the North Labrador Coast was not the best in the world. Fog, sleet, snow and freezing rain boggled the minds of every navigator when gearing up for the flight to Europe.

Most flights were solely depending on radar or gyrocompass beacons. To disrupt this system would cause havoc for crews aboard these giant bombers. Something would have to be put in place to scramble these systems. Maps of the route were quickly assembled at a meeting with Goring, the head of the Luftwaffe. Ice and snow conditions were considered.

It was decided a tower would have to be put in place somewhere. The decision finally was to put a station in place somewhere along the North Labrador Coast near Cape Chidley, the northernmost part of Labrador.

What would then be needed was someone familiar with Labrador.

This person would monitor the flights of aircraft flying the north coast and determine when to turn the radar scrambling devices on. To have the scrambling devices on continually would not be wise. The threat of being discovered would be too great.

Commander Karl Hausser read the classified memo calling for such a man. After he studied the memo and gave it a lot of consideration he knew he was the person most qualified for the job. He knew about Labrador. He had been born there. He could speak the Inuit language. Having grown up as a Moravian he would be able to disguise himself as a Moravian missionary. He knew enough about their religious ways to pass as a minister. He was prepared to take the job and expressed his feelings in a letter.

After much consideration the military board decided to give Karl the position. The project he would be in charge of was deemed as a weather station under the code name 'Kurt.'

CHAPTER 41
Grenfell dies

Freddy Frieda was living a very contented life at his home in Hopedale. He had built a new home for his family. His mother and sisters lived with him. Whenever he went to the Turnivik Islands or to the trap lines he took his family with him. Freddy was a much respected man in Hopedale and the surrounding areas.

After he returned from the war he never attended the Moravian Church again. No matter how much he was persuaded, he refused. He would tell everyone he never wanted to see another German, whether they were ministers, popes or generals, not after what the German captain had done to his comrades at Lille, France.

His wife and mother tried to persuade him to attend funerals of his relatives. He refused. He was asked to attend programs at Christmas and Easter. He refused to do that as well.

Many years after the war, Dr. Grenfell still went to Hopedale. On one occasion he invited Freddy to attend a church service with him.

Freddy refused, saying, "Dr. Grenfell, every time I see a German I can hear the screams of our men in my ears as the captain blew their brains out. I suppose I'll even hear it when I'm dying. It's branded on my memory. The captain's hand with the tattoo on the back reaches for me at night, holding a pistol. I can hear the click of the hammer. I still hold my breath, waiting as he gets ready to fire a round into the head of the Irishman. I can see the two young Dutchmen. He shot one in the back and I can hear his screams as his body hit the floor. The memory of those men torments me every night. It's a nightmare."

"Freddy, you were traumatized by the war and I think some treatment would be in order," said Dr. Grenfell. "We've had to treat a lot of war veterans around the Northern Peninsula. Hatred is something that leads to violence and the results are sometimes devastating. Treatment can help."

"I know, Doctor. The war was a terrible experience and I do try to block it out of my mind. Maybe thoughts of it will go away. Hopefully, I'll get over it."

"If you continue to have problems, please seek help," Grenfell advised.

He thought for a few minutes then said, "Freddy, I'm not expected to make many more trips this way. In fact, this could be my last one. My health hasn't been good these days. My legs are failing me. The war has left its toll on me too."

Freddy knew the elderly gentleman was getting tired. A lifetime battling the elements of Northern Newfoundland and Labrador, being pulled by dog teams, adrift alone with husky dogs on ice floes, the worry of having to beg governments, countries and rich merchants for assistance to buy medicines to treat the sick, had all taken its toll. And above all, running a field hospital on the battlefields of France had contributed to bringing this great man to his knees.

Freddy looked fondly at Dr. Grenfell and said, "I've changed my mind. I'll go to church with you tomorrow. You're the only one I'd do it for. I can't refuse you."

"I'm proud of you, Freddy. I'll meet you here tomorrow morning at ten forty-five. We'll go together."

"I'll be here," said Freddy.

Later that evening as a storm approached, Dr. Grenfell received a telegram from a man at Makkovik, Labrador, thirty miles to the south. The man's wife was dying in childbirth.

Grenfell had to rush to her aid.

He never returned.

This would be his last trip to Hopedale and the North Labrador Coast. He died in 1940. His death occurred two years after the passing of his wife, Anne.

CHAPTER 42
Martin Bay

During the winter of 1938 the news on the BBC was not good for anyone who had been through World War One.

Germany was again stirring up trouble with the countries close to her border, particularly Poland. As the world looked on, it became apparent Germany would plunge Europe into war again.

Hitler was prepared to do anything to achieve his goals.

He wanted to establish German as the dominant nation in Europe and as the leading economic, political and military power in the world.

One of his plans was to control the North Atlantic.

In the event of war he would prevent any supplies and equipment coming to England, France and the Baltic region. His plan for the North Coast of Labrador was in place. He was prepared to disrupt the flight of any heavy bomber coming to England or anywhere else in Europe to engage in a war with Germany.

Before the war started in 1939, Hitler and his Nazi Party tolerated organized religion. However, after the war started, Hitler became very hostile to all organized religions unless he wanted to use them for his own purposes. And then no one had the right to oppose him or they would suffer the consequences. Organized religions were afraid of the rising German dictator. The Moravian Church was no exception. Everyone lay low and kept quiet.

After hostilities officially started and England declared war on Germany, the Moravian missionaries along the Labrador Coast were again suspected of spying for Germany.

At the beginning of the war, and even before the war, submarines were sighted lurking around the inner bays along the Labrador Coast and around the Northern Peninsula of Newfoundland. Fishermen hauling cod traps near Cape Bauld lighthouse, the most northerly point on the Northern Peninsula, saw periscopes protruding from the water less than a hundred yards away. At one point an unmarked submarine surfaced close to a fishing crew.

When reports of submarines reached St. John's, the Newfoundland Government became concerned about boats and mail passenger steamers travelling along the coast. Reporting teams were organized along the coast and supervised by the Newfoundland Rangers. One such group was in the Hopedale area. The Ranger stationed there in 1941 was Earl Brazil. War veterans were asked to serve on these teams. That was how Freddy Frieda became a member.

****

When Karl was growing up in Hopedale, he would go to the Turnivik Islands for weekly trips with the Frieda family. It was a time he enjoyed. While there, he would see Newfoundland fishing schooners from the south coming into the harbour all decked out in their canvas. It was a sight he never forgot.

After he became a German naval commander, with the responsibility of secretly building radio communications towers on the Labrador coast, he realized these schooners could be the answer to accomplishing what he was required to do. No one would ever suspect a fishing schooner was owned by the German navy.

In mid-summer of 1938, a fishing schooner similar to the type used by Newfoundland fishermen crossed the Atlantic with two thirty-three foot towers in eleven-foot sections, and enough material to construct a small cabin.

The material was landed deep in Martin Bay, near Cape Chidley, Labrador. The boat was skippered by none other than Commander Karl Hausser.

Karl had no fear of fishermen catching him constructing the towers.

The fishermen were not in the bay. They were usually on the offshore islands. His only concern was discovery by Labrador natives who used the inner bays for hunting.

But Karl was clever enough to hide the material he was using in an area where hunters never frequented, close to the outside cliffs.

In less than a week the project was completed. The towers and a makeshift cabin were in a very desolate spot, behind a small hill hidden from the ocean, with the towers and detecting antennas facing south by west.

All the material used was stamped 'Made in Canada' and garbage was left lying around, indicating the towers were built and owned by Canada. That was the disguise.

****

During the early summer of 1942, the Moravian supply vessel *Harmony* arrived in Hopedale with supplies for the mission. Everyone was delighted to see the ship. She was a welcome sight.

People loved the Moravians. They had been coming to the Labrador for over two hundred years. They were the only source of comfort, especially when it came to healthcare, education and spiritual needs.

The Moravians were well aware that Hitler was dangerous. He was against organized religion and that was a great concern. But it was when he began interning and killing Jews that they really became scared.

The religious leaders at the time were baffled when they realized ninety percent of the German population was behind Hitler and his henchmen.

When Karl Hausser told the people in charge of the Moravian Church he was going to Hopedale, Labrador, as a missionary, no one questioned his authority. He was, after all, a German officer.

Karl's job was to go into Hopedale under the disguise of a missionary, set up a radio communication system, and listen for sounds of aircraft overhead. He would then radio the towers which in turn would pick up the signal and scramble the radio signals, disrupting their radio triangulation systems. This would create a massive problem for pilots flying in bad weather. All they could rely on then was sight. Every pilot would soon be staring at an empty gas gauge.

Germany also used the towers near Cape Chidley as a means of communicating with its submarine fleet that was lurking around North America, especially around Northern Newfoundland.

When the Germans were informed by their spies that the United States was about to build an air force base in Goose Bay, Labrador, where their fleet of heavy bombers could refuel, they decided to stop or at least delay the project by sinking the heavily laden ships carrying material for the construction of the base.

Communications between the submarines and German naval command went through the 'Kurt' towers at Martin Bay, Cape Chidley, Labrador. In 1942, 'Kurt' helped two submarines near Cape Bauld attack a convoy of cargo ships enroute to build the base at Goose Bay. That same year, a German submarine sank the Newfoundland Government passenger ferry *S.S.Caribou* as it crossed between Nova Scotia and Newfoundland. One hundred and thirty-six people lost their lives in the sinking.

CHAPTER 43
Brother Figgs

World War Two was raging in 1942.

Fishermen along the Labrador coast were seeing submarines almost every day. Reports by the Newfoundland Government said they were German submarines.

The people along the coast were scared. The home defense warned them to cover their windows whenever a light was on during the night. Also, they were to report immediately any sightings of strangers roving the countryside. People were expecting German soldiers to tap on their doors any night to kill them.

The Moravian supply vessel *Harmony* arrived in Hopedale on June tenth. Everyone in town, except the men who were away fishing, was there to greet the new arrivals.

Several strangers were aboard the ship. Some were missionaries going to places further north. Others were new people coming for the summer months only. Usually these were young men and women who worked with children and came as medical volunteers.

Karl Hausser, who was to be the key person using a radio system at Hopedale, stepped onto the wharf sporting a grey stubby beard. He was introduced as Brother Figgs, who would be relieving ministers in various parishes along the coast.

Karl stood for a few minutes and stared at the harbour and the Moravian Church.

He noticed the small village had grown slightly from the time he was a child. He heard dogs howling in the distance and noticed several huskies roaming the wharf. He thought things had not changed much since he left.

Then he thought about Freddy Frieda.

There was no doubt he must have longed to be back again in this little village, his home. Too bad he didn't make it. Too bad he ended up dead and buried in Lans, Austria.

"I suppose the people never knew what happened to him, just that he was killed in the war. Too bad I won't be able to tell them where he's buried," he thought as he looked across the harbour. He also thought about Aunt Nancy and wondered if she was still living. He would find out.

Karl met the Moravian minister in charge and was welcomed to Hopedale. The minister had received a telegram telling him when the new pastor, Brother Figgs, was arriving.

Karl pointed at the *Harmony* and said, "I have a folding kayak aboard. This should be a good place to use it. I bet there are people here that have never seen one like it before. It's a new German invention."

Karl told the minister the first workable folding kayak was built in 1905 by Alfred Heurich, a German architectural student. He said the kayak was made commercially successful by Johannes Klepper, whose factory was at Rosenheim, Germany. Klepper kayaks were introduced in 1906, many years before hard-shell boats were commercially produced.

The minister listened with interest as Karl told him about the kayak and then said he doubted that anyone in Hopedale had ever seen one that folded up.

"They make their own here in Labrador," the minister said. "I don't know what they would think about a kayak that folded up."

As they walked toward the Mission headquarters, Karl asked the minister if he listened to the war news very often. The minister shook his head.

"No," he said. "It's too depressing to turn on a radio. In fact, it's almost frightening to look through the window these days. You don't know if you're going to see Germans in the front yard. Every week there's a report of someone seeing a submarine in one of the bays."

"They may not be German submarines. The Americans have them all over the place too," said Karl.

"Whoever they are they have no business around here," said the minister.

"I have a very good radio with me," said Karl. "When it's set up properly it can tune in to most foreign radio stations. It's possible we could get up-to-date news every night."

"The only news I want to hear about the war is that it's over and done with," the minister exclaimed.

The Moravian Mission looked much the same as it had when Karl had lived in Hopedale as a boy. The only change was a different colour paint on the two sheds that housed the supplies.

Karl looked at the church steeple and figured it was high enough to erect an antenna that would give him good reception. He would drive an iron stake in the ground and attach a copper wire as a ground for the antenna.

"Do you have a wind charger?" he asked the minister.

"Yes, it's at the front. We have a fair amount of wind around here, enough to keep our batteries fully charged for all our needs."

"What about the radio?" Karl asked.

"It's on rechargeable or wet-cell batteries. It's too cold to have anything else here, especially in the winter time," the minister said.

"That's great, my radio should work fine here," said Karl.

"The message I received did not specify how long you'll be staying in Labrador. Do you plan to stay for the winter?" the minister asked.

"No. I'll be returning to Germany when the vessel makes its last run in the fall. I suppose it'll be around the last of September," said Karl.

"Yes, around that time unless the war interferes," the minister said.

Karl didn't want to comment on the war. He had a job to do and didn't want to jeopardize it.

The minister continued, "When the *Harmony* leaves tomorrow, my wife and I will be leaving for Germany. There are a few more ports of call it has to make further north before returning. We'll be busy tonight as I have to get you briefed on everything here. Most of the paperwork is up to date, the medical records are the most important."

When the two men reached the house, Karl was welcomed by the three workers on site and the minister's wife who invited everyone to come sit down and have tea and a cake made especially for the new pastor.

After tea was served, Karl asked questions about what was happening around the area.

"Are there any military personnel in this area?" he asked.

"We never see military personnel here but there is a Ranger stationed here now," the minister replied. "Constable Earl Brazil is very young, but he does his job well. He came here after the fishermen reported seeing submarines along the coast. He does patrols too."

"Does he have a patrol boat?" asked Karl.

The minister shook his head. "No," he said. "He usually hires a boat belonging to one of the fishermen, a member of the home guard named Freddy Frieda. Freddy is a veteran of World War One. I don't really know Freddy. But he and Earl patrol the inner bays together. Sometimes they're gone for as long as a week."

Karl was taken by surprise.

He had not expected to hear the name Freddy Frieda.

There had to be two Freddies, he thought.

This couldn't be the one he had seen in Lille. This couldn't be the one whose grave he'd seen in Lans.

It's not him, he thought to himself.

But his mind was racing and his father seemed to appear before him.

"You'll pay someday, Karl. You'll pay for it all," his father's words echoed through his mind.

"Is there something wrong, Brother Figgs?" asked the minister, staring at Karl.

"No. No. I had a little reaction from the tea, nothing serious," said Karl.

"As I was saying," the minister continued. "This Freddy Frieda isn't very friendly with the Mission. I would advise you to stay away from him. Since returning from the war he seems to hate all Germans who come to Labrador. It's got something to do him being a prisoner in Austria during the war. Although he practically grew up in this church in Hopedale he hasn't entered the door since he came back from the war." The minister paused. "There's quite a story being told about his escape."

Karl left the table and walked outside.

The news about Freddy had stunned him.

But Karl was certain no one in Hopedale would recognize him. He'd left the community when he was eleven and now he was close to fifty. Freddy had last seen him in 1916 when he was twenty-three. He didn't recognize Karl then. For sure he wouldn't recognize him twenty-six years later, with a grey beard he could hide behind. No, there was no need to worry about Freddy. There wasn't a chance in hell he would recognize him.

During the evening and late into the night, Karl was briefed about the operations of the Mission.

A couple of babies would have to be christened.

Two couples were getting married in August.

And, as usual, the Grenfell Mission hospital ship would be arriving soon.

Karl would have to entertain Captain Travize and the traveling nurse.

The minister guaranteed Karl he would have a wonderful summer in Hopedale. He noted the fishing was excellent, and said that would be especially so with his kayak.

Early the next morning, the minister and his wife boarded the *Harmony* and left Hopedale.

As soon as he was alone, Karl's first priority was getting his radio transmitter in place and tuned in.

His job was to stop the bombers flying to Britain and to sink every allied ship sailing across the Atlantic. He wanted to do it all in the name of Hitler and the Nazi Party.

Although Karl was convinced he would never be identified as the interrogator in Lille or the Hopedale-born son of Albert and Maria Hausser, the story about Freddy Frieda and his escape made him uneasy.

He thought about how he had been outfoxed by the young Inuit.

And he thought angrily how the Austrians in Lans had helped Freddy, even erecting a cross on his fictional grave.

"And now here I am on foreign soil. If Freddy discovers who I am I have no defense except a pistol and no way of escaping except in my kayak. A submarine might not get to me in time. I think I'm in great danger," he mumbled to himself. "But after we win the war, I'll get even supposing it's the last thing I do."

CHAPTER 44

Ranger Brazil

At the Moravian Mission, Karl had four on staff beside himself, two German students who hated Hitler and the German Army, as well as an elderly woman and a young girl from Hopedale. The older woman did most of the outside work. She was very talkative and knew everything about everything.

The staff noticed Karl spent a considerable amount of time talking on the radio. They also heard a lot of crackling noises coming from the church steeple. Karl made many trips from the front veranda to the room under the steeple and then he would talk to someone in German. They also noticed he was always scanning the sky with binoculars. The older woman became suspicious and asked Karl what he was doing. He told her he was doing a weather report for the Newfoundland Government. He said the minister before him was supposed to do it but didn't know how. She wasn't convinced but kept quiet.

Ranger Earl Brazil, Freddy, and two other men were doing patrols along the coast, south and north of Hopedale. Several submarines were sighted but no positive identification was made. However, it was suspected they were German submarines. It wasn't until August 1942, when a convoy of American cargo ships was attacked near Cape Bauld, that Canada and the United States started to take things more seriously.

During the latter part of August, people became more and more nervous. Ranger Brazil had a radio at the Ranger station and several men, including Freddy, would go there and listen to the war news on the BBC and the NBC, (Newfoundland Broadcasting Company). It seemed Germany was winning the war.

One day Ranger Brazil received a report about a suspicious noise coming from the steeple of the Moravian Church, a crackling-scratching kind of sound. The elderly woman who worked at the Mission said it sounded like static from a radio. The Ranger was told it was nothing more than the batteries being charged by the wind charger and nothing to worry about.

Freddy and the rest of his six man civil defense crew were suspicious of Brother Figgs the minute he arrived. Although Freddy had not seen him, enough was said about him and his activities to make everyone around nervous. Some said Brother Figgs looked like the devil himself. The two German students said they were afraid to sleep in their single rooms. They said Brother Figgs seemed to be up all night, in and out of the house and on the radio. Many mornings he would get in his kayak and go paddling around the harbour. He would be gone for hours.

Freddy hadn't gone fishing on the Turnivik Islands for two years. The threat of submarines caused his wife and children to be nervous when traveling on the water so he decided to stay in Hopedale and become a paid member of the home guard. His wife went back to work at the Hudson Bay store.

Freddy knew there was always the threat of something happening if he was to come face to face with crew members from a German submarine. He had seen a submarine on the surface of the water near the Turnivik Islands and a periscope from another submarine was sighted off the mouth of the harbour. For sure there would be shooting if he and a submarine had an encounter. He had a new .32 special rifle that was a ten shooter. He carried it fully loaded wherever he went. It never left his side. This was war.

During the winter of 1942, Freddy and his wife Mary adopted a young Inuit baby from a nearby village. The baby became the pride and joy of the family. Whenever Freddy was at home the baby was in his arms. During the spring and summer Freddy and his wife talked about having the baby christened. Freddy talked to the Ranger and asked if he had the authority to christen children. He said he didn't. Freddy asked too about completing the adoption papers and was told the child had to be christened before the adoption papers could be completed.

"There shouldn't be any problem adopting the child," Ranger Brazil told Freddy. "You get the baby christened and fill out the paperwork. Get it sworn to by a justice of the peace and the baby is legally yours."

"I'm not going to take the baby to the church here in Hopedale to have a German christen her. No matter what happens, I vowed I'd never enter the church again as long as a German is in charge," Freddy said.

"If that's the case you'll never legally adopt the baby. The law says the baby had to be christened before you can adopt her and I don't have the authority to christen her," said the Ranger. "Forget about what happened to you in the war and get the baby christened."

"That's hard," said Freddy. "I can't stop thinking about the German captain with the tattoo on the back of his hand. I see him holding his pistol, and getting ready to shoot me."

As the summer rolled on, Mary kept complaining to Freddy.

"We have to get the baby christened," she insisted. "If not we will have to take her back to her relatives in Island Harbour. I'm not going to raise this child to eight or ten and then have someone come and take her away from us. If we can't adopt her then we have to take her home."

Freddy kept saying it was impossible for him to stand in front of a German and have him christen the baby.

Mary finally said unless he went to church the following Sunday and had the baby christened he would have to return her to Island Harbour. She said firmly if he didn't, she would.

"The baby is not leaving this house come hell or high water," Freddy said angrily. "She's ours and she's not leaving."

"Well, you'd better be prepared to get her christened Sunday morning, and I don't care if you have to face the devil himself," Mary said.

Freddy knew his wife meant it. He had three days to make up his mind. But he swore the baby would never leave Hopedale except over his dead body.

****

Ranger Brazil had to go on a patrol Saturday morning. He had a report about a submarine sighting in the Nain area. He told Freddy to stay home for the christening on Sunday. He said Freddy would be paid overtime for the trip even though he wasn't coming. Brazil said all he wanted was for the baby to be christened.

On Saturday afternoon Freddy told his wife he was prepared to go to church for the christening.

"I know I'll be sorry for doing it after it's over, but for the sake of the baby I'll do anything," he said.

Mary was happy. She loved the child as much as Freddy did and she wasn't concerned if he never went to church again after the baby was christened and the adoption was complete.

"Thank God it will be done on Sunday," she said. "I'll go to the minister and give him the necessary information."

Mary went to the church office and found it locked. She then went to the living quarters and knocked on the front door. One of the German students opened the door. She introduced herself as Ilse and invited Mary in. Mary introduced herself and said she wanted to see Brother Figgs. She said she and her husband wanted to have their baby girl christened on Sunday morning.

"That's lovely, Mrs. Frieda," said Ilse. "I'm sure Brother Figgs will be very happy to do it. Wait here please. I'll ask him to come and see you. It should only be a few minutes."

Brother Figgs was a bearded man of medium height and very skinny. He stared at Mary and asked her what she wanted.

"We have a baby girl three months old who has not yet been christened. We would like very much to have her christened at the service tomorrow morning if that okay with you, sir," Mary politely replied.

"Are you married?" he asked in a condescending manner.

"Yes, I have two children," Mary said. "They are partly grown up. We want to adopt the baby, but the law says we must have her christened before we proceed with the adoption papers."

"That's fine," said Brother Figgs. "You'll have to give me all the details: the baby's names, date of birth, the sex of the child and the name of you and your husband. Give the information to my assistant and make sure you and your husband are at the church at eleven o'clock tomorrow morning, sharp." He said nothing more as he turned his back and walked away.

Ilse took the information from Mary and discovered she was a clerk at the Hudson Bay Store.

"Yes, of course," Ilse smiled at her. "I remember seeing you there. Your husband is the one who went to the First World War and was reported missing. We've all heard the story."

"My husband is Freddy Frieda and, you know, most of the stories told about him are exaggerated. He wouldn't hurt a fly," said Mary.

Word soon spread that Freddy was going to church to have the baby christened on Sunday morning. Every person in Hopedale was planning to be there.

CHAPTER 45
The Christening

Freddy Frieda was not a large man, but he was in excellent shape. He had broad shoulders and large hands that were hardened and calloused. He was a hard worker. He spent his summer months in the fishing boat hauling salmon nets and trawling for cod, except for this summer when he was with Ranger Brazil looking for submarines.

During the fall and winter, Freddy walked the country trapping, using snowshoes. Some days he walked as much as twenty miles. He often said he was never hungry.

"I eat because the hands on my watch tell me it's time to eat," he would say. People said he was never afraid, and he was known to have a heart of gold. And, if Freddy said he was going to do something, it almost took an act of God to change his mind.

Freddy got up early Sunday morning, wishing this day had never come. To face a German in Hopedale was like facing one on the battlefield in France, as far as Freddy was concerned. He wasn't sure how he was going to react when the time came.

The baby slept between him and his wife, the same as the other two children did when they were babies. He got out of bed, went to the kitchen and started the fire. Then he put the kettle on.

It was close to the end of August and he could feel the chill in the air. The time for hunting caribou was fast approaching. He was like every other Labradorian. He felt the glorious feeling of the open barrens in his bones. However, the thought of what he had to do this morning made him unhappy. He groaned when he thought about it.

He peered through the window and noticed frost on the ground. As the first signs of smoke rose into the outside air from his stovepipe his dogs began to bark. He pulled on his pants and shirt, put his feet in a pair of rubber boots, and went outside. In the nearby shed he got a fish prong and gave the dogs seal meat, enough to keep them quiet. His neighbors could now have a few more hours sleep. When he went back inside the house the kettle was boiling and he moved it to the back of the stove. Then he heard the baby calling and went to the bed and picked her up.

"Susie, Susie, we'll go out in the kitchen and I'll mix a bottle of milk for you, " he said as he gently patted her back. "Maybe I'll give you a double portion. This is the morning you have to face the Germans, I think I'd rather face old Mussolini than look him in the face over there," he said as he prepared the baby's bottle. "Dad's girl will have her name today. Susie Mary Frieda." The baby, who was now four months old, seemed to understand what he was saying and she started smiling.

As Mary prepared breakfast, Freddy was silent.

Every time he looked at the baby he thought about Julian.

The last time he saw him he was a baby in Jackie's arms. He was now twenty-five. Freddy hoped he wasn't a soldier in the German Army. God bless them and keep them all safe, he whispered as he said a brief prayer for Julian, Monica, Jackie and Olivie.

After breakfast, two of his hunting buddies came to his house. They'd heard he was going to church with the baby and they weren't happy about it. One told him about the noise in the church tower, and the fact that Karl was continually on a radio talking to someone in German. His buddies were suspicious of what was going on at the church.

"You know what happened during World War One. They collected all those fellows and put them in jail for spying. The same could happen now. That new pastor is a damn spy," said one of the men. His name was Joseph.

"I think he should be shot," said the other fellow, whose name was Allen. Then he winked at Freddy.

Mary became upset.

These two men were hunters and were capable of almost anything, even shooting someone. She wanted them to leave. She didn't want them putting ideas in Freddy's head. Mary had no intention of letting Freddy change his mind about going to church.

Freddy noticed Mary was perturbed and told the men he'd see them later. Then he checked the time and grinned at his wife.

"In the name of God, Mary," he said. "It's time for me to get my Sunday clothes on and get on the move."

"Susie is ready and so am I," Mary smiled. "We'll leave for church in ten minutes."

In ten minutes all was ready. Freddy stepped out onto the dirt road and headed for the church with the baby in his arms, a frown on his face, and hatred in his heart.

CHAPTER 46
A spy is discovered

When a man is forced to do something he doesn't want to do, it doesn't take much to upset him. Freddy was a very mild mannered man. All his life he was a good example to the people of Hopedale. His family had never heard him swear or curse.

However, as he walked the two hundred yards from his home to the church, he slipped on a rock and stumbled. Without hesitation, he cursed. Mary was shocked. It was the first time she had ever heard him swear.

As they walked along, Freddy saw crowds of people going to church. Some women stopped Mary and commented on the lovely baby girl. There was no doubt the church would be filled to capacity this morning.

****

Karl was so busy sending messages and listening for planes that he almost forgot about the Sunday Christening.

On Saturday, when he finally opened the information sheet his assistant had prepared, his eyes went wide in surprise. The first line read Parents of Child: Frederick and Mary Frieda, Hopedale, Labrador. He dropped the paper and rang the bell, summoning Ilse. She quickly rushed in.

"Yes, Brother Figgs. You rang for me," Ilse looked flustered.

"This Christening, are you sure the correct names are on the paper? How old is this Frederick Frieda you have listed here?" he asked.

Ilse looked at the paper. “I don’t know his age, sir, but the names are certainly correct,” she said. “It’s Mr. and Mrs. Frederick Frieda. And the baby is a little girl they want to adopt. The baby has to be christened before the adoption papers can be completed.”

“Do you have any details about this Frederick Frieda?” Karl tried to sound nonchalant.

“Oh yes sir, he is a very distinguished gentleman, but not very fond of our church. It apparently has something to do with him being a prisoner of war in Austria during the First World War,” Ilse explained.

After Ilse left, Karl looked at his hands and asked himself what he should do. He was shaking.

“I’ll have to go through with this in the name of the Fuhrer. Heil Hitler,” he said to himself.

Karl wondered again if he would recognize Freddy and if Freddy would recognize him. He felt confident Freddy wouldn’t know who he was.

Karl was awake all night. His conscience bothered him. Here he was in Hopedale as a German spy, pretending to be a minister in the very church where his father and mother had preached. He decided to carry his pistol inside his church robe in case something happened on Sunday. No one would see the gun under his robe. There was always the chance he might have to defend himself. He needed to have his gun close by.

****

As Freddy walked up the steps to the church he stopped and looked up at the steeple. This church is where he’d spent many of his younger days.

Coming here with his father and mother on a Sunday morning had been wonderful. His mother with her shining trumpet in her hand, dressed in her Sunday best, and his father smiling at everyone.

Nancy, his mother, was here today, and so were his sisters Blanche and Sarah. Everyone turned and looked at Freddy when he walked in the door.

Yes, it was true.

Freddy was inside the church again. The organ was playing as Freddy and Mary were called to bring their baby to the altar.

"We have a baby girl to be christened this morning," said the lay reader, "Brother Figgs will perform the ceremony."

As the organ played and the people sang the hymn 'Bring in the Children' Freddy had a flashback to Austria, and sweat rolled down his forehead.

The door opened from the inside office and Brother Figgs walked out on the platform wearing his church robe.

He carried a Bible in one hand and a crucifix in the other. He walked to the pulpit and placed the Bible on it. He waved the crucifix and placed it on the pulpit too.

When the people and the music were silent, Karl slowly walked to a small table and read from a ledger announcing the details of the christening. First, the names of the adoptive parents, then the date of birth, and finally the child's given names. When this was done, he came for the baby in order to baptize her at a sprinkler near the inner altar.

As Karl walked towards Freddy and Mary, he looked directly at Freddy. Freddy's blood ran cold as he looked into Brother Figgs' eyes.

He knew he had seen those eyes before. But where? Where could he have seen Brother Figgs? Where?

For a moment is mind was blank.

He couldn't think.

Karl walked closer.

He stopped less than three feet away and reached towards Mary for the baby.

As if in a dream, Freddy saw the hand, the right hand. It was coming towards him. On the back was the tattoo with the cross, drawn in blue ink with a red stripe down the center and letters on each side.

As quick as a cat reaching for its prey, Freddy's right hand snaked out and caught Karl's right wrist.

The church was silent as everyone looked on in astonishment.

Karl felt as though his arm was caught in a vice. Freddy's grip was paralyzing. Still holding the arm tightly, Freddy slowly brought the hand closer to his eyes and stared at the tattoo. He saw the initials.

"A and M," he bellowed. "My God, it's the Butcher of Lille."

Freddy flung Karl's hand away from him.

"You bastard," he roared. "You're the one who shot our men. You killed our men. You shot them down in cold blood."

Freddy reached for Karl's throat.

"I'll kill you, you bastard," he screamed with rage.

Karl's robe bunched in Freddy's hand as he lurched back.

Freddy reached for him again, but this time Karl reached inside his robe and drew out his pistol.

"Get back or I'll blow your head off," Karl yelled as he backed up, keeping the gun pointed at Freddy.

People grabbed their children and scrambled to get out of the line of fire.

The church was in turmoil.

Women and children were screaming, jostling against one another as they tried to get outside.

It was a scene of total pandemonium.

Karl was going to pull the trigger. He had nothing to lose now. He tried to pull the trigger to shoot Freddy but couldn't. He heard his father's words resonate in his head: "If you harm a hair on Freddy's head a curse will fall on you, Karl."

Seeing Brother Figgs in apparent distress, several men in the front row seats quickly jumped up and held Freddy by the arms.

This gave Karl time to rush back to the office and lock the door behind him.

Freddy became hysterical.

He was like a mad man. No one could calm him.

He kept yelling, "He shot our men. He shot our men in cold blood. Just blew their brains out in front of our eyes because they wouldn't talk. He shot them down in cold blood. The hand with the tattoo pulled the trigger and killed them. He's a killer, a cold blooded killer."

Freddy shook off the men holding him and ran for the door. He pushed through the crowd until he got outside then raced to his house.

"I am going for my rifle. I'm going to shoot him. Stand back," he roared. "The Butcher of Lille cannot live. The bastard has to die."

Mary couldn't believe what was happening.

She passed Susie to Nancy before she raced after Freddy.

Nancy and Sarah and Blanche were speechless as they looked at her in shocked disbelief.

They couldn't understand what had come over Freddy. It seemed that he had gone insane. He was a crazy man.

All the men standing around knew Ranger Brazil was out of town. It would be up to them to stop Freddy.

If they didn't, he would surely shoot Brother Figgs.

Freddy had his rifle on the rack in the kitchen. Taking it down, he quickly put five shells in the magazine.

"He shot our men. He's the captain who shot our men. He shot them in cold blood," he was saying when Mary came in alone.

Mary was horrified.

"My God, Freddy, what are you going to do? Put the rifle back on the rack. Please Freddy. This is Sunday. In God's name, put the rifle back," she begged. Then she tried to wrestle the rifle away from him.

It was no use.

Freddy pushed her away.

She could tell by the look in his eyes that something terrible had come over him. She had never seen such hate in his eyes before. This wasn't her Freddy Frieda. This was a madman.

Freddy stepped out on the road, rifle ready. He headed for the church.

The men of Hopedale weren't warriors. They were hunters and trappers. They could outsmart and stop any animal from a weasel to a polar bear. Now, they had to somehow stop one of their own. They had to stop Freddy.

They formed up along the pathway that Freddy had to walk on and waited. When he showed up with the rifle in his hands and started to walk between them the men closed in and overpowered him. They got him on the ground. Freddy was screaming to be let loose, but they held him down. One man cut off someone's clothes line and they used it to tie Freddy's hands and legs before taking him back to his house.

****

Karl was frightened. What could he do? Who could he turn to? Where could he go?

He knew the pistol he had was no match for the marksmanship of the Inuit hunters and there were no other guns of any kind around the Moravian Mission.

What could he do?

He realized with a sense of doom that he was on his own.

He looked at the tattoo on the back of his right hand and cursed. That damn tattoo. That's what gave him away. He'd never dreamt Freddy would have remembered it from the time he was captured in Lille. What a fool I was to let him go, Karl thought. I should have shot him then. I should never have let him go.

He rushed to the radio and put a call through to one of the submarines that was somewhere along the coast.

The closest submarine was five hours away.

He ordered it to proceed immediately to an area just north of Hopedale to pick him up. He said he was in grave danger. He gave the grid reading.

Karl knew he had to get out of Hopedale right away. My only hope is to get to the kayak and away from the harbour, he thought. He was confident that no one would catch him in a kayak. He quickly removed the priestly robes and his Sunday suit and threw them on the floor. He put on his work clothes and rubber boots and checked his watch. It was 12:35.

He stuffed most of the important papers about the Cape Chidley operation into a bag, grabbed his radio and his paddle and headed out the door.

He checked to see if Freddy was coming his way with a rifle.

Seeing no one, he dashed to the wharf.

He saw several groups of people along the road and guessed they were still in shock from the proceedings in church less than an hour ago. He unlocked the supply shed door and opened it. He got his kayak and carried it to the water. The wind was northwest. It was a fair wind out through the harbour.

"At least something is in my favour," he thought.

****

After half an hour or so, Freddy began to calm down.

He started to realize the trouble he had caused in the church.

Several of his closest friends were with him. Two of them, Joseph and Allen, were the best Inuit sharpshooters in Hopedale, men who had spent their lives shooting wild game.

They believed Freddy when he told them about his fellow soldiers, how they had been shot by the German captain in Lille. But they said that even though the captain was posing as Brother Figgs and carrying a pistol and might have deserved to be shot, it wasn't worth giving the church and the community a bad name by shooting him inside the church.

While they were talking, someone came in and said that Brother Figgs was headed out the harbour in his kayak, paddling at full speed.

Freddy got furious and demanded to be untied but no one would release him.

Joseph picked up Freddy's rifle and said, "You won't be needing this. I'm sure you won't mind if we borrow it for a while. We'll bring it back when we're through."

Joseph then leaned in close to Freddy and whispered, "How many bullets are in the rifle?"

"Eight," said Freddy.

"It's enough," said Joseph.

Joseph and Allen left and walked away from the house.

Nobody paid attention as they strolled casually towards the barrens.

They were sure they knew where Brother Figgs was headed and they knew where they should go to cut him off.

The two men had spent their whole lives on this narrow strip of land. They knew every crook and cranny. They knew the wind and tide and what men feared when they were out on the water.

The wind was picking up and they knew Karl would have to stay close to the shoreline if he didn't want to get blown off land.

The men crept up on a barren knoll not far from the ocean. They looked like two men stalking a polar bear. They sat and waited patiently.

They were sure they knew exactly what the German spy was planning.

He was going to be picked up by one of those German submarines.

That was the plan, they thought.

But Joseph and Allen had other ideas as they walked along the north side of the cove.

"Look," Joseph said. "He's coming around the point. I'll have the first shot. You take the second."

'You take the man. I'll take the kayak. One shot each," Allen replied.

"Good," said Joseph, as he pumped a round into the chamber.

"Three hundred and fifty yards, Joseph."

Joseph raised the sights, "Three notches, hey," he said.

With his elbows on his knees, Joseph took aim and fired.

The bullet hit Karl Hausser in the back. He immediately tumbled headlong into the water, overturning the kayak.

Joseph handed the rifle to Allen.

In a matter of seconds another round exploded.

The kayak broke into pieces and swiftly began to sink.

The two men waited a few minutes for any sign of life.

Nothing moved.

Someone who was on the road in Hopedale came and whispered to Freddy that they had heard two rifle shots. Freddy felt a great sense of relief.

"Untie my hands," he said coolly. "The war is finally over for me. This has been a good day."

The ropes were taken off his hands and ankles and Freddy quickly returned to normal. At last he was free in his own home.

During the late evening a submarine was spotted not far from Hopedale harbour. It cruised up and down the shoreline several times then disappeared. People suspected it was searching for Brother Figgs who had disappeared in the kayak and hadn't returned. They figured he had been recovered from the ocean.

The next day, Akna, the elderly woman who worked at the Moravian Mission, was told to clean out Brother Figgs' room.

She knew about the situation on Sunday, and how the minister had attempted to shoot Freddy in the church, and then disappeared afterwards in his kayak. He hadn't come back.

She found a small testament in Brother Figgs' clothes bag.

There was writing on the first two blank pages. The first page read: "To our darling son, Karl, on your tenth birthday. May God bless you and keep you. Love, Mutter and Vater."

The second page was inscribed with the names: "Albert and Maria Hausser, Hopedale, Labrador."

Shocked by what she'd read, she quickly put the testament into her pocket and left the house. She went directly to Freddy's place.

"Mary, is Freddy home?" she asked.

"No, he's outside, not far away."

"Tell him to come in, I want him."

"Not another yarn I hope. We've heard enough in the last while. I hope it's all over," said Mary, somewhat fed up.

"I have something to show him," said Akna.

Mary called to Freddy to come inside.

"Akna has something to show you. She says it's important."

Freddy came in and smiled at Akna.

'What's up now, darling?"

"I searched the bags belonging to Brother Figgs, or whatever his name was, and found something interesting. I think you should see it."

Akna took the small testament from her coat pocket and handed it to Freddy.

"I found this in one of his bags. Have a look at what's written inside."

Freddy read what was written on the first two pages and then put his hands to his face.

He looked shocked.

"Dear God," he said in a whisper to himself. "Is it possible this was the Karl I grew up with here in Hopedale? He must have recognized me in Lille the day he interrogated me and shot the rest of our men. Probably that's the reason he didn't shoot me that day. Perhaps that's why he sent me to a prison camp instead. He must have known all the time who I was. Maybe he could have shot me in the church on Sunday, but again he didn't. Why? Why didn't he shoot me?"

Freddy realized this was a question that would forever remain unanswered.

Ignoring the two women, he put his elbows on the table and looked out the window.

The sun was setting, casting an orange glow across the bay.

He let out a long shuddering breath.

Still whispering to himself, he said, "Twice he could have shot and killed me, but he didn't. I had one chance and I had him killed."

Freddy stood up and went over to the woodstove.

He removed the stove cover then ripped the two front pages from the testament and threw them in the fire.

The women looked at him but said nothing.

"The evidence is destroyed," Freddy said as he continued to whisper to himself. "No one will ever know the truth. No one will ever know it was Karl who was killed in Hopedale. It was Karl."

Freddy's last words sounded almost like a prayer.

* * * * * * * *

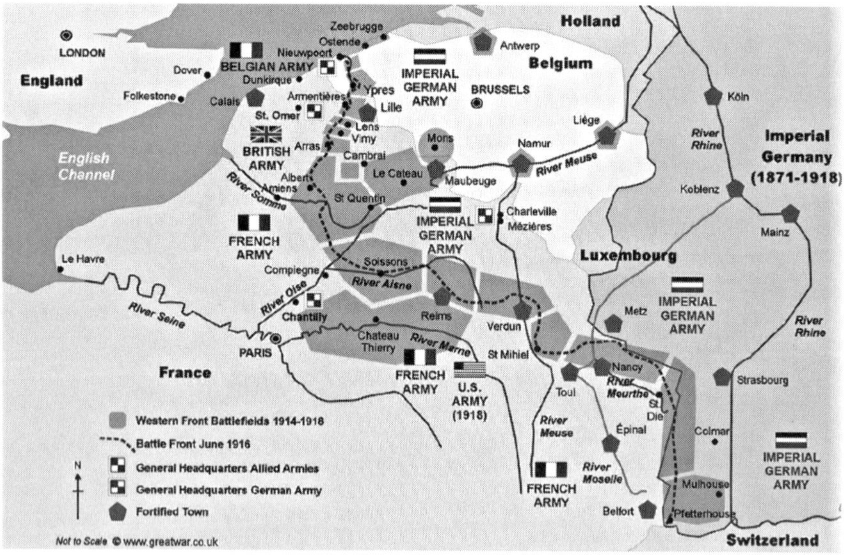

Western Front Battlefields 1914-1918

Emily's funeral: Her father Charley is there with his wife, not her mother, and Jimmy is there with handkerchief in his hand. Little girl is Emma.

About the Author

Earl B. Pilgrim, Newfoundland and Labrador's favourite storyteller, was born in Roddickton in 1939 and still lives there with his wife Beatrice. He and his wife have four grown children.

Earl started his working career in the Canadian Army where he got involved in the sport of boxing and went on to become Canadian Light Heavyweight Boxing Champion.

Following his stint in the Army, he worked as a Forest Ranger with the Newfoundland and Labrador Forestry Department. Nine years later he became a Wildlife Protection Officer with the Newfoundland Wildlife Division.

Earl has won many awards for his work, including the Queen Elizabeth II Golden Jubilee Medal; the Safari International Award; the Gunther Behr Award; and the Achievement Beyond the Call of Duty Award.

Earl and his son, Norman, have a wilderness lodge in the mountains of the Cloud River near Roddickton. They offer big game hunting for moose, caribou and black bear in the fall and snowmobiling in the winter. During summer, guests can fish for salmon or trout. The area where the lodge is located is one of the most successful on the island for all of these endeavours.

Earl can be reached by calling 709-457-2041, cell 709-457-7071 or e-mail earl.pilgrim@nf.sympatico.ca.

Web address is www.boughwiffenoutfitters.com

Other great reads from Earl by DRC Publishing:

The Day of Varick Frissell
The untold story of a daring young American film maker who was aboard the *SS Viking* the day she sailed to her doom from St. John's harbour.

The Sheppards are Coming
Read about the daring exploits of Brig Bay natives Kenneth Sheppard and his sons Tom and Carl as they defy the law on Prohibition in their schooner *Minnie Rose* – with success but not without consequences!

The Day Grenfell Cried
The true story of what happened when Dr. Wilfred Grenfell helped the poor people of northern Newfoundland and Labrador. Grenfell's compassion brought him into conflict with powerful fish merchants and almost broke his heart.

Marguerite of the Isle of Demons
An exciting true story of a French princess abandoned on a desolate island off northern Newfoundland in the 16th century. A moving fast paced story of survival against all odds by Newfoundland and Labrador's favourite storyteller.

Jump Ranger Jump
In May of 1943, Newfoundland Ranger Jack Hogan was one of four men who jumped from a burning airplane over the Northern Peninsula of Newfoundland. Hogan and RAF Corporal Eric Butt were the only survivors.

Drifting Into Doom
In January 1883, Howard Blackburn, a Nova Scotia native fishing out of Gloucester, Mass, and his dory mate, Thomas Welsh, a 16-year-old from Grand Bank, NL, went adrift from their schooner *Grace L. Fears* while fishing off the Burgeo Banks.

Beyond The Call
The tales of Doctor Baxter Gillard are true stories which will be enjoyed by everyone, especially those who love wilderness adventures.

The Place Called Quirpon
The story of Neil Dewar is an incredible one and well known to old timers on the Northern Peninsula of Newfoundland and Labrador who heard it passed down through the generations as the Narrative of the Shipwreck and Sufferings of Neil Dewar.